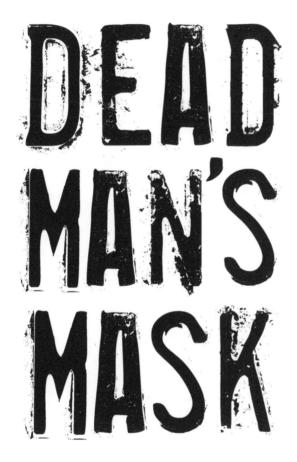

DEAD MAN'S MASK

Shawn McHatton

D0234237

ISBN: 978-1-4834-9064-9 (sc)
ISBN: 978-1-4834-9063-2 (e)

Library of Congress Control Number: 2018910312

Lulu Publishing Services rev. date: 09/18/2018

CONTENTS

PART III: THE SHOWDOWN

PROLOGUE

Daniel Raggel sat alone deep in the woods. Or, to put it more accurately, Daniel sat alone next to a dried-up tributary of the Mad River on the outskirts of Waterville Valley, New Hampshire, as he slowly began to die. Daniel had been in New Hampshire for the better part of a week, and things had started out great. But Daniel had learned a valuable lesson too late: it is unwise to break a blood oath.

Now in his midforties, Daniel owned and managed Talandoor's, one of the most prestigious antique furniture stores on East Fortieth Street in Midtown Manhattan. Daniel had seen and touched items of obscurity that most people only dreamed of seeing up close, let alone having the means to buy. Daniel had sold an antique couch allegedly owned by George Washington himself for $19,000. Research only suggested and had not confirmed that the first president had ever rested his ass on that seat, making this a terrific sale. Daniel also successfully brokered the deal to sell the rumored very first grandfather clock ever built, originally gifted to King Charles II of England. This item went to a wealthy collector in Austria for nearly $200,000, and Daniel's smooth negotiation skills netted him 20 percent of that arrangement. In short, Daniel either bought or negotiated sales for some of the most impressive antique collectibles that ever existed. His lifestyle earned him the luxury of enjoying a loft, nearly fifteen hundred square feet, above his store, where he threw parties and rubbed shoulders with other prestigious dealers in the metropolitan area. Although exciting and somewhat remarkable, Daniel's secret underground business remained his true passion.

Daniel graduated from Mill River Union High School in North Clarendon, Vermont, where he had been born and raised. He loved the television show *Friday the 13th*, which surprisingly enough had nothing to do with the movie franchise of the same name. Instead, the show told stories about a collectible shop that housed magical items that were often cursed. At a crossroads in his young life, Daniel needed to decide whether to go to college or just get a job as most of the locals did. His aunt Linda had given him a $1,000 bond to spend on either a car or something else that would be of equal importance to a young adult. Daniel chose the latter option (defining for himself what would be as imperative as getting his first car) and used half of the money to buy a strange dagger with both sides of the blade rippled like gentle waves in a lake. Daniel had bumped into the seller while standing in line at the concession stand in the Cumberland County Civic Center in Portland, Maine, as the two waited to grab a beer before a Whitesnake concert. Daniel's new friend, Mitchell, said he had recently relocated to Maine from Colorado. Mitchell told Daniel that a high-ranking military officer who also served as a priest of Lucifer had previously owned the dagger and had used it to sacrifice children during rituals that took place in a secret underground base. This tale fascinated Daniel, and he met Mitchell a week later in nearby Westbrook, Maine, to finalize the deal and purchase the item. Daniel had no idea whether the dagger had any supernatural powers like the items in his favorite television series did (although Mitchell had told him that he had had some far-out experiences a few times when he touched it). Daniel didn't care either way. He wanted to own something that the general population could never say they had owned, a one-of-a-kind item that told quite a tall tale all by itself.

Daniel stayed in touch with Mitchell and formed such a strong relationship with him that he used the leftover money from his aunt's bond to move to Maine, where he became Mitchell's business partner at his pawnshop.

Daniel learned an incredible amount from Mitchell very quickly. He marveled at his smooth salesmanship, watching him buy a Timex from one guy for two dollars and then sell it to the next guy for twenty. And Mitchell's hideous appearance—short and fat with greasy black hair along with an acne-riddled face—made this an even more impressive feat. "It's not about what you're selling," Mitchell had told Daniel during one of his training sessions, "it's about how you're selling it. Tell the potential buyer an engaging story, and the item will sell itself." Daniel agreed and heeded his mentor's advice, practicing his storytelling with each and every sale. The two rented a house down the street from the store, providing Daniel with an opportunity to pester Mitchell with questions every day.

Daniel kept the mysterious dagger in a small chest underneath his bed and took it out nearly every night before bed to study it. Although he never noticed any magical powers radiating from the blade, an unidentifiable sensation that coursed through his body when he held the weapon resulted in him developing a passion to acquire more mystical items.

Daniel had his chance eight years later after Mitchell got busted for selling a brick of coke out of the pawnshop in a sting late one Saturday night. Luckily for Daniel, he had never gotten involved in that element of Mitchell's business and had been at the movies with a date that night. After the bust, the two agreed to sell the shop and split the proceeds, as by that point, Daniel and Mitchell were equal partners. Mitchell used his portion of the money to pay for his defense attorneys, and Daniel never saw or heard from him again, as he used his share to relocate and open a furniture store in Lower Manhattan, reasoning that moving to the big city would increase his chances of getting his hands on more obscure items.

Daniel opened Daniel's Drawers on Crosby Street, a clever play on words further enhanced by his sign that displayed a dresser with a pair of underwear sticking out of the top drawer. Soon after, he moved into a small studio apartment above the store. In the early days of the store's existence, Daniel sold inexpensive furniture, the kind that IKEA would proudly display when they went on to dominate the industry in years to come. But Daniel couldn't have cared less about what he sold; his main focus remained on continuing to develop the skills that Mitchell had taught him. Over time, antiques started making their way into the shop: a hundred-year-old desk from Maine here, a rare Aztec bowl there. While Daniel found the dialogue with his customers quite interesting, he found the items in his store to be quite boring—that is, until someone brought him something interesting in February 2002.

Like the rest of America, Daniel had been overwhelmed by the events of September 11. But the tragedy hit New Yorkers even harder than everyone else, especially those who worked or lived in Manhattan at the time. By chance, Daniel had been visiting his parents back in Vermont during the event. He had decided to extend his vacation into the following week, horrified at how close the attack had been to his own shop. Upon returning to the city, it amazed him to find that the people who were normally so hostile and aggressive toward one another were now holding out welcoming arms to help their fellow neighbors in any way possible, as if they had suddenly all been thrust onto the same sports team and now shared a common alliance. Daniel took part in this as well, offering up to 50 percent off all his store items to families who had lost loved ones in the tragedy. And in February 2002, one such customer returned the generosity.

Ethel Millonocket, a seventy-year-old woman from Queens, had lost her husband, Larry, because of the North Tower's collapse. Larry had worked as a semiretired janitor, cleaning the restrooms in the tower in order to gain some extra spending money for the couple. Sadly, he had been on the fifty-first floor during the building's demise and could not escape. Ethel came to Daniel in February 2002 and asked him to buy Larry's olive-green La-Z-Boy recliner, as it pained her to stare at it every night and not see her husband's skinny behind firmly planted in the seat. Daniel happily agreed and hired a laborer to go to Ethel's apartment and pick it up. While cleaning it back in the shop, Daniel found an onyx stone ring with a gold band wedged between the cushions. Because of its light weight, Daniel reasoned that it had little financial worth but likely had personal value to Ethel. He called Ethel upon discovering it and planned on finding a way to get it back to her, but she surprised him by saying, "Keep it. I'm surprised he wasn't wearing it that day. It's another one of those things I just can't look at around here. It's not worth much; maybe it will yield you the gas money for the moving truck."

Not being one to refuse free things, Daniel thanked her without argument. It shocked him when he put the ring on his right index finger and found that it fit perfectly. But Daniel would be in for a much bigger surprise three days later when he discovered what the ring actually did.

Daniel could not believe when he discovered that he had worn the ring for three days straight. He certainly remembered putting it on but had seemingly lost track after that. This startled him greatly, as he did not usually wear jewelry and should have been bothered by its presence. On this third day, he learned why it had not. During work hours, Daniel normally waited to use the bathroom in the privacy of his studio apartment. But on this particular day, the store had been quite busy, and the 7-Up he had chugged a couple of hours earlier needed to make a hasty exit. Daniel used the small bathroom he had set up for the store customers, a unisex bathroom with a urinal and a stall. As Daniel approached the urinal, he could not hide his surprise when he saw a five, a ten, and two one-dollar bills on the floor, seventeen dollars in total just sitting there for the taking. Two more times over the following three weeks, Daniel found money in public bathrooms, once while out to dinner and again while meeting a colleague for drinks. By the end of that month, Daniel had found nearly a hundred dollars lying around in bathrooms, all while wearing the ring.

When David finally connected the newfound cash to the mysterious ring (a connection he easily made after taking it off for two weeks and finding no money and then putting it back on for two weeks and finding close to forty bucks), his interest in mystical items reached an all-time high. Daniel had to laugh when he thought about Ethel's husband choosing to go back to work after having retired. *Now I know why,* Daniel thought as he had a private laugh. But Daniel had a problem: he had nobody to talk to about the ring's ability. He did not have a lot of friends, as he did nothing but focus on building his business. This included girlfriends as well. Being tall, dark haired, and handsome had yielded Daniel plenty of action when he chose to indulge in it, but he always distanced himself from forming relationships in order to keep his focus on work. But even if Daniel did decide to talk to someone about the money-finding powers of the ring, he did not think that anyone would actually believe him. Daniel decided to hold on to his little secret for the time being and continued to wear the ring, resulting in more cash grabs in public bathrooms. Six months later, Daniel got his wish about having someone to talk to about the ring—and much more.

Late in 2003, Daniel decided to attend a furniture-and-bedding conference in Tampa, Florida. There was at least one a year, usually held in hotel conference rooms in various cities all over the country in order to allow salespeople to network and learn more about soon-to-be-released products. Daniel occasionally attended them, not because he cared about the changes occurring in the furniture world but because of his interest in networking with other like-minded people, especially considering that he did not socialize as much as he should. This particular conference would last three days, and Daniel attended the entire event, shaking hands and making new friends each day. And as he sat in the Marriott bar on the second night after the day's lectures had ended, Daniel met someone who would forever change his life.

Daniel had been sitting at the bar by himself, casually working on his third Seagram's and Seven as he watched the mind-numbing broadcast of a preseason Tampa Bay Lightning hockey game. A strange man with long black hair and a beard and mustache of the same color, both greased to points, pulled up a seat next to him. He wore a dark trench coat and a black suit so outdated it actually looked vintage and pretty cool. Daniel let out a small laugh after studying his features.

"Wow," Daniel said, "you look just like Robert De Niro's character in *Angel Heart*." Immediately, he regretted making the statement, fearing that his intoxication would make it sound like an insult instead of a compliment. Much to Daniel's relief, the strange man turned to him and smiled as he removed his purple-tinted sunglasses, revealing eyes that at first looked silver in color but then somehow shifted to a dark blue.

"That's great," the man said with a chuckle. "That's exactly the look I was going for. My name is Ben. Let me buy you another round."

Daniel thanked him and nodded in approval as Ben ordered him another drink while getting a Jack and Coke for himself. The two made small talk for close to five minutes (mostly about Daniel's store) until Ben noticed Daniel's ring and pointed at it. "That seems a little dull for your type of personality, doesn't it?"

That statement surprised Daniel, as he had changed after the day's conference into jeans and a T-shirt to go along with his Adidas sneakers; he could not have looked more casual if he tried. But intoxication caused him not to have complete control of the words coming out of his mouth.

"You wouldn't believe me if I told you what it did," Daniel said in a hushed whisper, looking around in order to make sure no nearby patrons could eavesdrop on their conversation.

"Oh, you'd be surprised," Ben answered with a wry smile. "I've seen just about everything."

"I find money in public bathrooms when I wear this ring," Daniel blurted out. He could not believe that he did, but he also could not get himself to be upset by it. The sensations in his body went beyond intoxication—almost like being under a spell.

Ben continued to smile. "That's a very special ring you got there," he said. "I've heard of it. It's called a Robin Hood ring. It was crafted by a very poor and very angry man about sixty years ago. The money that is 'found' is actually relieved from wealthy people, although, for the life of me, I have no idea why the hell it only works in public restrooms. Wouldn't you think that if this guy was going to go through all this trouble that he would make it so the item would work somewhere other than where people took smelly dumps all day?"

"What do you mean, you've heard of it?" Daniel asked, sober enough to pick up on the comment. "You already knew about this ring? Are there other items that have special powers like this does?"

"You ever see that show from the eighties, *Friday the 13th*?"

"Yes!" Daniel answered, so excited that he nearly spilled his drink. "That was my favorite show back then!"

"Well, that 'fictional' show, along with a lot of others, is based in reality. There are several enchanted items out there, and there are several people who use these items regularly."

"I don't understand. I can't deny that something special has occurred since I found this ring. But actual magic? How could magical items possibly exist in the twenty-first century?"

"Oh, I don't know," Ben answered, taking a moment to pull a hearty tug from his Jack and Coke. "A deal with Lucifer, maybe? Listen, pal—I'm in the furniture game, just like you. But unlike you, it's only a front for me. The real money is in the items like the one you're wearing on your finger. There's a lot of money to be made in this business, and my New York guy recently … retired. That's a huge market just going to waste right now. How would you like to fill that seat? Hold on. Let's back up. Let me be completely honest with you: this is a lifelong commitment. My colleagues take this line of work very seriously, and they would die to protect its secrets. I'll make sure you're trained and that you have help to set up your secret shop. If you like any items you buy, you keep them for yourself; selling them is always up to you. And, of course, our people will hook you up with buyers for the items you choose to sell. But you gotta swear to keep the names and identities of those you meet in this business a secret.

We live by our own code and manage our own judicial system, if you get my meaning.

"I'll tell you what," Ben said as he stood up and threw a hundred-dollar bill on the counter, telling the bartender to pay it forward to cover any more drinks that Daniel wanted, "don't answer tonight. Take some time, go back to New York, and I'll have someone find you in a week or so to get your decision."

Daniel did just that, and a week later, he received a sealed envelope from a bicycle messenger. When he opened the letter, he found what appeared to be very old parchment with ink penned as though it had been written with a feather quill, inviting him to a 2:00 a.m. limo pickup the upcoming Saturday for an in-person 3:00 a.m. meeting. No name or signature or phone number had been listed. But by this point, Daniel had made up his mind: he would go. He loved his ring and still had not taken it off, gladly grabbing tens and twenties from bathroom floors (and he still had to laugh about Ethel's husband, Larry, as he had been in the perfect place to use it, at least up to the horrific moment of his death). He wondered what kind of other mystical artifacts there could be out there. Daniel still had the mysterious rippled dagger, but upon finding the ring, he had slowly lost interest in it and stashed the case housing the blade away on a shelf deep in his bedroom closet. The dagger did not seem to have any obvious powers, so the ring received all of Daniel's attention.

And when that Saturday arrived, Daniel dressed in a dark-gray Armani suit with black loafers and caffeinated himself enough to endure an all-nighter. Sure enough, he found a limo waiting for him outside, right at two. A driver in a chauffeur's outfit, wearing sunglasses even at that hour, climbed out of the front seat and opened the rear door, gesturing for Daniel to climb inside after telling him that they were heading for Queens. Daniel followed his instructions and found snacks and alcoholic beverages waiting for him. He played it cool, deciding not to drink anything, wanting to maintain a professional demeanor. They made it to Queens in thirty-five minutes, thanks to the light traffic of the wee morning hours. Once there, they drove into an industrial section of town full of old buildings with dim streetlights illuminating their outer walls. As Daniel studied his surroundings, the limo driver rolled down the window that separated the front and back seats. "We need to wait until five minutes 'til three," he said to Daniel, peering through his dark sunglasses while looking in the rearview mirror.

"Fine with me," Daniel responded.

When that time finally arrived, the driver retrieved Daniel from the backseat and escorted him down a dark alleyway between two of the large warehouse buildings. The driver reached into his pocket and pulled out a small flashlight. It surprised Daniel that there were not any alley cats or remnants of cardboard boxes, garbage bags, or anything else one would normally find in a New York City alleyway. It made him uneasy. *Am I going to die tonight?* Daniel wondered, having just realized how mysterious Ben had been the night they had met. *Now's my chance,* he thought. *I could probably outrun this guy and get the fuck out of here.* Growing up in Vermont, Daniel had been an active, outdoorsy child. Upon moving to the city, he shifted that focus to the gym, doing light weightlifting and intense cardio at least four days a week. He believed that he could get himself out of this situation if he acted quickly. But some sort of internal energy gently nudged him to continue on. As such, Daniel decided to keep going, not wanting to spend the rest of his life selling midpriced dining room tables and recliner chairs.

Finally, they reached an iron door. The driver reached into his pants pocket and pulled out what looked to be a skeleton key. He opened the door, stepped inside, and held the door for Daniel to do the same. Daniel took another deep breath and followed.

Once inside, Daniel found himself in a small, narrow hallway dimly lit by what appeared to be fluorescent-green lights stretching across the top of the walls. But the lights did not behave as normal fluorescent lights; instead of flickering, they seemed to pulsate, as if they glowed at various degrees of strength based on timed intervals. Daniel did not have much time to examine them, because after a brief walk, the hallway ended at an elevator. The limo driver walked up to the call button labeled B and inserted the same key he had used before. The elevator took a long time to get to their level, making Daniel believe the elevator to be old and slow or that perhaps the basement resided deep underground. Finally, the elevator doors opened, and the driver stepped inside, waving Daniel in to join him. The glowing green light of the hallway reflected eerily off his sunglasses. Daniel cautiously walked into the elevator, his dress shoes clopping on the tiled hallway floor and sending echoes rattling throughout the chamber.

Once inside, the driver pulled out what looked like a small crystal that pulsated with nearly the same color as the hallway lights. As soon as he did so, the elevator doors shut, and the descent began. Thankfully, Daniel found that all the exercise he had done slowed his heart rate, as he may have otherwise passed out because of the overstimulation that he had been dealing with at that moment.

Eventually, the elevator came to a stop and dinged before the doors opened. As Daniel followed the limo driver into the hallway, he found himself in a large, rectangular room lit by evenly spaced torches on the walls. The black-and-white checkerboard floor remained empty except at the other end of the room, where a gold throne resided. A man with shortly cropped curly hair wearing a dark suit with a bowtie sat on the throne. He had his legs crossed and clutched a silver cane that ended in a wolf's head with red gems for eyes. The limo driver led Daniel over to about ten feet from the throne before walking over to the left side of the throne and standing against the wall. The man uncrossed his legs and leaned forward, putting his weight on the cane.

"Good evening," the man said after taking a moment to size Daniel up. "Thank you for coming, and thank you for dressing up. I like a man who takes opportunities to better himself very seriously. My name is Harry Houdini."

Daniel could not help but let out a small chuckle. *Fitting*, he thought, as both the man's suit and hairstyle looked to be about a hundred years out of date.

"That's great," Daniel said. "Like the magician. Your likeness is uncanny. Good work!"

"My likeness is due to my actual-ness. I am the one and only Harry Houdini. I did not die, as was reported. As to how I avoided death and still live nearly a hundred years later, this is not information you are yet worthy of hearing. Suffice to say, I've conducted some very important business for my employer over the years in secrecy. Now, let us get back to why you are here tonight."

Daniel nodded. For all he knew, this man had security watching his every move by means of hidden video cameras. He did not want to offend the man and end up in the city dump after having been chopped into several pieces, nobody the wiser as to what had happened to him. As such, he decided to shut his trap and listen.

"Several things portrayed in movies and television as fantasy are in fact based on reality," Houdini continued. "A perfect example of this is magical items. The ring you wear now is one such item, so I'm sure I do not need to convince you as to how real these items are. Now, I could lecture you for hours as to how and why these things exist. So instead, for tonight's little chat, I'm going to skip ahead and get to the meat of our conversation. Many of these items have become lost over time. As such, they end up in the hands of mundanes, the typical ignorant human population that would have no idea what the hell they were actually holding if I myself sat in front of them telling them. There are others similar to you, who indeed know what they hold, and they have a great passion to possess even more of these items. I am a leader of a very large group of these people. Our purpose is to retrieve these items from the idiots who don't understand what they've got and either hold on to them for our own personal use or sell them to approved customers in our network. Ben has told me that you are an individual who shows great promise and that you deserve to be a part of our organization. So here tonight, I give you one such invitation. You must decide tonight, and regardless of your answer, you must keep what you have been informed of thus far a secret, else your life be in peril. So, Daniel Raggel, would you like to join our organization?"

Daniel stood mesmerized as he listened to the man's old, outdated accent, which would certainly match that of the era Houdini would have lived in. He did not need long to answer.

"I gladly accept," Daniel said. "I've been given a small taste of what a life like yours has to offer, and I want more. I want to be one of you."

"Excellent," Houdini responded with a crooked smile. "Welcome to the club. You will be one of us, and you will be well taught in the ways of owning and dealing magical artifacts. All that is required of you is to swear on your life to keep these actions a secret from outsiders, as well as to provide us with a gift."

The limo driver emerged from the shadows and withdrew a dagger from an inside coat pocket that looked exactly like the rippled blade currently residing in Daniel's bedroom closet. *That cannot possibly be my dagger, can it?* Daniel wondered.

"This is indeed your dagger," Houdini said, somehow seeming to read Daniel's mind. "Do not worry; we did not go to your apartment to take it but instead summoned it by means of a different magical item. We did so because we know how important this item is to you. We know that it is your very first magical item purchased. In truth, we have been watching you from the moment that you bought it from your former dimwitted business partner. On a related point, Mitchell used to be one of us, but he did not come to us first before selling you the dagger, therefore breaking our sacred rule. As such, he died six months after beginning his prison sentence. And that brings me to my next point: you need to allow your thumb to be cut and let some of your blood run onto the floor as you say, 'I swear to always do what I am told as well as to withhold my membership of our order as a secret, now and forever.' As far as our gift, we will claim the dagger from you, as we know how to use it and have things planned for it."

Daniel needed a moment to process the emotions overwhelming him. If he said no, would the limo driver stab him in the back with his own dagger? *It's either this or selling ugly fucking couches for the rest of my life*, Daniel thought.

"I accept all your terms," Daniel said as he extended his thumb and allowed it to be cut open before reciting the required oath.

Less than a month after Daniel's mysterious meeting in Queens, he had been given a brand-new shop named Talandoor's (a name that Houdini insisted upon) in Midtown. Both the shop and the loft that came with it were much larger than what he had left behind down the street, and although the ground-level shop appeared to be relatively the same size as his original furniture shop, his new shop had a secret store in the basement, Daniel's very own *Friday the 13th* personal collection of magical items. And thanks to Houdini's help, it did not take long for Daniel's store to get a decent supply of items. After providing him with trainers (mysterious, but regular-looking fellas) to teach him how to buy and sell in this market as well as how to have enough fortitude to handle the powerful items coming his way, Daniel began his dream job. He never saw the mysterious man calling himself Houdini again and had only talked to him occasionally over the phone. Instead, he received help from the nameless trainers. "Focus on what you are being told, not on who is telling you," one man with sandy blond hair and a mustache told him. Considering the fact that Daniel had just been given an opportunity that most people could only dream about, he did not complain.

Daniel's made six figures in his first ten months and had even made a cool million twice over the following several years. On the surface, he appeared to the public as a high-end antiques dealer who bought and sold and even brokered deals at auctions for other collectors. And quite literally below the surface, Daniel developed a collection of magical items for himself. The large, cube-shaped basement had walls, floors, and ceilings constructed from some ancient material that Daniel could not identify, with crystal glass cases scattered throughout. A magical source illuminated the chamber when he walked into certain parts of it, just as a motion-sensor-activated light would. The lights even changed colors, if one knew how to do it, and Daniel's trainers told him he would learn the ancient magic that operated such features of the secret room at a later date. "This basement is magically warded at the highest possible level," one of his trainers told him as they toured the large underground room. "The magic of the items you store down here cannot penetrate these walls. But this does not apply to you. You need to know exactly what you are doing when you handle each item. The untrained and unaware can end up dead, fast. Do not fear; we will train you on how to handle each one." And they did. While the mysterious trainers (six in all, coming and going at various times) opened doors to help Daniel grow the main business of Talandoor's, they also submerged him deep into the underground network that dealt in magical artifacts. And Daniel loved every minute of it.

Their first brokered deal helped him buy a real-life djinni lamp for a reasonable $75,000, a second-century item crafted from bronze that had been discovered in modern-day Iraq. Similar to how the lamps were portrayed in movies and television shows, rubbing the lamp would, in fact, summon a djinni, who would grant the summoner three wishes. "This is an ancient artifact, and you need years of training before you're ready for it," Trainer C (Daniel started naming his trainers with letters from the alphabet in the order that he had met them) told him.

"For now, we will secure it in a case, where you can admire it from a safe distance until that time comes." The basement had several other cases of various sizes, and Daniel retired Ethel's ring, deciding that he no longer needed to scrape dollar bills off dirty bathroom floors. Daniel placed the ring in a smaller case at the other end of the room and visited both the ring and the djinni lamp regularly, proud of his accomplishments.

A year later, Daniel had added two more items, a seventeenth-century golden goblet that would refill itself with wine all on its own and a yellow clown suit that gave its wearer the power to charm children into performing reasonable tasks that were not life-threatening. Daniel had no interest in testing the suit's powers, as, in truth, it creeped him the fuck out. But at that time, he had a strong desire to increase his inventory, and he gladly stashed the suit on a special rubber mannequin in a large case near Ethel's ring. He had a chance to buy the alleged Spear of Destiny, the weapon that pierced Jesus Christ as he died on the cross, from some guy in Indiana for a mere $250,000 but remained skeptical of its authenticity, no matter what his trainers had told him about the credibility of the seller. Daniel enjoyed taking the slow and steady pace to buy artifacts and did not want to blow all his savings too quickly. And just when he thought that things could not get any better, he fell in love.

Daniel met Tessa in early 2013 when she seductively strutted into Talandoor's looking for an antique dresser for a guest bedroom in her house across the bridge in Jersey. Daniel found her long, curly red hair and sharp blue eyes attractive on her tall body. He soon learned that her charisma and comeliness were enhanced from being a witch of the white light. This excited him, as he now had an ally he could let into his world who could help him manage his secret business.

Daniel knew this would be dangerous territory; after all, he had taken a blood oath, swearing on his life that he would never reveal the secrets of his trade to an outsider. Therefore, he waited several months in order to find out if their relationship seemed as though it would last. And when it did, Daniel invited Tessa into his world, one step at a time. Regardless of his blood oath, he believed this action to be his right to take. Why should he be left alone with mysterious trainers and a guy calling himself Harry Houdini, whom he had not seen in years? Daniel decided, all on his own, that he deserved to

xx

be happy. And he came up with the perfect cover to pull it all off: he would hire Tessa as his salesperson for the nonsecretive part of Talandoor's.

"I can keep a secret," Tessa said with an alluring smile as Daniel explained his covert operation. "I have to. There are others in my coven, and some are well known, even famous. I am a master of secrets, and I can even help you determine the authenticity of the items you are buying."

Daniel liked the sound of that, reasoning that Tessa might even be able to teach him things that his trainers could not.

Daniel had the smart idea of telling his trainers about her, as he thought it would be suspicious if he did not. So one day, as Trainer D helped him try to sell an Etruscan pen that wrote in blood, Daniel told him about Tessa, saying that she would help him run the furniture business so that he could delve deeper into his clandestine work.

"That's fine," Trainer D said to him. "Just don't tell her about what goes on downstairs. Remember, you took an oath, and an oath such as that cannot be broken without the direst of consequences."

It did not take Daniel and Tessa long to accomplish great things together, both with the store's work as well as with their personal relationship. Daniel truly loved her, and Tessa appeared to love him back. She kept her house in Jersey but often stayed with Daniel in his upstairs loft. The two even talked of having children after a union ceremony (as Tessa did not believe in church marriages). Daniel decided to give her Ethel's ring as an engagement ring, telling her to make sure that she never wore it on days when the trainers were expected to visit. Things were going great with the two of them, until 2018.

Daniel had to admit that of all the magical items passing through his hands, the one he had purchased in August 2018 enthralled him the most. He did not understand why; he just seemed to bond with the artifact. But deep down, he knew of another important reason: Daniel had made his first unsanctioned purchase by buying the magical item. He had been told to log all his transactions in a journal maintained by his trainers, who would then either authorize or deny the transaction. Even though he had yet to be denied the purchasing or selling of an item, he wanted to keep this particular purchase to himself. For the last year, Daniel had been browsing the dark web, looking for more items to buy and sell, and found this particular one for sale by a mysterious seller calling himself Big Bear out of Wyoming. Daniel purchased the item for five bitcoins, the equivalent of nearly $60,000 (on that particular day). Believing he got a steal, Daniel could not wait to get the magical item in his hands.

After the relic had been delivered, Daniel knew he needed to get out of the city in order to test its capabilities (not to mention, he certainly did not want to use it anywhere near where his trainers could be watching). At first, he thought about going back to Vermont. He had not been home to see his parents in over a year because of the store being so busy, and this would have certainly been a good excuse to do so. But Tessa convinced him otherwise, indicating that in the same way one should not mix business with pleasure (even though the two of them did exactly that), it would not be wise to mix family and magic. So, after browsing online to find a great place to use it without having to travel too far to do so, Tessa suggested Waterville Valley, a quaint little town in the middle of New Hampshire.

"It's a great tourist place that's also remote," Tessa said, telling Daniel that she knew of it because one of her coven members had grown up in the area. He agreed, and the two decided that they would head up the weekend after Labor Day, as the summer rush both in his store as well as at vacation spots would be over.

Once the time arrived, they rented a small one-bedroom town house and drove for nearly six hours to start their vacation.

Monday went wonderfully for Daniel. The artifact helped him reach a new state of perception he had never known to be possible. But by the time he had woken up Tuesday morning after accidentally falling asleep in the woods, the excruciating pain in his stomach made him realize that something terrible must have happened. On Wednesday, Tessa had left Daniel after leaving a note and taking their only vehicle back to New York (or perhaps to New Jersey; Daniel had no idea if she had ended their relationship as well). On Thursday morning, Daniel found himself lying next to a dried-up branch of the Mad River on the outskirts of town, staring up at the sun as it cascaded through the leaves that had turned red and orange. He clung to the magical artifact in his left hand, being in too much pain to do anything else. Late Thursday afternoon, Daniel watched his life flash before his eyes: growing up in Vermont, the pawnshop in Maine, and

Harry-fucking-Houdini sitting in some mystical lair in Queens (by this point, after everything that had transpired, Daniel believed him to indeed be the famous magician). Daniel laughed as he choked on his own blood. He died while watching rats eat his exposed intestines after the lining of his stomach exploded.

PART I
THE VALLEY

CHAPTER 1

"I'm busy, Mom!" Devin yelled from his bedroom. "Tell them to go away!"

After saving all year, Devin finally had his prized possession sitting in front of him on his desk: a brand-new Lego *Millennium Falcon*. Devin's plans for this late-September Saturday afternoon were to do nothing but assemble it into its glorious completed perfection as he blasted Youzed Panteez, a new glam metal band from Maine that had quickly become one of his favorites. But his mother's persistent nagging diverted his attention elsewhere.

"But they're already here!" Devin's mother shouted from downstairs. "Come tell them yourself!"

Fucking dickholes, Devin thought as he shoved his desk chair back and stared helplessly at the chaotic mess of Lego pieces stranded in front of him. *They knew I would be working on this today. Why can't they leave me the fuck alone?*

Devin grabbed his iPhone and turned off the music as he left his bedroom. As he made his way downstairs, he reflected on all the recent changes in his life. The new school year had just started, and Devin and his companions downstairs—Corey and Matthew—were now freshmen at White Mountain Academy, a small private school.

Devin had been playing bass for most of the year, and after he had nagged Corey and Matthew all summer to take a break from BMX riding on the half pipe in the parking lot next to Waterville Valley Village, they eventually joined him in his musical pursuits, Corey taking up drums and Matthew helming the vocals. They needed a band name and, more important, a guitar player. Devin knew just the right person for that role, but he also knew that it would take far more persuasion than his friends had required, so he remained patient while he formulated a plan.

Devin wanted a complete band ready to play Youzed Panteez's "Hangin' 'n' Bangin'"—pretty much the only song of theirs tame enough to play without getting them expelled—at the academy's talent show in November. Youzed Panteez would be playing the Expo in Portland, Maine, in October, and Devin's coworker at the bike shop, Dale, indicated that he would be able to not only get them tickets but take them to the show as well. A lot of variables needed to be in place to pull this off. Getting the tickets and the ride would be much easier than convincing all their parents to allow their children to go to a show of such debauchery with an out-of-towner not very well known among the adults.

As Devin ambled down the hardwood stairway of his family's two-story town house on Bobcat Way in Waterville Valley's neighboring town of North Sandwich, he hoped that his dipshit friends were interrupting his fantastic day to discuss either the band or the upcoming Youzed Panteez concert.

Heavenly smells of warm apples and spicy cinnamon greeted Devin once he descended the staircase. After his mother had let his friends in, she puttered off to the kitchen, where she continued to assemble and bake her award-winning (locally, at least) apple pies. Although she sold most of what she made at Mary's Market, accompanying the handcrafted candles that she made year-round, the family insisted that at least two pies were kept for them to devour. They considered this a somewhat enjoyable consolation prize, as although the pies always tasted amazing as a result of Devin's mother experimenting with new ingredients to add some originality to her craft (this year, a small dash of honey and vanilla extract caused the house to smell even more incredible), the family barely endured the labor required to make it all possible. Devin's mother required them to travel to North Haverhill each September for an apple-picking Saturday morning, which they had returned from less than three hours ago. She sold this tradition as having two benefits: they were able to eat some of the delicious pies, and, more important (to her, at least), they would engage in valuable family bonding time while picking the apples. Devin would much rather hang out with his friends and play his Jackson JS1X Minion bass guitar than spend over two hours in the car and two hours in an orchard with people he had to see every single day. Devin's mother would blab about local town gossip while his father would talk about the woes of his auto shop, often mentioning how he had to take out second mortgages on both the garage and the town house to put his kids into the private academy. Devin's older sister, Mandy, would lovingly reply, "If you only had one kid, you guys wouldn't be in this situation."

Devin would rather endure his parents' painful conversations than spend any time with his sister. Now starting her junior year at the academy, Mandy spent the majority of the car ride and the time at the orchard on her phone, talking to girls about boys or with the boys themselves.

Devin found Corey and Matthew waiting in the living room. Corey's untucked dark-blue, long-sleeved, button-up shirt and faded gray sweatpants made him look like a complete slob, and his dark, curly hair crammed underneath his backward bright-red Angry Birds baseball cap only added to his disarray. Matthew sat in Devin's father's recliner under the cuckoo clock and looked like he would be leaving from there to join his father cutting trees out in the woods. In a red-and-black flannel shirt with jeans and work boots, he twirled his black Oakley sunglasses in one hand. His sandy-brown hair had grown almost to his chest, and although his voice still needed some fine-tuning, his frontman image did not.

As Devin approached the two, Corey jumped up from the couch. "Hi, Devin!" he said.

"What are you twats doing here?" Devin answered. "You know I had the Falcon project today. We can practice tomorrow. Now kindly go fuck off somewhere so I can get back to work."

"That's what we're here to talk about," Corey responded, glancing between Devin and the kitchen. "We bumped into a Masshole on our way to Grizzly's Bar to grab a burger. Apparently, he played bass with the cover band there last night. He's leaving tonight and can't take the bass with him. Something about his girlfriend demanding that he sell it once he gets back home. The guy would rather sell it to someone up here so he can spend the cash before his bitchy girlfriend can. It's a Fender Jaco Pastorius, and he's willing to let it go for only two hundred!"

That tidbit of information caught Devin's attention, as that bass model could fetch nearly ten times that amount.

"I suppose I can take an hour break to check that shit out," Devin said. "I'll grab my bike."

"Great," Corey said as Matthew rose from the chair to stand beside him. "We'll meet you outside."

Corey's tone sounded weird to Devin, and he noticed that Matthew had remained oddly silent. *If they're fucking with me right now, I'll cut their balls off,* Devin thought.

Devin decided that his silver running pants were good enough for this trek and grabbed the matching jacket from the closet, along with his blue Puma Street Cats, before making his way into the kitchen. He found his mother molding the crust around one of the pies, her dark-blue "Kiss the Cook" apron somehow remaining immaculate. Devin liked that she at least kept herself busy while his father religiously worked six days a week; he went straight back to the garage after returning from apple picking. Devin's mom looked like an older version of Mandy, having dark blond hair with a few hints of red running to her shoulders and just enough makeup to be ready to greet visitors, which, other than Devin's or Mandy's friends, they never received on the weekends.

"I'm gonna step out with the boys for a minute," Devin said before hugging his mother from behind and kissing her on the cheek.

She smiled but kept her focus on crafting the pie crust. "That's fine," she responded. "Just be home for dinner. I'm not sure how long the family pie will last after your father gets home."

Devin nodded to the back of his mother's head and proceeded through the door that led to the garage. He pushed the button to open the garage door and squeezed by his mother's olive-green Subaru Outback to make his way to the opposite wall where he racked his bikes. But as he reached for his treasured black Eastern Traildigger twenty-inch with camo seat and rims, he noticed that Corey and Matthew were on their mountain bikes instead of their BMX bikes. Corey shook his head and pointed at the Framed Marquette Alloy black-and-white mountain bike mounted next to it. *Fine,* Devin thought, *whatever gets these dipshits to go away faster.* He could have argued the fact that by going to the village, they would only be riding the streets and thus could jam on their BMX bikes, but he did not want to waste time squabbling with the two fools. Devin had gotten his beautiful mountain bike for a fraction of the cost once the bike shop no longer wanted it, a superior machine compared to the SE Big Mountain twenty-one-speeds his friends were riding. Perhaps he could find an opportunity to rub that fact in their faces along their short journey.

After lining up next to each other, the gang rode off. Upon making their way to Valley Road, the main road that led to larger civilizations elsewhere in New Hampshire, Devin began turning his bike right in order to take the shortest route to Waterville Valley Village. "No, not that way," Corey said.

"What the fuck is wrong with you?" Devin said. "Why the fuck are you being so weird? And why were you talking so loud at my house? Do you have Hank shoved up your ass or something?" Devin certainly hoped that Hank the hamster did not reside in his friend's posterior. It would be Devin's turn to take care of the class pet a week from Monday, all part of some initiative to teach the students how to nurture and care for something other than themselves.

Corey and Matthew both stopped riding.

"We needed your mother to think that's what we're about to do," Corey responded somberly. "We're doing something else, something very serious. We're on the mountain bikes 'cause we're heading for the Mad River Trail."

"Why the fuck are we going there?" Devin asked, angry about being led even further away from his Lego project.

"Can't tell you," Corey answered. "Gotta show you."

Devin looked at Matthew for more clarity, but he only nodded. After a brief moment of silence, Corey took off, heading left while Matthew quickly followed. Devin sucked in an annoyed breath before falling in line, wondering what in the fuck they could be showing him that deserved such an elaborate cover story.

The gang made their way down Tecumseh Road before reaching Garage Way, where Matthew lived, a street full of town houses that looked very much like Devin's neighborhood. Milly, a nosy, crusty old lady who worked at the post office, lived at the end of the street. She often shook people's packages and asked them what they were mailing in a tone insinuating offense at having to process something so unimportant. The kids struck back at her nasty attitude by traversing through her unmowed backyard in order to join up with the dog path that eventually connected to the Mad River Trail. By the time Milly would run out of her back door as she angrily shook her fists and yelled at them, the gang would already have blasted through her yard. On this day, no hostilities greeted them from the house as they plowed through Milly's unloved, overgrown backyard. After a short jaunt on the well-kept dog path, the trio joined up with the Mad River Trail.

Devin loved Waterville Valley in September. The summer hiking tourists were gone, and the winter skiing tourists had not yet arrived. The trail that they were on, which would normally be full of amateur hikers who desperately tried not to get lost after drinking too much at Grizzly's Bar, contained nothing but the crunchy leaves of maple and beech trees along with a heavy dose of spruce needles sprinkled on top due to an early fall. The dense canopy of the looming forest rejected most of the persistent rays of sunlight, adding an extra chill to the air.

The fresh air reinvigorated Devin, reluctantly making him glad that he had allowed his friends to drag him out of the house. He always enjoyed journeying along the Mad River Trail, especially when the tourists were long gone. The trio meandered at a mediocre pace next to the Mad River, watching as it bubbled and gurgled along past them. They soon reached Devin's favorite part of the trail, where they had to traverse narrow beams of wood stretched across a small gulch before arriving at a handcrafted stone staircase that looked to be straight out of an *Elder Scrolls* game. Devin pretended to be a heroic knight on his way to slay a mighty dragon as he championed the stairs with his bike on his shoulder (which helped him take his mind off carrying a large mountain bike up the damn stairs). After continuing their journey along the trail for a short jaunt, Corey held up his hand.

"We're going here, up Black Bear Brook," Corey said.

A small tributary off West Branch Mad River, Black Bear Brook got its name from the numerous black bears that roamed its banks. But "brook" may not have been an accurate label for a normally dry riverbed, as usually, its water came from overflow that had not yet dumped itself into the Mad River during heavy snow-melting or rainy seasons. Only the locals knew about it, and fewer still could locate it when it was dry. The Mad River Trail did not extend to Black Bear Brook, causing Devin to grimace as he followed his companions and began heading up the mostly dry, rocky riverbed.

Even with his rugged mountain bike, traversing the terrain quickly proved to be miserable. Running over (or into) rocks of various sizes sent jolts up his shins and forearms, and he occasionally got stuck in the few remaining muddy parts of the riverbed. "Are we almost there?" Devin yelled.

"Almost," Corey responded.

After a couple of minutes of horrendous riding, Corey stopped the group again. "Look," he said, pointing. Devin saw pillars on each side of the riverbed composed of rocks of various shapes and sizes stacked one on top of the other. They balanced precariously and looked as though they would fall over with the slightest touch.

"What the fuck?" Devin asked, perplexed. Instantly, he became uneasy, as the structures reminded him of the evil creations he saw in *Blair Witch*.

"I remembered these from when we were playing Skyrim," Corey said. "They're called cairns. They are meant to mark a pathway in difficult terrain. Speaking of that, we can leave our bikes here. It's a short walk the rest of the way."

"How did you even find this place?" Devin asked. "What the fuck were you doing out here?"

"Looking for a Chikorita," Corey answered. "There's one out here somewhere."

"Who the fuck still plays Pokémon Go?" Devin said.

"Fuck off," Corey responded. "It's still on fleek to play it."

"The kind of kid who still says 'on fleek' is the kind of kid who would still play Pokémon Go," Matthew said to Devin through a half smile, having taken off his sunglasses to examine his surroundings further.

"Shut up, both of you," Corey said. "I was looking for the fucking Chikorita earlier today and stumbled upon this shit. I couldn't believe it, so I went to Matthew's house first, 'cause he was closest. I convinced him to follow me, and then we went to your house to convince you. You guys are not gonna believe what you're about to see!"

"And just what is that, exactly?" Devin asked, running out of patience after nearly tripping over a large rock.

"This," Corey said as he pointed in front of him.

After climbing a small knoll, Devin looked in amazement upon a circle of cairns, most of which were taller than he was. Some of the large rocks at the base of the cairns were so enormous that Devin thought they must weigh more than the three boys combined.

"How ... how is this possible?" Devin asked as he marveled at the stones spiraling into the sky around him. He desperately wanted to touch them but feared that he would cause them to topple. Devin could no longer hear the river below him or even the birds chirping above him. The stillness of the air did not seem natural, and it sickened him. The unusual structure had no place in a healthy forest normally full of living beings. It looked like a Stonehenge made of cairns, tainted and just plain wrong.

"Well," Corey said as he pointed to the leafy earthen floor in the center of the cairns, "I bet he knows. Or knew." Devin looked to where Corey pointed and let out a small scream. He stumbled backward, directly into one of the large cairn pillars, and gasped as the rocks on top awkwardly swayed. He shielded his eyes in order to avoid staring at impending death from above until he had the courage to look again. Once he did, he saw Matthew standing over the center of everyone's attention.

"Ladies and gentlemen," Matthew said, "I believe what we got here is a dead body." He took his folded sunglasses and poked the body.

"What in the fuck!" Devin yelled as he started shaking.

"I don't know what happened," Corey responded, "but I know from watching *CSI* with my mother that this guy only died a day or two ago. His face looks fresh, and the bears would have certainly eaten the rest of him by now."

Devin could not help but take a closer look after hearing Corey's comment about "the rest of him." The dead man's abdomen had been torn open, the entrails hanging out. Judging by the tiny paw prints in the dried blood on top of the man's torn, dirty T-shirt, rats and mice had begun eating his stomach. Devin wondered what scared them off and could only come to the conclusion that the cairn stones had something to do with it. He quickly became nauseous and thought that, maybe for the first year ever, he would not be eating any of mom's annual apple pie.

"Fuckin' hell," Matthew said. "I watched a drunk moron accidentally cut off part of his leg with a chainsaw one time, but this is way beyond that."

"We need to tell Chief Hannon," Devin said. "We need to go tell him and get the fuck away from here—now."

"I agree," Corey said, "but don't forget who found him. I'm the hero here. I wanted to give you guys a chance to see him before the body is taken away, but don't forget that this is my discovery." Corey put his hands on his hips.

"Whatever, weirdo," Matthew said. "I've seen it, and I don't wanna see no more. I'm with Devin; let's get the fuck outta here." With that, Matthew shook his long mane and began trekking down the rocky creek bed back to their bikes.

Corey quickly flashed a "Look what I just did!" type of smile at Devin before following suit. Boldly, Devin took one more glance at the body. The man looked slightly older than his father, with dark-brown hair and eyes that vacantly stared up toward the sky, as if his soul pleaded to be taken to the heavens and far away from this place. He looked as though he probably had good looks and a fit body while living, making Devin cringe even more as he thought about what could have possibly happened to cause the man's fatality. Just before Devin turned to walk away, he noticed something. The dead man tightly clung to something in his left hand in a state of rigor mortis, which had remained partially hidden among the sticks and fallen leaves that had collected around his body. Devin had nearly missed the bland object that seemed to blend in with its surroundings. But he did not, and the "thing" somehow seemed to call to him on an intuitive level. After making sure Corey and Matthew were not watching him, Devin quickly bent down and pried it from the man's hand before stuffing the item into his jacket pocket. He zipped the pocket shut and rejoined his friends, not mentioning the fact that he had just pilfered from the dead.

CHAPTER 2

What had been a pleasant ride into the woods proved to be a dismal trek back into town for the trio. Nobody spoke, not even Corey, which may have been a first. The cool autumn air had now turned cold, biting at any exposed skin as they traversed on their bikes. Upon exiting the ravine of Black Bear Brook, Matthew hit a dry patch and skidded out, painfully sliding on his legs after falling off his bike. The beautiful woods of Waterville Valley, normally calm and welcoming, suddenly seemed hostile and abrasive to the gang.

And Devin's misery far exceeded that of his friends, thanks to the strange item secured in his pocket. He had not been able to identify it; it looked to Devin like some sort of old slingshot, with the sack that held the projectile now being withered and old, while the elastic that would propel it had the texture of gritty leather. Or, Devin thought, the object might be the remains of a pouch, with some of the sack having eroded away. Devin tabled his investigative thoughts to keep his focus on getting out of the woods without anyone noticing what he had taken. He had enough awareness to notice that his perception of his surroundings had changed since first touching the strange item, so he needed to keep his willpower up in order to avoid becoming overwhelmed by that observation.

Once out of the woods, the gang proceeded along the dog path past Milly's yard until they reached Tripoli Road, which, after a short trek, led to TAC Way, the location of the police station. The three knew they needed to hurry because of the late hour. Years ago, the Waterville Valley Police Department had been reduced to one person, Chief Hannon. Although he often remained on call when his office hours were over, he did not work all the time, and when the chief did not work, all police calls were routed to the Plymouth Police Department. Surprisingly for a bunch of fourteen-year-olds, the boys actually had a decent relationship with their local police officer and held no interest in taking a matter of such great importance out of town. So, once they were on Tripoli Road, the gang made their way with haste to Chief Hannon's office in order to get there before he went home.

Upon seeing the chief's black Chevy Trailblazer in the parking lot, Devin knew that they had made it on time. They just needed to figure out how to get past the chief's dipshit assistant, Shane. After a brief discussion, the group decided that they would bully their way past Shane while being sure not to talk about anything important in front of him. Shane remained bitter about not being funded to go to the police academy and would often discuss police business with those he should not, so they knew that they needed to keep him in the dark regarding this matter at all costs.

Devin and his friends ditched their bikes and ran through the glass doors, where they found Shane and his immaculate desk in the center of the lobby. A large hunting knife that he kept unsheathed sat on the left side of his desk, perhaps to look intimidating in the absence of a gun (and Devin had no problems admitting that it intimidated him). A cloud of stale cigar smoke drifting from the office behind it contrasted Shane's spotless workspace. He and the other two boys hastily followed the smoke trail, circling around Shane's desk without even acknowledging his presence. As soon as they began their evasive maneuver, Shane stood up and made sure his dark-blond hair remained in perfect position as he walked around his desk in order to impede their path. His khaki pants with complementary brown loafers and a sky-blue polo shirt with the police department's logo on it did not have a wrinkle in sight. The grumpy assistant angrily waved his finger in Devin's face as they approached him.

"You three," Shane said angrily. "What are you doing here? He's about to go home. What could you possibly want to talk about that deserves his immediate attention?"

At this point, the trio still proceeded forward at a rapid pace. Devin considered keeping up the tempo and aggressively charging Shane as though it were third and seven for the Pats and Shane served as a defensive lineman on the hated Jets. Perhaps if they ganged up on him and all ran into him at the same time …

"We have important business to discuss with the chief—now,"

Matthew answered boldly, pulling Devin back to the present and out of thoughts of a sport he had never even attempted to play.

"Is that so?" Shane asked as he glared at them while stepping in front of Matthew. "That is a decision for me to make, not a bunch of children. So, like I already asked, what are you clowns doing here?"

"An unimportant secretary with nothing to do all day," Corey said. "You're just living the dream, aren't you?"

Shane's face turned dark red. "I'm not a secretary, you little shit," Shane said as he approached Corey while grabbing a magazine from a table in the lobby. He rolled it up and raised it over Corey's head with a menacing look in his eyes.

"That's enough, everyone," Chief Hannon bellowed from behind them as he stood in his doorway, smoking a cheap cigar (Devin had no idea what cigars cost; he based that assessment on the terrible smell). "I have ten minutes left of my shift. I suppose I can let these fine young gentlemen take the remainder my time."

With that, Shane reluctantly stepped aside while waving the rolled-up magazine in Corey's direction with a *this isn't over* look on his face. Devin exchanged a quick glance with Corey and Matthew, indicating to them the need to make haste to safety at once.

"I don't know why he got so upset by that," Corey whispered. "There are male secretaries on tons of shows that my mother watches nowadays."

"Shut the fuck up and remember why we're here!" Devin responded, still a bit off from the object he had secretly stashed away in his jacket pocket.

The three hastily proceeded into the disaster area also known as Chief Hannon's office. The rank cigar smoke caused each of them to cough or gag (or both). Piles of books and papers were everywhere, stacked chaotically in a manner that undoubtedly made sense to nobody, including the chief. And on top of several stacks of papers were Styrofoam cups full of musty dirt and earthworms, most of which were long dead. The worms complemented all the fishing pictures that covered the walls of the office quite well, displaying Chief Hannon holding up various types of fish that Devin could not identify even if his life depended on it. Although the ugly fish left something to be desired, the pictures were actually a welcome sight compared to the rest of the walls, as all the parts not covered by pictures exposed the fake wooden panels that were most likely thirty years out of date or more. Devin had no idea why the chief's office had not gotten the renovation that the rest of the department had received, but at this moment, he had much more important matters to discuss, so he took a step in front of his friends and toward the chief's desk. "Chief Hannon, we have something very—"

"Nuh-uh," Chief Hannon responded.

"But, Chief ..." Devin protested.

"Nope," the chief said as he pointed to Devin's right. "You know what you need to do."

Devin sighed, knowing that they were wasting time and he needed to give in and get it over with. He had no fucking clue as to why the chief insisted that Devin and his friends do this whenever they visited his office (which, thankfully, they did not do often), and he often wondered if the chief made adults do it as well. Regardless, Devin walked past Corey, who smiled at him while sweeping his arms in an *after you* type of gesture and let Devin make his way to the wall. Once there, Devin reached up in between two pictures of fish to touch the plastic button in the middle. As soon as he did, he jumped backward, as though he had just set off the timer for an explosive device. In a way, Devin thought that that might have been more desirable than what happened instead, as the plastic fish above the plastic button started squirming and flopping around as though having some sort of fucking plastic seizure.

"Doooooooodoooooodoooo, dooodooooodooooodooodooooodoooo-dooo! Don't worry! Dooodooooodooooodooooodooooodooodooo, be happy! Dooooodoooodooodooooodooo, don't worry! Be happy!" Devin winced and considered plugging his ears, while Corey clapped and sang along with the plastic fish's heinous tune. Chief Hannon banged his hand on his desk while pointing at Corey.

"See," the chief said, "this one gets it! Aren't you in a better mood now? How can you not be in a better mood after hearing that?"

"I'm in a better mood!" Corey yelled as he took off his baseball cap and ran his fingers through his thick, curly hair.

Devin glared at him, quickly settling Corey down.

"Chief, we have something very serious to discuss," Devin said, once the annoying plastic fish finished its seizure and died. "I'm gonna just come out and say it: we found a body."

Chief Hannon shifted in his seat, causing the chair to squeak loudly in protest. Not exactly fat but not thin either, the chief sported a hefty frame of muscle blanketed by a slightly excessive amount of fat. But his dress did not match the messiness of his office, as his uniform consisted of neatly pressed dark-blue khakis and a matching button-up shirt with the police department logo on his shoulders and his badge above his right breast. He loved his smelly fish and his smelly cigars, but the gang came to him because he took his job seriously. After a brief moment of contemplation, Chief Hannon spoke.

"Dammit," he said while slamming his fist on his desk, causing a nearby cup full of worms to topple over and spill their squirmy contents. "I told Dave to stop putting rat poison in the damn dumpsters! I know we have a problem with the bears gettin' in them, and I told him I would take care of 'em! Just tell me where it is, and we'll have it removed."

"No," Devin answered, and as he did, he heard a door shut behind him. He turned around and saw Matthew standing behind him, having shut the chief's door. *At least somebody else besides me gets it*, Devin thought. "No," Devin repeated. "Not that kind of body." He paused, and all three of the kids stared at Chief Hannon, who stared back at each of them while he stroked his dark-red handlebar mustache.

"Drunk and passed out, sleeping it off," Chief Hannon said thoughtfully. "Or fell and hit his head after slipping on a wet rock while crossing the river. Or sleeping in the woods in order to get away from an angry wife."

"No," Devin repeated.

Chief Hannon shuffled some of the loose papers around on his desk. After distracting himself as long as he could, the chief spoke again. "We haven't had this … It's been years, long before any of you were born since this last happened. Tell me, where is … it?"

"I found it at Black Bear Brook," Corey said. "I was looking for a Chikorita and stumbled upon it. I showed these guys first but only to make sure I wasn't imagining anything before coming to you and wasting your time. As soon as they confirmed that I was seeing what I thought I was seeing, we came here immediately. Judging by my expert opinion as a result of watching so many crime dramas with my mother, I would estimate that the body is two or three days old." Corey crossed his arms in triumph, as if he had just solved the entire case.

"Assuming that whatever that 'thing' you said you were searching for was some meaningless kid thing," Chief Hannon responded, "I need to ask you all a very important question: did any of you alter the crime scene in any way?"

"No!" Devin shouted, and as soon as he did, he panicked, clutching his windbreaker tightly around his waist while hoping that he did not give the truth away.

"None of us were in the mood to be near that thing," Matthew interjected from behind Devin, saving him from the scrutiny of the chief's gaze. "And to be honest, the rats have gotten at it a bit. That's not anything we care to see. Not to mention, there are some … weird things around his body. We think they are called cairn stones, something so large that we have no clue how they could have been put there. We want nothing to do with this and are leaving this in your good hands now, Chief."

"Listen," the chief said while once again rising from his desk and pointing a stern finger at all three of the boys. "As you know, this type of thing does not happen around here, ever. Because of that, I need some time to get my arms around this, and by that, I mean you tell nobody. And that means nobody. This includes your friends at school, your online friends, and even your parents. I need a few days to examine the scene and determine a cause of death. I can't have the locals panicking in the meantime, making this out to be something bigger than it is. Most likely, this was some dumbass tourist who tripped and fell and hit his head before bleeding out. So, I need your word, right now, all three of you." Devin glanced at Corey and Matthew as they all returned his gaze. Devin could not help but wonder if the chief would believe "natural causes" were the cause of this guy's death once he entered the circle of cairn stones that were stacked several feet high. Devin would leave that for him to decide.

"We swear that we will keep this between the four of us," Devin said while Corey and Matthew nodded in unison.

"Good," Chief Hannon said as he made his way from behind the desk to stand next to the boys. The terrible smell of his cigar only added to his intimidating persona. "I'll be calling upon you if I have questions. And don't worry; when this case becomes public, I will not only credit you with the discovery, but I will also inform everyone that I required your silence so that you don't get in trouble with your parents and all."

Devin looked at his two friends as the chief walked in between them and opened the door after grabbing his hat from the hat rack. "Workday's done, Shane," the chief said. "Time to go home. Boys, thanks for stoppin' by and telling me about the sighting of the mama bear and her cubs. I'll make sure I warn any tourists left in the summer condos out that way. Have a good night."

Devin did not wait to see what reaction Shane had on his face as a result of hearing this fictitious story, leading the way for his two friends to get outside and back to their bikes as soon as possible. After riding out of the parking lot and back onto Tripoli Road, Devin put up a hand to stop his two friends.

"Do we agree to follow his rules?" Devin asked. In reality, he did not want to do it just because the chief said so; he wanted to limit the risk of anyone finding out about what he had in his pocket.

"Dude, my mother would freak if she found out we just poked a damn dead body," Corey said.

"Yeah," Matthew responded, "we're just starting freshman year. We got a lot goin' on as it is. Let's give the chief some time to see what comes of it. We can always blab to someone else later if we wanna."

"Besides," Corey said, "we have no idea what the fuck those cairn stones are there for. I don't wanna tell someone to go out there and then have them end up like that guy. I wouldn't sleep for months if I was responsible for something like that."

Devin nodded, impressed by the ethical wisdom of Corey's statement.

"All right," Devin said, "we agree. Good. Now, I'm gonna go home and get back to work on the *Millennium Falcon* and see if I can forget all of this." But based on the object in his pocket, which he once again clutched from outside of his jacket, he never would forget, and his life would never again be the same.

CHAPTER 3

Devin stepped into his house, which now smelled like a mix of apples and meat, remembering that his mother had started a beef stew dinner in the slow cooker as he left. Once in the kitchen, he found his father, now home from work, shoving apple pie into his mouth. He had not even changed yet, still wearing his one-piece, zip-up dark-blue mechanic's suit, with a name tag sewn into the right breast and "Tim's Auto Shop" written in white cursive letters across the back, an outfit and logo designed by Devin's mother. Devin could not believe that his father could eat so much and still remain stick thin. As Devin watched his father greedily stuff his face, his mother emerged into his field of view. She began whacking his father with a wooden spoon. "You are a mess!" she said. "Get out of my kitchen and go clean yourself up!" Devin's father winked at Devin as he stood up before departing the kitchen, flashing a look similar to that of a young child causing mischief. "And you," Devin's mother said, looking directly at him, "why do you smell like cigars?"

"Chief Hannon caught us while we were riding around," Devin lied. "He made me promise that you would get him a pie." *Thank God I thought of that so quickly,* Devin thought in a near state of panic.

"You tell him that he can buy one at Mary's Market, just like everyone else. Did you end up getting the bass from that guy?"

"No. Looks like he changed his mind and ended up heading home before we had a chance to talk to him." Sweat began forming on Devin's forehead as he told his mother one lie after another. *I better get used to this,* he thought. *I better get used to lying to everyone, about everything.* "I'm gonna get back to work on the *Falcon* until dinner is ready."

Once in his room, Devin shut the door behind him. He realized that constantly grabbing at his jacket pocket might have looked suspicious to his ever-perceptive mother, so he decided to change out of his tracksuit into green Adidas shorts and a black Youzed Panteez T-shirt. But before he threw the outfit into a pile of dirty clothes, he took the special item out of his pocket, finally having some privacy to examine it. Both the pouch section and the leather straps were very dry, so much so that Devin half-expected it to crumble in his hands. As he touched it with his flesh once again, an energetic pulse radiated into his hands and all through his body. The energy seemed to grant him some sort of enhanced perception of the world—though he could not identify exactly how.

As Devin sat on his bed caressing the strange item, he knew he had to be careful. He wanted to continue to carry it around with him in an attempt to identify it but also knew it would be risky to do so near his mother, who seemed to be able to sniff out just about anything on him. He decided that he would hide the item while at home. This would also prove challenging, as his mother did not allow a messy room. After a quick look around, he found the shoebox that his Pumas had come in and decided that would be a good place to start. He took a yellow Waterville Valley T-shirt that he had gotten from Mary's Market over a year ago and used it to line the inside of the box. After blanketing the strange item inside the T-shirt and sealing the box up, Devin found a cozy spot under a stack of sweatpants in the storage cube organizer within his closet to hide the box in. Then he shut the closet door and prepared to head downstairs for dinner. Being away from the item filled Devin with separation anxiety, as if a part of him yearned to return home in order to be complete. These emotions confused and panicked Devin, so he quickly made his way downstairs, believing that a good meal would clear his head. It did not.

CHAPTER 4

On Monday morning, Devin found himself in the backseat of his mother's Outback as she took him and Mandy to school. The second week of his freshman year had begun, and that would normally be enough to keep a fourteen-year-old lost in thought. But between the strange item that he now possessed and the stern request from Chief Hannon to keep the discovery of a dead fucking body low key, Devin could not stop his head from spinning. Luckily, Corey and Matthew did not attempt to contact him on Sunday, giving him the entire day to bond with his new possession. But it had not proven to be an easy day to attain privacy. His mother, a full-time homebody, had been busy in the kitchen all day continuing her apple pie baking, while his father had spent most of the day on the couch, pounding beer and watching football while sneaking off to get some pie scraps whenever he could. Even his sister, Mandy, had been home all day, spending it in her bedroom across from Devin's, FaceTiming and texting her friends. This actually proved to be beneficial for Devin, as it gave him an excuse to keep his bedroom door shut as he blasted heavy metal music. While Devin pretended to spend the day fucking around with his Lego *Millennium Falcon* (which he actually did for a bit, in order to keep up appearances), he spent most of the afternoon studying the strange item he had removed from the dead body. Devin still could not describe the sensations, but "bonding" seemed to be a fairly accurate way to explain his newly formed relationship with it. The bond grew stronger with each moment that he touched the item, but Devin still did not understand the nature of the bond and believed the only way to discover that answer lay in spending as much time with it as possible.

As Devin sat in the backseat of his mother's car, he kept his hand covering the zipped-up pocket of his dark-blue fleece jacket, which safely held the item. He could have left it tucked away in his bedroom closet but did not like the thought of having it out of reach while he sat in school. Although he could have easily (and certainly would have preferred) to ride one of his bikes for the two-mile trek to school, his mother insisted on driving both of her children. "It's good bonding time for all of us," his mother told him and Mandy when Devin had griped about it the previous week. "Besides, winter comes fast up here, so you may as well get used to spending time in my company."

But Devin knew that his mother also had another reason. White Mountain Academy housed grades six through twelve, and school started at 7:30 sharp for each grade. But as a private school, the school did not really care if the students were there or not, because, as Devin's father had stated to him and his sister about a hundred fucking times, "They already have my money, kids, so unless you wanna be grounded for life, you better be there, all day, every day." By taking the children to school every day, Devin's mother fulfilled his father's insurance policy to make sure that he got what he paid for. Devin looked at the beautiful three-story log cabin school building large enough to house at least fifty as his mother pulled into the circular driveway. While the first floor housed the gymnasium, cafeteria, and multiple fully equipped music rooms, the second floor held classes for grades six through eleven. The seniors had the top floor all to themselves, allowing them to look down on everyone from their ivory (or at least, wooden) tower. The entire freshman class consisted of one other student besides Devin and his friends, some kid named Jacob whom they did not know very well. Jacob's father worked as some sort of lawyer who made more money than all their families combined. Jacob spent his time doing whatever the fuck rich kids did. But Devin's thoughts quickly shifted from Jacob to the other freshmen when he saw Corey and Matthew standing at the top of the driveway, seemingly waiting for his arrival.

"Oh, look, Devin, your friends are waiting for you," Devin's mother said, stating the obvious. She beeped the horn and waved at them once she had stopped the car, causing them to awkwardly return the wave as they stood with blank expressions. As soon as she parked the car, she started applying eyeliner as she looked at herself in the visor mirror.

"Come on, Mom," Mandy said in an annoyed tone as she climbed out of the passenger seat.

Devin's mother did not break her locked gaze from the mirror. "Mandy," she said, "there may be some teachers or other parents nearby silently judging me. Soon enough, you'll be middle-aged just like I am now, and you'll realize how important it is for everyone to think that you're the hottest mom in town. None of the other mothers would admit this, but trust me, vanity is the center of all adult women's lives."

"Gross," Mandy said before exiting the car and slamming the door.

Devin nervously said goodbye to his mother before climbing out of the backseat. As his mother finished applying her makeup and drove away, Devin made his way toward his friends. He became nervous, wondering if they had already blabbed about their discovery in the woods or, even worse, suspected him of having removed something from the dead body. Devin clutched the outside of his jacket pocket to reassure himself that the item remained safely inside. Upon being certain, he walked with more confidence in his step. His friends stared at him with blank expressions, which made Devin uneasy.

"What's wrong?" Devin asked.

Matthew put his flannelled arm around Devin's shoulder and gently guided him away from the school's entrance.

"I'm sure your head is spinning like ours are," Matthew said after ensuring no eavesdroppers were nearby. "Me and Corey were talking and decided that we need a distraction, and the best one we came up with was to start having more band practices."

"Great!" Devin said, relieved that they were not about to report something horrible to him. "We can start practicing regularly during Creative Studies this week. Let's talk to Principal Jeffries and get permission to use the music rooms after hours on a regular basis. When can you two start staying late?"

"Oh, no," Corey said as he waved his finger an inch in front of Devin's face. "In order for us to be really into this, we need a complete band. So you know what you need to do. Get her on the DM and smash that shit already."

"Fuck you!" Devin yelled a bit louder than he intended to. "I'm not trying to smash her."

"Whatever your story is," Matthew said, "get her on board and complete the band, so we can keep our shit together. Besides, don't you think practicing your smooth talking is a good idea right now?"

Corey laughed, but Devin decided to stop the senseless argument. Although he had the bass covered and Corey and Matthew had the drums and vocals covered, respectively, the band lacked a guitar player. And Devin knew the best person for the job: Li Lee.

Devin had met Li the past July 4 during the fireworks celebration at Corcoran Pond. He just happened to be standing next to her, sipping a Mountain Dew, as the fireworks were about to start. At first, he took her as one of the regular summer tourists who had made their way into the village. But after briefly conversing with her, Devin learned that Li and some of her family had just moved to the area. Her father, a semiretired dentist, had opened an office above Mary's Market that he would work in during the spring, summer, and fall before taking the winter off to ski. Li had told Devin that she would be starting her junior year in the fall at White Mountain Academy. Devin had a crush on her from the very first moment he saw her. Her tall, athletic build and shoulder-length black hair made her really cute, magnified by the fact that she played three instruments, including guitar. And her being Chinese attracted Devin to her even more. All the other Waterville Valley residents (and even most of what Devin had seen of the rest of New Hampshire, for that matter) were Caucasian, and Li being of a different ethnicity on top of being a musician made her quite alluring. Despite the fact that his friends seemed to notice his attraction to Li (as first pointed out by Corey when Devin could not shut up about her for the entire week after he met her), he knew he needed to figure out if she would join them in their musical efforts.

Devin pulled out his iPhone and sent Li a Video Snap, asking her to meet him at lunch with a crudely drawn guitar covering his image, hoping she would understand his message. He had gotten her contact information after boldly asking for her number during their first meeting, under the guise of, "Hey, I know you're new here, so you can have me be your tour guide and stuff." Soon after walking into the school with his two companions, Devin heard his phone ping and looked down to find a texted response saying, "Okay." Devin smiled, and Corey noticed. He mouthed, "Smash! Smash!" through his smile until Matthew smacked him upside his head, knocking his baseball cap off.

Devin and his two friends made their way to the freshman classroom and joined Jacob, who had already claimed his seat. Devin would have believed the classroom to be normal, never having been in a different school system since sixth grade, if it hadn't been for his father's reaction during orientation the week before school started: "Wow, I never had this!" and "You sure are lucky; my desk always had someone else's gum and snots stuck to it!" Most schoolrooms did not look like a home, as Devin's schoolroom did. The log cabin walls showed through wherever a painting or bookshelf did not cover them, and on the left side of the classroom, a cozy fireplace waited to warm them during the cold winter months. Luscious green plants sat in pots on the floor and hung from the ceiling, and Hank, the freshman hamster, ran around on his wheel in the cage at the back of the class. The morning class schedule involved English, math, and science, and after an hour lunch, expanded religion and philosophy (which involved courses ranging from traditional Christian texts to esoteric practices to nearly everything else in between) filled the early afternoons while physical fitness and Creative Studies, a period in which students of all grades could comingle and work on art or music, ended the day.

Devin could not focus during the morning classes, continually grabbing his pocket, sometimes not even noticing until several seconds after doing so. He had continual thoughts of hunger to the point that they annoyed him and he wondered if some of that came from being nervous about having to talk to Li at lunchtime.

When lunchtime finally arrived, Devin joined Corey and Matthew in the cafeteria, a room that Devin's father had called a "restaurant" during the orientation. The school's dining room boasted an indoor and outdoor structure, circular in shape with a large spruce tree directly in the center, its top triumphantly growing through to the outside. Heating lamps surrounded each table for the cold months, and several pictures of the school's ski teams dating all the way back to its opening in 1971 lined the walls. A master chef ran the kitchen and provided the children with high-quality, organic meals along with the typical burgers and fries, which Devin and his friends chose to eat on this particular day.

Just after they sat down and began devouring their grub, Devin's phone vibrated. He had received a text that read "meet me outside," from Li. Devin ignored the laughs and gestures from Corey as he got up and made his way outside the school's entrance, where Li waited for him. She wore a long-sleeve purple shirt over black jeans and boots and had two silver necklaces on. She stood staring at her iPhone in a case seemingly made from dark-blue glitter. As Devin approached her, he could smell a gentle perfume that had hints of honey and citrus peels.

"Hey," she said, looking up at him. His heart beat faster as her soft brown eyes met his. He had not seen her since July 4, as she and her family had to return to their old residence in San Francisco in order to finish their relocation.

"What's up?" Devin asked, hoping that his hair had just the right amount of scruffiness to look cool.

"You tell me," Li said, gently chuckling. "You are the one that wanted to get together."

"Oh yeah. How did the rest of your move from San Fran go?"

"It was fine. Is this what you wanted to talk about? I gotta go eat before lunch is over."

"No problem," Devin said, nervously clutching at his jacket pocket. He saw that Li noticed him doing so, which made him even more anxious. "Hey," he said, "I remember you said that you played guitar when we chatted on the Fourth. Me and my friends are forming a band to play a song or two at the talent show in November. We need a guitar player. Are you up for it?"

"I don't know," Li answered, sneaking in glances at her phone. "What kind of music?"

"Hard rock," Devin responded, not wanting to tell her Youzed Panteez's name in the hopes that she did not Google them and find "Chinese Take-Out" as the first song that popped up, a song about ordering a Chinese escort from Craigslist. "I'll send you some songs."

"Okay. I'll check them out and let you know within a few days. Is there something wrong with your jacket?"

Devin looked down, mortified that he had grabbed at the pocket so hard that he nearly tore his jacket off.

"Fleece," Devin responded as he scratched himself in an exaggerated manner. "Makes me itchy."

"You may wanna get that checked out," Li said as she began walking inside. "Don't forget to send me the songs."

"Okay!" Devin said as she walked away. After letting her walk alone for a few moments (so that he did not appear to be chasing her down like a creepy stalker), Devin made his way back to the cafeteria to finish his lukewarm burger and fries. He ate it all and grabbed a second helping as he and his friends made small talk about their new band. Devin liked that he and his friends were being so cool with everything. It had only been two days since they had seen a dead body; not everyone could handle that sort of stress.

After lunch, Devin made his way back to the classroom. As the afternoon classes dragged on, the relentless thoughts of hunger returned. Devin did not know what to make of this; he had gone back for a second hamburger to ensure that he did not have to deal with hunger pangs for the rest of the afternoon. But as the hours crept by, the thoughts not only persisted but also became stronger. Just before the Creative Studies period started, Devin heard a clear message.

"I'm so hungry," he heard a voice say inside his head, causing him to nearly fall out of his seat.

"Who ... who is this?" Devin projected back into the thought-voice, as best as he could.

"It's me, Hank," the voice responded. *"The pellets are stale, and I'm starving."*

Devin did his best to quietly and casually turn around. Once he did, he saw Hank's beady eyes staring directly at him from within his glass cage.

CHAPTER 5

Chief Ted Hannon hastily made his way to his Trailblazer once the boys had left the office. He made sure Shane had driven away before he departed. He needed to be certain that he appeared to not be in a rush. It had been quite a while since he had needed to do an acting job such as this, so he hoped that he appeared calm enough to pull it off. After climbing into his truck, he threw his officer's hat into the passenger's seat and grabbed his cell phone before speed-dialing a number.

"Yeah, it's Ted," Chief Hannon said once the recipient of his call answered. "Are you at the shop? Okay. I'm on my way. Need to talk about something very serious, so please make sure everyone's out. In fact, close early. I'll explain everything as soon as I get there."

Ted hung up and headed down Tripoli Road before jumping on Route 49, heading toward Thornton. It would take him about ten minutes to get there, so he had plenty of time to clear his head and focus. He did not fire up a cigar, nor did he turn on the country music station, deciding instead to think about his next course of action.

Chief Ted Hannon had a deep passion for serving as the sole police officer of Waterville Valley, but his career aspirations certainly did not start that way. Born in 1962 about twenty-five miles away in Plymouth, where he was also raised, Ted initially wanted to become police chief of his much more urban hometown. He had a good childhood, born the middle child between two sisters of an ordained minister at Plymouth Congregational and a receptionist to NH Paper, Inc., the local paper mill. Leaner and more athletic in his younger years, Ted had a great high school career as an offensive tackle for Plymouth High. Although he'd had a lot of friends, had gotten good grades, and had a promising future ahead of him, Ted had one large roadblock that started in his childhood and carried over into adulthood: Samuel Reed.

Two years Ted's senior, Samuel Reed (never Sam and always

Samuel, unless one wanted to receive a beating) served as the all-star quarterback for the football team. Ted never had any interactions with Samuel outside of football, never bumping into him in the halls or running into him at social events. For some reason that Ted could never fully understand, Samuel despised him. Ted had spent hours of his younger years racking his brain in order to determine if he had ever said or done anything that deserved such a harsh reaction from Samuel or maybe if even his family ever had. But Ted could never come up with an answer. Samuel's father worked as an insurance salesman and often traveled all over New Hampshire, so he and his family were rarely, if ever, in church. Admittedly, Ted not only understood that but also wished that he had that kind of "get out of church free" pass. His father's repetitive, monotonic sermons seemed to drag on forever and pushed Ted away from God rather than bringing him closer.

Ted often wondered if Tabatha, his older sister, may have been involved with Samuel somehow. Ted questioned Tabatha repeatedly about the matter, and she always denied there being any kind of problem between the two. Ted realized that sometimes kids just didn't get along, and there were no obvious answers as to why. But things became problematic for Ted when Samuel's unexplainable hatred toward him carried over into adulthood.

Apparently, Samuel also had childhood dreams of becoming a police officer, which surprised many, including Ted. The entire school knew that Samuel had received a scholarship to the University of Maine, but a lot more people than just Ted were surprised to hear that the mister-popular, all-star quarterback instead chose to enroll in the newly opened police academy down in Concord. Samuel graduated and returned home to Plymouth to join the police force and rapidly climb its ranks. Ted did not know of any cops in Samuel's family, and there weren't any in his either, as he had developed his own passion to become an officer from watching *Adam-12* as a child. But still, it seemed strange that Samuel did not at least try playing quarterback in college first. Being tall, blond, blue-eyed, and strong, Samuel looked like a "tough guy" cop. He skipped a potential career in football and instead returned to Plymouth as a member of the police force, along with a fiancée, Jenny Milbrook, a beautiful blonde in her own right. And by the time Ted took his own turn to go through the academy and return to Plymouth as a police officer, Samuel had already made sergeant, outranking him and, even worse, giving him orders.

Thanks mostly to Samuel, the beginning of Ted's career as a police officer had been fairly unpleasant. As his superior officer, Samuel often assigned Ted the lowest or most boring of assignments—directing traffic at roadblocks, working speed traps on rural, less-traveled roads, and so on. While rookies did normally get the low-level assignments, a good cop did not usually have to endure that treatment after the first year. And if things in the department were not bad enough, in 1992, when Chief Franklin announced a sudden retirement because of undisclosed health issues, Samuel, a lieutenant at the time, became chief. Ted finally made sergeant in 1997, even with Samuel running the entire show, and just before he accepted a lieutenant role in Glendale, Arizona, in 2003, Samuel called him into his office to have a conversation that took Ted by surprise.

"Listen," Samuel had said. "I'm sure you know where Waterville Valley is. Probably have even been there before. They have a police force up there. Technically, it looks as though it's a stand-alone operation to the town's residents, but for reasons I can't get into right now, they actually report to our department in secrecy. Now, regardless of how our conversation ends, I'm going to count on the fact that you're gonna keep this information a secret, as your career depends on it. Anyway, they're an operation of about six, and their chief just accepted a job in Utah. I'm recommending you for the role, so I need to know right now: do you accept?"

Ted gladly accepted and after skipping the rest of the ranks became chief of police in Waterville Valley three weeks later.

Things started great for Ted in his new job. He had married two years prior, a beautiful woman named Eleanor, who had relocated from Massachusetts to take a job as part of the faculty at Plymouth State. They kept their modest, two-bedroom home in Plymouth, and Ted made the reasonable commute to work from there. But as soon as the next phase of his career started looking promising, things changed. In 2005, Samuel informed Ted of "necessary" budget cuts and laid off two of his officers. Additionally, they had to stop renovations of the Waterville Valley Police Department that were in progress, coincidentally finishing everything except the renovation of Ted's decades-outdated office just before ceasing the work. And just when things seemed like they could not get much worse, in 2006, Ted discovered that Eleanor had been having an affair with an ex from back home. He found out in the most unfortunate of ways when he walked in on the two in his own bed after coming home from work early one day. They agreed to divorce, and Eleanor left Ted the house without incident, as she wanted to return to Massachusetts and move on as soon as possible. This devastated Ted, as he had been both wanting and willing to start a family at this point. This devastation necessitated an immediate change, so he sold his house and bought a small, one-bedroom condo on Bear Brook Lane in Waterville Valley, deciding to live where he worked and start life anew.

True to his word, Samuel laid off more of Ted's staff, and by 2007, he had laid off the rest. So that he did not have to do everything alone, Samuel provided Ted with an assistant, Shane. Within weeks, Shane quickly proved to be a snotty, pretentious jerk, fresh out of college and somehow believing he should be in line for Ted's job. Shane held zero credentials for being a police officer, and therefore, Ted did not understand why Samuel would issue him someone so volatile and flat-out wrong for helping him manage the administrative portion of his job. Ted wondered if Shane served as Samuel's pawn and if Samuel would be using him to monitor Ted. Even the town's board of selectmen, which proved to be quite helpful at integrating Ted into the town, had been disbanded, sold to the public as an action that would offer the residents and businesses a tremendous tax break. Coincidentally enough, these positions were now absorbed by the selectmen of Plymouth, another position that Samuel held. Even though Ted's personal life and career were rapidly becoming a laughing matter, he did have one bright spot: his buddy Freddy.

Ted met Freddy soon after moving to Waterville Valley. Ted loved fishing; it served as his Zen way of getting his mind off the complications of his life. Soon after settling into his new home, he found Freddy's Bait and Tackle Shop and stocked up on gear. The two immediately bonded over fishing, and Freddy's level of enthusiasm on the hobby put his own to shame. They began fishing together at all the local rivers and took annual summer vacations to fish Lake Winnipesaukee. Once, they even journeyed to Portsmouth to fish the Atlantic. Freddy proved to be a great friend for Ted. He had a couple of years on him; a bit of a leaner, taller body; and salt-and-pepper hair with a matching mustache accompanied by glasses so thick that Freddy would certainly be blind without them. As much as they bonded over water creatures, the two had another interesting thing in common: Freddy used to work in law enforcement.

Freddy originally hailed from Philadelphia. Like Ted, he had had a childhood passion to work in law enforcement. But unlike Ted, Freddy had come from a family of police officers, his father and grandfather being retired cops. Freddy followed suit and quickly climbed the ranks, becoming a detective in Philly's Fifth District. His messy personal life of one failing marriage and a second one about to follow the same course did not stain his exceptional police record, at least until 1997. Freddy's second wife of less than a year, Beth, could not keep coke out of her nose. Freddy loved her (or at least tried to) and desperately wanted to avoid having a second marriage fail, so in order to keep their relationship intact, Freddy fed his wife's habit. Whenever he worked a case in which cocaine had been discovered, Freddy would skim just enough to keep Beth high and shut her up for a while. It worked until Freddy learned that his partner had been watching him break the law and eventually ratted him out. Freddy got fired, and his wife, unable to find a use for a man who could no longer score for her, immediately filed for divorce. And even worse, Freddy's family disowned him, naming him a disgrace to both the badge and their last name (which Ted did not even know, as Freddy never talked about his lineage). Freddy decided that he needed a change and randomly picked a spot on a map to relocate to, the Waterville Valley area. He packed his car and, knowing that his soon-to-be ex would get the house anyway, painted "Gone Fishin'" across the garage door in red paint. Freddy started a brand-new life in New Hampshire, well received by both the tourists and the locals.

Ted took a breath as he pulled into the driveway of Freddy's shop. He noticed that Freddy had cleared away any customers and had the "Closed" sign hanging authoritatively in the window. Ted hoped that nobody would notice him being there. He pulled around to the back of the shop, where the one-room shack that served as Freddy's home resided. He parked next to Freddy's old silver Bronco, the same vehicle he had used to leave Philly in his rearview mirror. Ted stared at Freddy's home after climbing out of his truck. The shack remained in a sad state of affairs, with the red paint faded to the point that the brown of the wood showed more than the color of the paint in many of the spots. Several tiles had chipped off the roof and fallen all over the ground. Ted could even see a large piece of plywood covering what would most likely be a sizable hole in the roof. Although Freddy clearly did not have much money, whatever he did have seemed to go into the bait and tackle shop, as it had fresh white paint on its walls (which Ted knew for certain, as he had helped Freddy paint it just a few months prior), and the entire building appeared to be in good shape. Ted did not know why Freddy did not just move into the shop, but how his friend chose to live his private life did not concern him. He tried the back door of the shop and grumbled to find the screen door latched shut. Ted then made his way to the front and found the door to be unlocked despite the sign indicating otherwise. He opened the door and made his way inside, causing a bell to jingle.

As soon as Ted stepped into the shop, Freddy emerged from the office behind the counter, dressed in waders, tan overalls with a matching fishing hat covered in lures, and rubber gloves that he wore while gutting fish. He quickly grabbed two fishing rods that were nearby leaning against the wall, one in each hand, and shook them rapidly as he stared at Ted from behind his thick glasses. "Freddy's ready!" he yelled with a large smile. Ted turned around to make sure nobody had pulled into the parking lot behind him, as two enormous windows on each side of the door covered the front wall of the shop, allowing anyone in the parking lot to easily see inside the store.

"I wish I was here to surprise you with a fishing adventure," Ted said somberly. "But I'm not. I really need your help with something. So please leave the gear behind but take those," Ted said as he pointed at Freddy's rubber gloves. Freddy stared at Ted through his thick glasses before putting the fishing rods down and taking off his boots, overalls, and hat.

"Whatever you need, pal," Freddy finally answered.

"Great," Ted responded. "I'm parked out back. Please, let's go, now. I need your help with something before the sun sets. I'll go back to my truck and give you a chance to lock up before you meet me outside." Freddy nodded as Ted made his way back out the front door and around the back to his truck. After a few short minutes, Freddy emerged from the back and climbed into the passenger seat after picking up Ted's hat and hanging it on the gun rack. Ted took off as rapidly as he dared to.

The two friends drove in silence. After heading back toward Waterville Valley, Ted drove to Tripoli Road and past TAC Lane. He drove until he found one of his speed trap hiding spots. Once there, he pulled off the road and parked behind the small cluster of pines and birch, where he often would sit in the summer to nail speeding tourists. He grabbed a couple of flashlights from the back of the truck and began leading Freddy through the woods. They did not have a path to follow, so he hoped that he knew his unmarked route as well as he thought he did. If he walked too far and overshot his destination, then he would reach the river and be able to guide them from the other direction, so it did not matter too much, other than for the sake of not wasting valuable daylight. "Can I ask where we're going now?" Freddy said.

"I'm trying to backdoor our way in to where Black Bear Brook starts," Ted responded. Freddy seemed content with the answer and clutched his rubber gloves in silence, so Ted proceeded forward. Within ten minutes, he found his destination.

"What is that?" Freddy said as they crested a small knoll and saw an astounding sight.

"They're called cairn stones," Ted answered. "I had no idea; I had to look them up to see what they were. If we came in from the other side of the brook, you would see that they are spaced out in order to guide whoever was meant to come here to this exact spot. Thank God the hiking tourists are all gone, as they surely would have found them."

"How did you find this?" Freddy asked.

"I was sitting in the speed trap hideout and walked into the woods to go number two when I stumbled upon it," Ted lied, not wanting to tell anyone, even Freddy, about the kids making the discovery, at least for the time being. "I need you to go inside the circle of standing stones and take a look at what's in there."

Freddy obeyed Ted's request and made his way inside the circle of cairn stones. As he stared at the ground, he put his rubber gloves on, indicating to Ted that he had seen the dead body. *I'm glad the kids told me the truth and described the scenario accurately*, Ted thought, as he had yet to see this for himself.

Freddy stepped out of the cairn circle and approached Ted. "Dead two or three days," he said after taking off his gloves and then his thick glasses in order to rub his eyes. "Animals gnawed at his stomach; rats, probably, based on the paw prints. But something, or probably someone, had killed him before then. Have you called this into Samuel yet?"

"No," Ted replied sternly. "And I'm not going to."

Freddy put his glasses back on and stared at Ted with an authoritative glare that he had never seen from him before. "Listen, Ted," Freddy said, sounding somber. "I'm gonna be honest with you. You're my best friend in this entire town, probably in the entire world. I love our fishing adventures. And I know that even though you don't talk about it much, you have disdain for your superior officer. And I'm here to tell you right here, right now, get over it and do your damned job. This is not the time to hold a grudge. This man did not die from a recreational activity; he most likely was murdered. And look at these stone pillars. Who built them? And how in the world were they stacked so high without using heavy machinery that would have been heard for miles? This is serious. You need a full police department that's staffed with detectives to investigate this."

"You're a detective," Ted answered candidly.

"No, I am not," Freddy answered sternly, still staring at Ted through the fat lenses of his glasses.

Ted reached into his pocket and pulled out a small Bible.

"What are you doing?" Freddy asked.

"I'm going to deputize you. Hold up your right hand."

"Ted," Freddy said, this time in a comforting tone as he put a hand on Ted's shoulder, "you're not a sheriff, and this is not a Hollywood movie. You can't do this. Call it in."

"Listen," Ted responded with his own authoritative tone, "I know what this looks like. I know this looks like a bitter cop who hates his boss and thinks he can become the town hero and save his career by solving the first murder case in decades. But I promise you this is not like that. There's a lot I haven't told you yet. Something's up with Samuel and how he runs the department, and honestly, I think Shane secretly reports to him, watching my every move on Samuel's behalf. I know it may not make sense; hell, I don't get it yet either. But I'm going with my gut here. And my gut says that somethin' is not right. Like you, I've grown to love this town. Can we risk lettin' them screw it up before we, the ones who truly care about this town and would do anything for it, have a chance to investigate this for ourselves?

"Look, you're right. Setting up these stones seems like an impossible task. And did you notice how still the air is here? Notice how you don't hear the birds when you're near the pillars? Notice how it feels like the entire world is somehow wrong up here? Samuel's got it out for me; of that, I'm certain. He'll eventually fire me, maybe five years from now, maybe next year. Before he does, I'd like to do one good deed by savin' this town from whatever this is. Whatever heat comes down from this, I'll take it all. Now, I need to know: are you with me?"

Freddy stared at Ted. Finally, he held up his right hand. Ted smiled and swore him in. He knew that the gesture held no legal grounds; he needed to know that a person he trusted, a person he considered a friend, would see this through with him, wherever it led.

Freddy went back into the circle of stone columns in order to further examine the body.

"What did you find?" Ted asked.

"So far, not much. His left hand is clinched. It looks like he was either making a fist to fight something off or was holding something tightly. Has anyone taken anything from here?"

"Not that I know of," Ted responded, hoping that the boys had told him the truth about not removing anything from the crime scene.

"I can examine it more, but that will take some time. There aren't too many days left before the body starts to rot. Do you have a plan for that?"

"Yeah," Ted said as he pulled out the flashlights. "We wait until dark and then drag him into the back of my truck. Then we … store him in the private freezer you have in your office."

"Terrific. What if I had refused to help you?"

"Then, as the enforcer of law in this town, I would've commandeered your freezer and done it anyway."

"Terrific," Freddy said again as the two sat on flat ground nearby and waited for darkness to descend.

CHAPTER 6

Devin began questioning his sanity on the Monday afternoon of his second week of school. A fucking hamster had just talked to him! And just in case Devin had any doubt, he watched Jacob reach into the glass cage in order to pour out some dry pellets to get Hank through the night. As soon as Jacob reached his hand inside, Hank trotted over from the other end of the cage and tried to bite Jacob's finger.

"Hey!" Jacob yelled. "This thing tried to nibble my finger!"

"Ooh," Corey said as he turned around. "Is that your bae?"

Everyone except Jacob laughed, although Devin did not laugh much, as immediately after, he heard a familiar voice in his head.

"I told you," Hank said. *"These pellets are not food. Get me some real food, or else I'm going to eat anything that ends up in this cage. Even you."* Devin put his hands over his temples and squeezed his head tightly, hoping that if he caused himself a great deal of self-inflicted pain, then maybe the voice would go away. It did not work, so Devin finally gave in, understanding that hearing an animal talk to him must have something to do with the strange object sealed tightly in his jacket pocket. Devin realized that in order to learn what this mysterious item did, he would have to allow it to reveal its true nature in a manner such as this. He wisely reasoned that if voices from living things other than humans would be filling his head, then a small, defenseless animal might be a good one to start with.

"I'll do my best to get you something that tastes good when it's my turn to take care of you next week," Devin responded through the thought-voice frequency.

"You had better," Hank said, *"or else I will eat your finger."*

Devin tried to look normal as he left school with his friends. The three decided that they would start band practice on Thursday, allowing Devin time to hopefully win over their missing bandmate.

Devin rode home with his mother and sister in a daze as he continued to process all the craziness happening in his life. Once home, he stashed his stolen item in his new hiding place, tucked in the shoebox that he then, in turn, tucked under a stack of sweats in his closet. Devin wanted to get used to perceiving the world around him with the item as well as without and preferred to keep it as far away from his observant mother as possible.

When he returned to school on Tuesday, once again stashing the item in his zipped-up fleece pocket, he endured a day similar to Monday, with constant hunger pangs lasting throughout the day, as well as messages like *"Feed me!"* and *"How would you like to be trapped in a cage for your entire life?"* Devin tried to keep himself sane while also appeasing Hank, assuring him that he would feed him well next week and even promising to let him out of the cage for a while just to shut him up. Wednesday proved to be more of the same, and Devin looked forward to after school when he would be working at the bike shop.

Devin loved working at Barry's Bike Shop. It provided him with many great opportunities, including getting a killer mountain bike for a fraction of its cost. All the tourists were gone, and the frantic summer rentals had come to an end, making the job an easy one at this time of year. The shop would only be open for one more month (even though Snow Mountain offered fat biking in the winter, the bikes were rented from there, at the base), and employees spent this time of year tightening chains, fixing gears, and logging inventory before the season's closing. Additionally, Devin had a blast working with his coworker and manager, Dale. Devin started working at the shop, his very first official, paying job, this past May, and Dale had started the month before. Barry, the shop's owner, traveled the country while buying and selling foreclosed properties and businesses as a real estate mogul. Earlier in the year, he purchased a dock installation business in Mobile, Alabama, formerly owned by Dale and his brother. Dale and Barry became fast friends, and since Dale could not say that he had a great relationship with his brother, he gladly accepted the position of managing the day-to-day business of Barry's store while taking up residence in the loft above it.

Devin found Dale to be a really cool dude. Although about the same age as Devin's parents, Dale looked much younger with his long, flowing jet-black hair blanketing the black band T-shirts he always wore. He looked as though he could step into a heavy metal band at any moment (or perhaps had just stepped out of one) and had previously told Devin that he dabbled with drums here and there, making him even cooler. Devin looked forward to spending this Wednesday afternoon with Dale, working on bikes, listening to music, and clearing his head for a while.

After Devin's mother brought him home from school, he grabbed his bike and rode to work. He liked the fall air biting at his face and sharpening his senses as he hummed along the roadside at a quick pace. When Devin passed the ice rink and gazebo and entered the paved circular area where most of the village's shops were (a few shops and restaurants were tucked into the sloping hill like cozy animal dens in the back), he noticed that the doors on each side of the bike shop were propped open. He heard noises coming from within and, upon getting closer, identified it as Slayer's *Hell Awaits* album. Dale played it nearly every week. Devin preferred more of the hard rock subgenre of metal but had begun liking the album after hearing it repeatedly.

Clashing smells of brand-new rubber tires and pungent, heavily sprayed WD-40 greeted Devin as he entered the shop. He watched Dale screw new pedals on to a bike frame that he had secured in a vice on the workbench. He wore all black (as usual) and a Slayer baseball cap backward to keep the majority of his long-flowing mane out of his face. Devin liked that idea, as his own scruffy hair had become long and unruly, so he walked over to the merchandise table and grabbed a black with white pinstripes Oakley baseball cap and put it on his head before making a note on his timesheet of his purchase. Barry gave his staff a great deal of autonomy: if you wanted something, you took it and noted it as per the honor system, so its cost could be deducted from the next payroll run. *A well-spent thirty bucks*, Devin thought. Outside of Mountain Dew and Lego box sets, Devin did not spend much money on anything anyway.

"What's up?" Dale asked Devin over the volume of music blasting out of the stereo.

"Hey," Devin half-shouted. "What do you want me to do?"

"Grab that green Diamondback leaning against the wall over there and take it out for a spin. Make sure the gears shift well and the chain feels good."

Devin followed his boss's instructions, taking the bike outside and riding it around the plaza circle before going a bit further, passing the skating rink and then returning around the back of Cochran Pond. Devin had never swum in the nice little body of water because of the ominous words of his father: "I swam in that twenty years ago once; came out with leeches all over my feet and never went back in again!" Devin vowed that next summer, he would try it for himself to see if he would fare any better. In the meantime, he enjoyed the cool fall day. A blanket of puffy gray clouds covered the sky and threatened rain but did not seem like they would actually deliver on their promise. When Devin pulled the bike up toward the left door of the shop, he found Dale sitting on the doorstep, waiting for him.

"So, what's the deal with your little Youzed Panteez concert?" Dale asked. "Do you want me to set you guys up or what?" He had offered to get the tickets and take Devin and his friends.

"We still need a couple of weeks to talk to our parents," Devin responded, hoping beyond hope that when he did finally ask his parents for permission, he would not have to explain to his mother what "DP" meant, which the band constantly sang about. "The bike is great, by the way."

"Cool. Let's sit out here for a bit and enjoy the tunes. Sounds like you've earned a five-minute break," Dale said with a half smile. Devin pulled up next to Dale while leaning the bike against the small stone wall that housed a nice little garden. Before Devin could grab a seat on the wall, Marvin, Dave's assistant at Grizzly's Bar, came running around the side of the building. He clung to two garbage bags, one in each hand, as he jumped all over like a madman.

"Slaaaayyyeeerr!" Marvin yelled at Dale while jumping around a few more times before returning back from where he came.

Devin could have sworn that he still heard Marvin yelling, "Slayer!" as he ran away but did not believe that to be possible with the music playing so loudly. Meanwhile, Dale sat on the doorstep cracking up, and Devin reasoned that Marvin had probably done this garbage bag dance before.

"Slayer will do that to ya," Dale said in his southern accent as he leaned against the door frame while continuing to laugh. "Speaking of which, aren't you guys formin' a band? How's that goin'?"

"We're just getting started," Devin answered. "I'm gonna play bass, Corey will be on drums, and Matthew will sing."

"Wise choice. I haven't heard his voice yet, but that kid looks exactly like a guy from down south named Jesse James Dupree, from this band called Jackyl. Matthew looks so much like that guy he actually could be his son. You should check 'em out; they're on the mellower side of metal, just like you like it. In fact, didn't you say that Matthew works as a lumberjack? Jackyl has a song for that! That would be a perfect song for you guys to cover!" Devin made a mental note to check that band out. "What about your guitar player?"

"I'm still working on her. We're gonna all jam tomorrow, and she'll decide from there."

Li had sent a text to Devin earlier in the day, simply saying, "I'll try a practice with you on Thurs and decide after."

Devin had sent her YouTube links to "Hangin' 'n' Bangin'" and "Three-Day Party" and appreciated that she would at least give it a shot.

"Oh?" Dale said in a devious tone. "She, huh?"

"Yeah. Her name is Li. She moved here around the time you did. You'd recognize her—she's the only Chinese girl in town. She plays a few different instruments, including guitar. She's gonna show up at practice tomorrow and see if she wants to join us. Hopefully, she does."

"If I didn't know any better," Dale said, smiling, "I'd say that you like her as more than just a bandmate." Devin's silence seemed to answer his question. "Why don't you find out if she likes you back?"

"I … I don't know how to even bring that up with her," Devin said, staring at the asphalt walkway beneath his feet. "She's the first Chinese person I've ever met. I don't know anything about her culture. I wouldn't want to do or say something that offended her. Not to mention, she's older than me."

Much to Devin's surprise, this caused Dale to laugh. He rose to his feet and put a comforting hand on Devin's shoulder.

"Listen," Dale said in a supportive tone, "believe it or not, I was in a similar situation when I was your age. My first love was a woman of a different ethnicity. Not only that, she was also older than me. And I come from a place and time where this kinda thing could be dangerous. The world has moved on quite a bit since then, and up here is nowhere near as hateful as the South can be, so you got it easy on that front. But let me give you this piece of advice. Before she's Chinese, she's a woman, and based on my experience, if a woman really likes you, you'll know it. So, find out what she likes and either give her something nice or do something cool for her. It won't take you long to realize if she feels the same way about you."

"Thanks. That girl sounds really cool. Are you two still together?"

"No," Dale said somberly, taking his hand off Devin's shoulder and stepping away. "She died a long time ago. I've never really gotten over it, to tell you the truth."

"Fuck. I'm sorry I asked."

"It's okay," Dale said as he smiled again. "We had great years together. I'm so glad I embraced each and every day with her. I learned to love again, but it took a long time. So don't waste any, boy. If you like her, don't wait, because she may not wait for you to figure yourself out."

Devin thanked Dale for his sage advice, although he wondered about its relevance. As a small-town kid, Devin had little worldly life experience, and Dale, in contrast, looked like he had just finished a tour with a best-selling metal band (other than not having any visible tattoos, which were strangely absent on a guy like him).

After a short and easy workday, Devin climbed on his bike, still wearing his new hat. Luckily, the rain never came, so his ride home would be a quick and easy trip. Or so he thought.

As Devin lazily pedaled along the side of Route 49, a now familiar sensation tickled the inside of his mind. *"You,"* the thought-voice said, seemingly out of nowhere, *"stop."* Devin slammed on his front brake a moment before squeezing the back, nearly causing him to flip over the handlebars. He panicked and looked around, wondering if Hank had somehow gotten out of his cage or if he could now talk to him from far away without being able to see him. *"Over here,"* the voice said again, and as Devin followed the mental trail, he watched as the tall grass obscuring the small bushes of the ditch off to his right abruptly shifted before an adult calico cat casually trotted out from between the long grass blades. *"I'm Frank,"* the cat told Devin through the mind-link created by the object still safely tucked away in his jacket pocket. *"Take me home with you."*

CHAPTER 7

Devin could not believe that he had talked to two different animals over a forty-eight-hour period. For the last two days, he had been listening to a food-deprived hamster complain to him (all fucking day long, for that matter) about not having enough to eat. And now, as he rode his bike home from work on this late Wednesday afternoon, a pretentious cat that quite literally jumped out of the bushes accosted him. By this point, it had become clear to Devin that the mysterious item he had stolen from a dead man created some sort of telepathic link to animals—and not just one; a cat had joined the hamster on Devin's "friend list." Devin did not know if he would be able to just stroll into his home with a pet and demand that his family keep it, as his father, who had not allowed any animal in the house as of yet, would be a roadblock. But Frank insisted, saying that his "idiot" tourist owners from Connecticut had forgotten him, and he wanted to get some warm food and shelter, even if only for a couple of nights. Devin, in turn, wanted to take Frank in, in the hopes that the cat could teach him more about the mystical leathery object that he now carried everywhere.

Devin slowed his pace in order to allow Frank to keep up. He offered to carry the feline in one hand while walking his bike in the other, but the offer caused Frank to scoff. *"Do I look incapable of walking to you?"*

Devin watched as Frank strutted next to him as if he were on parade, both his head and his tail held high in the air. *Man, cats are dicks,* Devin thought.

"I heard that," Frank said. Devin flinched, realizing that he would have to be careful with his thoughts, clearly not yet knowing as to when he thought and when he telepathically communicated.

After what had turned into a slow trek home, Devin looked at Frank as they stood in the garage. *"Are you sure you don't want me to* carry you in?" Devin asked Frank through his thoughts. *"It may look weird if you just walk into the place like you already live here."*

"Are you sure you don't want me to claw your legs until they bleed?" Frank answered.

Devin sighed. As soon as he opened the door that led to the kitchen, tantalizing smells of rotisserie chicken, bread stuffing, and steamed green beans glazed in honey danced through his nose. Devin's mother stirred, shook, and cut up her culinary masterpiece to prepare it for the evening's feast. Her hair pulled tightly back into a ponytail and cooking apron remained immaculate, as usual.

Devin noticed rapid movement out of the corner of his eye and watched as Frank ran up to his mother's legs and rubbed against them. Devin panicked, wondering if she would scream. Instead, his mother put down the spoon and smiled as she picked Frank up.

"Oh, look at you!" Devin's mother said as Frank rubbed his face against hers. "What a beautiful cat! Where did you come from?"

"So, I can't pick you up, but she can?" Devin asked Frank.

"That's exactly right," Frank responded in a seductive tone as he continued to nuzzle his mother's face.

"Gross," Devin responded as he sighed. "His name is Frank," Devin said to his mother.

"How do you know that? I don't see a tag on him."

"Yes," Frank said slyly. *"How do you know that?"*

Sweat began to bead on Devin's forehead, realizing that he still had a great deal more to learn about how to manage his newfound animal abilities.

"I mean, he looks like a Frank," Devin responded, thankful for his quick thinking.

"Actually, I look like a Chester," Frank answered. *"But my idiot owners named me Frank, and now I am used to that."*

"Oh, who is this?" Mandy asked after making her way into the kitchen. She walked up to Frank and put her face against his as he still rested comfortably in their mother's arms, apparently not caring that it might smudge her makeup. Frank purred loudly as he went back and forth, nuzzling their faces.

"He followed Devin home from work," Devin's mother answered. "Devin's calling him Frank, which seems to fit."

"Can we keep him?" Mandy asked. "His colored spots are beautiful."

"*Indeed, they are,*" Frank said to Devin as he continued to purr.

"I don't know," their mother responded. "I'd be all for it, but we need to clear it with your father first."

And that went about as well as everyone expected, because as soon as Devin's father emerged through the front door in his grease-covered mechanic's suit, they got the answer they had all anticipated.

"No, no, no!" Devin's father said before his mother could even get her full sentence out. "The last thing we need is a dirty, smelly, shedding animal running around this house. No way!"

"*Excuse me?*" Frank said so loudly in Devin's mind that it sounded like a scream. "*Who does he think he is? And look who's talking? He looks like a filthy savage!*"

"He does take some getting used to," Devin answered in semiagreement.

"*Well, let's see if he gets used to this.*" At this point, Devin's mother had let Frank go, and he roamed freely around the kitchen floor. The calico cat made his way over to Devin's father and lifted his tail. Soon after, his father grumbled and turned away in disgust.

"Oh God! Smell that?" Devin's father said. "This is exactly what I'm talking about! Disgusting!"

Devin's mother and sister chuckled while Frank casually strutted back to them.

"Come on," Devin's mother pleaded. "He is so cute! Can we at least meet in the middle on this?"

"You have until the weekend to find him another home," Devin's father said after surveying the disappointed faces in the room.

"*Sorry,*" Devin said to Frank.

"*Do not worry,*" Frank responded, "*as that gives us time to work something out.*"

Devin joined his family at the dining table to enjoy the succulent dinner that his mother had prepared. Frank spent the entire meal under the table, rubbing against Devin's mother's and sister's legs, causing them to say, "Awww," as they reached down to pet him. He occasionally rubbed against Devin's, hitting everyone in the family save for Devin's father, who grumbled about how much Frank must be shedding all over them.

After finishing dinner, Mandy touched up her makeup and took their mother's car keys before leaving for who knew where. As his mother began cleaning the kitchen and his father sat lazily in front of the television while pounding Goose Island beers, Devin reached out to Frank.

"Hey, can I talk to you upstairs?" Devin asked.

"Talk to me here," Frank responded, lying on the tiled floor of the kitchen, casually flicking his tail back and forth as he watched Devin's mother scuttle around the room. She had recently fed Frank leftover chicken scraps to go along with a small bowl of almond milk, both of which he quickly devoured. *"Nobody else seems to hear us."*

"Well," Devin responded awkwardly, *"I want to talk to you upstairs because I want to show you something. In private."*

"Fine," Frank grumbled.

Devin made his way upstairs to his bedroom, and after a few minutes, Frank elegantly strutted in. Devin shut his bedroom door and sat down on his bed.

"Can you keep a secret?" Devin asked.

"Can you? After all, you are the human talking to a cat."

"Well, that's exactly what I wanted to talk to you about. I've only been able to speak with animals for a couple of days, and it's pretty obvious as to why." After quickly glancing at his bedroom door one more time, Devin unzipped the left pocket of his fleece jacket and pulled out the dead man's mystery item. Frank jumped up on the bed and crouched slightly as he studied the object, eyeing it like he would a cornered mouse. After a few moments, Frank walked up and lightly touched his nose against it. He jumped backward after letting out a strangled meow as if he had been shocked by a jolt of static electricity.

"Powerful," Frank said after shaking the energetic charge off. *"And somewhat tainted. Typical of human magic. I do not understand why humans think they can outdo Mother Nature."*

"Magic?"

"Yes. There is a lot of human magic in the world. I only know what I can intuitively sense. And I can clearly sense that this is some sort of magical item. But I am unsure what it can do or what it is actually for."

"It must be for doing something with animals because as soon as I took it, I started hearing animals talking in my head."

"Took it from where?"

"*Never mind that,*" Devin answered, not wanting to reveal the truth of the matter just yet.

"*Are you sure that's the reason you're able to talk to me now?*"

"*How else could I be?*"

"*Humans naturally have a link to animals, and some links are stronger than others. Some humans can forge this bond quite naturally, but that seems to be a dying art, as you now turn to technology instead of speaking with Mother Nature, as we do. Regardless of all that, be careful with this item. As I said before, human magic taints easily, as it is often unnatural and created for the wrong reasons. This strange item may have very destructive capabilities that you have not yet learned of.*"

"*I will definitely keep that in mind,*" Devin responded. "*Thank you, Frank.*" Devin pondered Frank's words as he spent the rest of the night in his room. He turned his phone off so he could focus on his Lego *Millennium Falcon* but wondered if he would ever finish putting the fucking thing together. After a couple of hours, Devin drifted off to sleep, only to be awoken by Frank pushing against his face rather aggressively.

"*Open your bedroom door,*" Frank insisted.

"*Uh, why?*" Devin mumbled.

"*Because I just heard the front door shut. Now I know your sister's finally home.*"

"*Are you friggin' serious?*"

"*Oh yes,*" Frank answered deviously, flipping his tail back and forth while standing next to the bedroom door. "*I have to be honest with you: the women in this family are much more enjoyable to be around than the men.*"

"*Did you … did you just wink at me?*" Devin asked as he opened the door. Frank did not answer as he trotted out into the dimly illuminated hallway and waited at the top of the stairs for Mandy.

CHAPTER 8

Devin went to school the following morning, having had to listen to his sister talk endlessly about Frank spending the entire night at the foot of her bed. He did his best to tune her out and keep his focus on what he had lined up for the afternoon. That day during Creative Studies would be the first official band practice, if they could truly call it that. Li wanted to play with them at least once before deciding whether she would commit to the project. Devin had his bass stashed in the back of his mother's vehicle and hoped that Li remembered to bring her guitar (he resisted sending a desperation text in order to find out). Corey and Matthew had it far easier, as the practice rooms were stocked with drums, cymbals, microphones, amps, and PA systems.

Devin's morning went relatively smoothly. Hank talked incessantly about food, but after having all night to hone his skills with Frank, Devin now knew how to turn down the volume of the animals' voices in his head. Lunchtime, however, proved to be a different challenge, as Corey approached Devin and Matthew at their cafeteria table.

Covered in sweat, Corey said, "I'm losin' it, guys. It's startin' to hit me now. I don't know how much longer I can keep quiet about this."

Devin understood. Having a better understanding of what the mysterious item (which he always carried with him) did, he knew that it distracted him from what the other two had to endure. If he had not been so busy talking to animals, Devin knew that he too would be having a difficult time keeping it together. After all, they were not traipsing around in a fictional setting like *Grand Theft Auto*, where deaths occurred on a regular basis; someone had died (or had been killed) in their very own small community.

"This is a lot for all of us to handle," Devin said while glancing at Matthew, who nodded. "And you're right: we should not have to carry this shit around anymore. So, let's do this: if we don't hear from the chief by Sunday, let's go to him. Let's tell him that this shit is far above our pay grade, and it's no longer our responsibility. Everyone agree?"

Matthew and Corey nodded.

Devin reasoned that having three more days might yield him an even greater connection to the magical object before having to adapt to whatever changes talking to the chief would bring.

Finally, after a boring and annoying afternoon of classes, the time for Creative Studies had arrived. Devin, Corey, and Matthew made their way downstairs and headed for Room B, which Devin had reserved for their practice. As soon as they were down the stairs and in the hallway, they found Li waiting for them in front of the door, dressed in blue jeans, boots, and a yellow Hello Kitty T-shirt. Her guitar case rested on the floor as she leaned against the closed door while scrolling through her phone.

"Punctual!" Corey yelled from down the hall. "I like that!"

Li briefly looked up from her phone before continuing to scroll away.

"Thanks for coming," Devin said as he walked up to her, trying not to appear clumsy while dragging along his bass.

The cozy room had soft track lighting scattered throughout the ceiling, and gray egg crate soundproofing covered the rest of the ceiling and walls. Corey made his way to the brand-new silver Tama Superstar drum set accompanied by Sabian cymbals, while Matthew claimed the mic. Li knelt on the dark-gray interlocking rubber foam pieces covering the floor as she snapped open her case and pulled out a hot-pink Ibanez Vai Signature model.

"Wow, that's really nice," Devin said, truly impressed by her instrument.

"So is yours," Li responded, showing some emotion for the first time as she gazed upon his Jackson bass.

Devin smiled, probably bigger than he meant to. But just as thoughts about Li consumed his attention, Corey started crashing away on the drums and cymbals, yelling, "This shit is straight Gucci!"

Devin immediately went over to a small table where a wooden bowl full of soft earplugs sat and grabbed a pair for everyone. Li could barely get the plastic bag open fast enough before pulling aside her hair and jamming them into her ears. Everyone else followed suit before Corey counted them off and the quartet made their way through Youzed

Panteez's "Hangin' 'n' Bangin'" and "Three-Day Party." After going through the two songs for about thirty minutes, Devin raised his hand in the air to get everyone's attention before nervously looking at Li.

"Well," Devin said to Li after taking his earplugs out, "what did you think?"

"Holy shit," Li said, "you guys are terrible."

Li's honest feedback cut through the room like a sharp blade. In reality, Devin knew where the weak link resided. He had his parts down fairly well (which were not that complicated in the first place), and Matthew's voice proved to be fairly decent, but Corey pretty much sucked. Devin knew that he did not practice much, especially after finding the dead body in the woods, and therefore, he did not judge him too harshly. Devin looked at him as he huffed and puffed with his Angry Birds baseball cap flipped backward, holding his tight curls in. For the first time in a long time, Corey did not have a witty comeback and remained silent as he stared at his shoes.

"But you can get better," Li quickly responded. "You have plenty of time before the contest. You just need to practice."

"I practiced four times so far this month," Corey said, sounding defeated.

Li could not help but let out a small chuckle. "I've practiced guitar about three hours a day for the last three years."

That explains why she's nailing Randee Ryan's guitar parts with ease, even the solos, Devin thought.

"But, hey, you have to start somewhere," Li continued. "So just keep going, and you'll all get there."

"But will you get there with us?" Devin boldly asked. "You're right; we all need practice. But we also need direction. Will you help us?"

"I'll tell you what," Li said. "Let's do this again next week. Show me that you are all taking this seriously and practicing outside of band practice. If next week sounds better than today, I'll do it."

"I think that's fair," Matthew said through the microphone, and Devin agreed. Even Corey nodded.

Devin and Li began packing their instruments into their cases, while Matthew started going through the lyrics without the mic. Corey began air-drumming along to Matthew's singing. Li once again returned to burying her face in her phone.

"Shit," she said. "My dad is still working. I need to get a ride to the village."

Devin could sense the gazes of Corey and Matthew upon him without even looking.

"My mother can take you," Devin answered. "We may need to stop at my place first if she needs to check on dinner, but she can definitely drop you off. Hey, that reminds me: does your family like pets? I had a stray cat follow me into the house last night. He's clean and in good shape, just must have been forgotten by his tourist owners. My sister wanted to keep him, but my dad's not gonna allow it. Maybe you guys can take him?" Devin secretly gleamed with pride, remembering Dale's advice of trying to do nice things for Li in order to earn her affection. *Maybe this will work,* he happily thought.

"You have a cat now?" Corey interjected with a tone that clearly indicated his surprise. Corey's comment caused Devin to panic, and he nervously squeezed his secret object from outside his fleece jacket pocket.

"I'll take a look at him," Li answered, saving Devin from having to respond to Corey. "My mother still hasn't fully relocated from San Fran yet, so our poodle, MonkeyBuns, is still out there. Long story, we may not be able to bring him here, so it would be nice to replace him if that ends up being the case. I have a little eight-year-old brother who loves animals.

"MonkeyBuns?" Corey yelled from behind the drums, causing everyone to laugh. Devin appreciated how Corey's wittiness reduced the tension by several notches.

"Yeah," Li said, still laughing and flipping her hair out of her face after looking at her phone, "that's what kind of name you get from an eight-year-old."

Once the room had settled down, Devin texted his mother, telling her that she needed to give Li a ride, as he may have found an owner for Frank in addition to finding a new bandmate. Devin's mother immediately responded, telling him that it all sounded great and that she would be there soon.

Corey and Matthew made their way to their mountain bikes secured in the rack outside of the school and departed for their homes. Devin tried to make small talk with Li by asking her what kind of music she liked as they sat on a bench waiting for his mother. Li responded by saying she listened to a few metal bands, her favorite being Symphony X, a band that Devin had never heard of. "They're like Rush, only heavier and faster," Li said. "When you get better at that," Li said, pointing at Devin's bass, "maybe we can try one of their songs."

Devin nearly jumped off the bench, excited at the prospect of spending more time with his crush. He vowed to put his Lego creations aside in order to practice more regularly.

Soon after, Devin's mother pulled into the school's circular driveway. Devin stashed the two cases in the rear and offered Li the front seat while he climbed in the back, already used to being a second-class citizen from all the times of riding with Mandy. Devin's mother introduced herself to Li and made small talk during the drive, saying things like "Oh, I think I've seen you around town before" and "Oh, we'll have to check your father's dentistry out; we're all overdue for cleanings" and "Get to Mary's Market and grab one of my apple pies before they're all gone!" Devin's mother talked so much that her conversation filled the entire drive to their house.

After they had pulled into the garage, Devin grabbed his bass from the back and led the way inside. He found Frank lazily lying on the living room couch while bathing in the day's last beams of sunlight that trickled through the sheer curtains.

"Oh, he's cute!" Li said. Devin's heart fluttered upon seeing Li inside his house. Li pulled out her phone and said, "I'm gonna take a picture of him and send it to my father."

"When was the last time someone wanted to take your picture?" Frank asked Devin as he stretched his legs out and began approaching Li.

"It never ends with you, does it?" Devin said as he watched Li stroke Frank's back and tail.

"Oh, I see. You like her. You like her, and you wish that she would touch you like this."

"Fuck off," Devin retorted.

"My dad already texted me back," Li said, breaking up the telepathic argument. "He said no problem. If you're willing to bring him over tomorrow night, my dad will also have you for dinner." Fluttering sensations once again raced through Devin's stomach as Li stared at him instead of his mother.

"Devin would love to," Devin's mother responded on his behalf. "I can take him and Frank—that's the cat's name, by the way—over at dinnertime and pick him up when you guys are done."

Li nodded and waved goodbye to Devin before following his mother back to the car.

"I believe a thank you is in order," Frank said to Devin, and Devin knew what he meant: if it hadn't been for Frank, Devin wouldn't have been about to embark on what could potentially, under a very loose definition, be considered a date.

"You know what?" Devin said to Frank. *"You're actually right. Thank you."* He smiled as he ran upstairs with his bass in order to begin an evening of heavy practice.

CHAPTER 9

Devin eagerly counted down the hours until he would be at Li's house. Frank seemed indifferent, once again spending the night at the foot of Mandy's bed. *"I may as well get one more night in,"* Frank told Devin through their telepathic mind link, to which Devin did not respond. Instead, he practiced his bass until he fell asleep, meticulously going through the Youzed Panteez songs that the band had played during the afternoon.

The following day, Devin had a difficult time concentrating at school, as this particular Friday offered several reasons for his thoughts to be all over the place. Hank the hamster incessantly demanded that Devin give him kale or romaine lettuce. Devin promised Hank special treats during his time to take care of him the following week and then did his best to block the animal's thoughts from his head. When the time to feed his own face had arrived, Devin joined Corey and Matthew in the cafeteria as they ate pork chops stuffed with apple slices. Devin told the two that he would be going to dinner at Li's house in order to give her the stray cat and mentioned that he would try to get a better read on her regarding her commitment to the band. Much to his surprise, Corey did not respond with a wise-ass remark, which concerned Devin. He once again raised the agreed-upon course of action, that they would find Chief Hannon Sunday afternoon and tell him that they had all had enough with his secret pact. Devin quickly began to like the plan. The more people who knew about the dead body, the greater the chance that someone else could have stolen the strange magical item from it, should that item ever be known to exist in the first place.

Once back home, Devin and his mother took a cardboard box from the garage and used it to transport Frank before heading to Li's. Frank resisted the idea at first, telling Devin, *"Don't you dare close the top and seal me in.*" Devin made a deal with him; he would keep the box open and sit in the backseat with him, appearing to comfort the cat while simultaneously hiding the fact from his mother that he could talk to Frank. Frank accepted his proposal and promised that he would stay in the box. Li's father would be scooting down from his office to Grizzly's Bar to grab a couple of pepperoni pizzas. Devin's mother would pick Devin up (and Frank, if necessary) after dinner. Devin gave her the directions to Li's house, having gotten a text from Li earlier in the day with her address. He knew the sizable log cabin on top of a big hill off Route 49 fairly well but had not realized that Li's family had bought it. The house could be seen from Waterville Valley Village down below, and Devin knew that the families who lived on top of the big hills were the families with money.

"Wow, this is nice!" Devin's mother said as she turned her car off the road and onto the open-gated driveway. Crushed gravel covered the entire driveway (which looked more like a small road because of its length and width) and thick trees that had lost their leaves for the fall season surrounded it as if in a protective manner. After ascending several hundred feet, the vehicle reached the log cabin home, easily twice the size of Devin's. A large welcome mat and a dangling "Home Is Where the Heart Is" handcrafted sign painted in blue greeted them at the front door. He heard loud heavy metal coming from inside, which ceased after his mother rang the doorbell. After a brief pause accompanied by shuffling footsteps, the door opened, revealing Li, dressed in sweatpants and a black tank top covered by a white skull.

"Come in," Li said. She immediately smiled upon seeing Frank.

The feline jumped out of the box and started trotting around the home as if he owned the place. Somewhat envious, Devin studied his surroundings. The front door opened directly into the living room, which had brown leather couches and chairs surrounding an enormous, flat-screen television mounted on the wall. A large picture window on the other side of the room had a partial view of the valley down below.

"This is much nicer than your house," Frank told Devin bluntly.

"No shit," Devin responded.

A small boy dressed in a one-piece dark-blue pajama suit jumped off one of the chairs and begin making his way toward Frank with a big smile.

"This is my little brother, Cheng," Li said.

53

"Hi, Cheng," Devin said while making his way over to him. "This is Frank. He's a calico cat."

"Spot!" Cheng yelled while rapidly patting Frank over his spotted sides. "He's Spot!"

"You hear that, Frank?" Devin asked, laughing through his thought connection to the cat. *"Your name is Spot now."*

"Don't worry," Frank responded. *"He'll call me Frank soon enough."*

"How do you know that?"

"Because you did, didn't you?"

Devin heard another vehicle pull up into the driveway before the front door opened, revealing a middle-aged Asian man slightly taller than Li, carrying two boxes of pizza.

"Hello. I'm Bolin," he said while making a beeline for Devin's mother in order to shake her hand.

"Hi. I'm Emily," she responded. "I was just dropping off my son and our newfound cat here. I'll come back in a couple of hours to pick him up—and the cat as well if he doesn't work out."

"Oh, I can see my kids have already taken a liking to the cat," Bolin said with a smile. His white collared dentist's jacket displayed his name on his left breast pocket with a dark-blue patch. "Why make two trips up and down our big hill? Stay for dinner!"

"Well, I guess I can have my husband and daughter heat up the lasagna for themselves," she responded as she pulled out her phone to send a text.

"Don't be upset," Frank told Devin. *"Your mother can keep Dad busy, which will give you some time to talk to Li."*

Devin agreed with the cat, and as they all sat down to pizza slices and Coke at a beautiful wooden dining room table, Devin proceeded to make small talk with Li, mostly about playing guitar. Devin did his best to keep up, as Li knew things even about the bass guitar that he did not know. Once everyone filled up on pizza and soda, Li's father spoke.

"Li, why don't you show your friend the Zen garden out back before it gets dark?" he said. "This will give me and his mother a chance to finish negotiating the deal for our new pet."

"Sure," Li responded nonchalantly to Devin. "Let's go."

The two made their way across the house and out through a sliding glass door that led to the backyard. Li grabbed a guitar case leaning against the wall on her way out, making Devin regret that he did not even think of bringing his bass with him. After shutting the sliding door behind them and taking a brief stroll, they arrived at a bench that overlooked a small reflecting pool with a three-foot statue of a religious icon that Devin had seen before but could not identify.

"This is cool," Devin said. "So peaceful. Do you mind if I take a pic?"

"I don't care," Li responded as she unsnapped her guitar case and began scrolling through her iTunes. Devin trotted around to the side of the pool in order to get a good angle for a photo while also ensuring that Li would at least partially be in it. He snapped a couple and then stopped in order to not look suspicious. The pics were almost portrait ready, as the shades of the yellow and red dead leaves on the ground added a warmth to the serenity of the pool (not to mention, Li looked stunning as she held her guitar in the back corner of the pic). Satisfied with his cleverness, Devin returned to take a seat on the bench and watched as Li played a really fast song on her phone. She picked along to it on her unplugged Ibanez, keeping up with it as easily as if she had written the song herself. "This is 'Iconoclast' by Symphony X," Li said.

"That sounds crazy!" Devin said.

"Well, you better get used to it. If you want me to stick around in your band, I can't play that easy shit all the time. I'll tell you what. If you're really serious, I'll teach you the bass lines to some of my kind of music. I'll show you how to play it, and I'll show you what you need to practice in order to get better at it."

"I'd say that's a deal," Devin said with a smile, and his smile became even bigger once he noticed that, for the first time, she smiled at him in response. The two stayed outside for ten more minutes until darkness surrounded them and Devin's mother came out to tell him that they needed to go.

"Everything's all set here," his mother said to him after everyone had made their way back inside. "We've found a good home for Frank. Now it's time for us to get home, so I can make sure your father didn't burn the house down while trying to use the damned microwave."

"*You know,*" Frank said to Devin, "*if you come see me, you get to see her as well.*"

"*I really like the sound of that,*" Devin said with a smile as he reached down to pet Frank one last time before leaving.

CHAPTER 10

Devin listened to his mother fill in some gaps about Li on the drive home from dinner after she told him that her father insisted on paying a hundred dollars for a recently homeless cat. Devin realized that his mother's nosiness benefited him greatly, as the more he learned about Li and her family, the more meaningful conversations he could have with her. Apparently, Li's mother had not yet been able to complete the move to New Hampshire before wrapping up business for her important tech job, which created tension in the household. As Devin listened to his mother talk about Li's family as well as her happiness at Frank finding a good home, he secretly sneaked in a few glances at Li's pic that he had taken while they hung out in her backyard. He smiled as he thought of Frank's suggestion: Devin could say that he needed to visit because he missed the cat, which would create a scenario of potentially spending more time with Li at her house. Devin reasoned he may even be able to take some bass lessons out back in the Zen garden after successfully negotiating a reason to get back inside her house.

Devin spent all day Saturday fooling around on his bass. He had even reached out to Li via text for his first lesson, asking for some tips on what to work on during a long practice. Li responded with a text that read, "Ditch the pick and play with your fingers!" Devin put his phone down and took a breath after leaning back. *That's gonna be some work*, he thought. He began playing scales throughout the afternoon and generated new calluses on his fingers. Devin hated to admit it, but he already missed Frank. Besides the fact that talking to Frank taught him a great deal about the mysterious object that he had stolen from the dead man in the woods, Devin had grown to like the calico cat, as it gave him someone to talk to in the house other than his annoying family.

When Sunday morning arrived, he texted Corey and Matthew

in order to make sure they were still on board with the plan. They both responded that they were and they were ready to move forward. After a simple lunch of a turkey sandwich and chips, Devin put on a black-and-gray Nike tracksuit (while of course sealing up the magical item in his left pocket, as he always did), grabbed his mountain bike, and headed for the top of TAC Lane, where they would meet before heading to the station.

Devin let the cool air invigorate him as he rode. The autumn sun added just enough warmth to make the breeze enjoyable. The valley did not have many weeks left before a brief fall would turn into a long winter, which would bring even more tourists than the summer did, as skiers from down south invaded in large quantities. Devin could not wait to come clean with the chief and push the burden back on him. Finally, with Li all but fully committed, the band had taken shape. Even Corey had gotten into it, texting Devin the day before that his mother would not only allow him to get a drum set but would also let him play it in the garage. Devin responded that he would ask if his coworker, Dale, would be willing to give him lessons, which he hoped would make Corey even more committed. And although he would not yet admit it, Devin eagerly awaited spending more alone time with Li as soon as possible.

Once at the top of TAC Lane, Devin found Corey and Matthew waiting. Corey wore his dark, curly hair slicked back without his usual baseball cap, surprising Devin. Additionally, he wore black jeans with a maroon, button-up, collared shirt, neatly tucked in. Matthew, dressed in his normal flannel, jeans, and work boots, saw Devin checking Corey out and shrugged his shoulders as his long hair gently blew in the wind.

"He wants Hannon to take us seriously," Matthew said.

"This is going to be good for us," Devin said. "The school year is underway, and our band is off to a great start. We'll tell Chief Hannon that we're done keeping his secret, and also that we're not gonna be the ones who discovered the body. Don't worry, Corey—the chief knows you did, and that's what counts. But we don't need the locals asking us questions all fucking school year about this. To the general public, we will not know any more than they do. We never saw the body or the crime scene for ourselves. Today, we wipe our hands clean. We're fucking done, and we're moving on. Agreed?" Corey and Matthew nodded.

Once in the police station parking lot, the gang saw Shane's blue Honda Accord but not the chief's truck. Devin grimaced, knowing that they would need to talk to Shane in order to find out when the chief would be back in the office. As Devin thought of what to say to Chief Hannon's jerk-off assistant, the three pulled their bikes up to the bike rack and walked inside the station.

The chief's door, normally left open for Shane while the chief ran around town, remained shut. Shane's brown eyes immediately locked onto the trio. Devin wondered why he wore jeans and a long-sleeve T-shirt instead of his normal soft-collared police shirt and khakis.

"What do you fucksticks want?" Shane asked as he rose from his seat and pointed at them with his hunting dagger.

"Whoa!" Corey said while throwing his arms up in a submissive motion. "Language, Shane! Language! And watch where you point that thing!"

"I don't have time for you little twats today," Shane said.

Devin noticed that he almost shook as he spoke to them.

"That's fine," Devin said calmly. "We're just here to have a brief chat with the chief. Where is he?"

"Who the fuck knows?" Shane said as he threw a stack of papers from his desk in the direction of the boys. "We're on call to Plymouth."

"So he won't be back today?" Devin asked. "Is he sick or something?"

"Why don't you ask him when you see him?" Shane said angrily. "Because you probably know more than I do. He left me a note saying he would be out of the office for a while. That's all that fucking asshole said."

"When was that?" Matthew asked.

"Four fucking days ago," Shane said.

Devin looked at Corey and Matthew, who shared the same silent question through their frantic gazes with him: *"Where the fuck did Chief Hannon go?"*

CHAPTER 11

Ted formulated a plan as he drove away from Freddy's store Saturday night, over a week before the boys would seek him out at his office (unknown to him). Immediately, they had gotten a lead: as they were placing the dead man's body into the back of Ted's police truck, Freddy noticed something protruding from the elastic band of his sweatpants. He grabbed it and pulled out a small key ring with a green rubber tag that read "Sly Fox Lodge." They both smiled, knowing where the man had most certainly been staying during his time in Waterville Valley. The town had several logging trails left over from its old days, and after the village had been designed to house tourists instead of loggers and farmers, the old pathways were used to further expand the tourist housing. In addition to an athletic trail equipped with an obstacle course, several condos and town houses were built on the obscure paths for the adventurous flatlanders who wanted to pretend they were big-time woodsmen and stay out of sight of civilization (as some were remote enough that they did not even have driveways connecting to them, and the guests would need to park in the village and trek out to their rooms from there). Some of the town houses were large, up to four bedrooms, which allowed those with big families to have space from each other that they would not have in two connected hotel rooms. Those who rented from the Sly Fox Lodge had money, as those rentals were far from cheap. And since Ted and Freddy knew that the man had been staying in one of the higher-end resorts, they also knew that he had the money to pay for it.

Before returning home, Ted swung by TAC Lane to drop by the office. Once surveying the parking lot for Shane's car, Ted discreetly locked himself inside the station. While on call during his required three nights a week, he would be contacted after any local 911 calls were made. On off nights, such as this, the emergency calls were instead routed to Samuel's police department in Plymouth. The Plymouth cops did not normally come to Waterville Valley save for a true emergency (which rarely ever happened, and even when they did, Samuel would usually "persuade" Ted to handle it). Still, the department had keys to Ted's facilities, and he did not want to take a chance of being spotted on a rare occasion in which Samuel's soldiers descended into his wooded community. Therefore, Ted proceeded in the relative dimness of the sparse nighttime security lights that kept the office just bright enough to ward off bored teenagers who thought it might be cool to break into a police station. After sneaking into his own office, Ted uncovered his trusted Rolodex atop his messy desk.

Ted resisted the age of technology as much as possible. He had a cell phone but only kept important local contacts in it. He refused to put every friggin' number of every friggin' person he had ever friggin' met in his entire life in it and, therefore, needed his Rolodex that night. As with several of the wealthier establishments of Waterville Valley, a corporate bigwig from Needham, Massachusetts, named Jay owned the Sly Fox Lodge. Jay rarely even came up to the valley, instead utilizing local contractors and handymen to take care of the smaller issues. Jay had Milly, the old grump who worked at the post office, hand out the keys to the guests of the lodge, as many were staying long enough to want a PO box to forward their mail to for the summer. Jay had registration set up through the website, which would trigger an email to Milly, telling her what room key to have ready and taking copies of credit cards to hold on to in case of damages and so on. Jay paid Milly under the table for her not-so-legal assistance. Ted turned a blind eye, considering it a federal matter and therefore none of his business. And the very nosy and very gabby Milly loved the arrangement. In fact, Ted knew about the whole ordeal because Milly talked to anyone and everyone about it, even him. He knew he needed to contact Jay directly for this matter in order to avoid her small-town antics.

"Hey, Jay, this is Ted, chief of Waterville Valley Police," Ted began his message after reaching Jay's voice mail. "Listen, I got one of your keys in my possession. Looks like you had a tourist in unit 137 that may have been up to some trouble. You know Freddy, who owns the bait and tackle shop? He said that some guy had come in and tried to steal some expensive fishing gear. Freddy chased him off, and in his hasty exit, the guy dropped your room key in Freddy's parking lot.

Freddy said that he had seen the guy in the shop earlier in the week, possibly scoping the place. So tomorrow, I'm gonna take Freddy to this guy's room and, under my supervision, let him see if the guy stashed any stolen items there. When you get a chance, please let me know the name of the guy you had in that room. Oh, and the most important thing here: I need to be very careful before officially accusing this guy of attempted theft and such. Until I get my own facts straight, I need to keep this away from town gossip, so do me a favor. Check this guy's info yourself and don't tell Milly. Thanks, buddy."

By the time Ted got home, he had received a text from Jay, who told him that he would have his information by tomorrow while keeping Milly in the dark. Content that things were going in the right direction, Ted went to sleep.

Shane's usual grumpy self greeted Ted when he went to work Sunday morning. He had been going through seemingly random papers on his desk and made no attempt to hide the fact that he had printed out requirements by the state of Maine to participate in their police academy. *Good,* Ted thought as he made his way into his office. *Please, Shane, for the love of God, leave for another job.* Out of spite, as soon as Ted opened the door of his office, he walked over to the wall and pressed the button to start the "Don't Worry Be Happy" singing fish, causing it to flail and gyrate as the song played. Just as he did when the boys had come into his office the day before, Ted pretended he did it for his own amusement. But in reality, he despised it as much as everyone else. Ted just liked hearing Shane grumble every time it played, claiming a small victory with his misery.

Just after lunchtime, Ted grabbed his police hat and told Shane that he would be going out on patrol. Instead, Ted made his way directly to Freddy's fishing shop and picked him up, as per the agreed-upon time. Ted had texted Freddy after messaging Jay the night before, telling him that they were going to investigate their lead. As soon as Ted pulled into Freddy's driveway, he emerged from his shed behind the shop, wearing a brown flannel shirt, blue jeans, and Timberland boots. He had also switched out his normal thick glasses for a similar pair that tinted in the sunlight.

Upon jumping into the passenger seat, Freddy looked at Ted from behind his tinted glasses. "It's secure," Freddy said, and Ted knew exactly what that meant: the corpse that the duo had stolen from the crime scene remained safely tucked away in Freddy's locked freezer. Ted headed out, and the two rode in silence.

After leaving Freddy's driveway, Ted headed back to his speed trap location off Tripoli Road and parked behind the patch of trees. But instead of heading for Black Bear Brook, they took a hard right to meet up with the old logging trail that led to Sly Fox Lodge. They could have taken a much more direct route, walking the trail that crossed the Mad River from behind the village, but Ted wanted to avoid all human contact, if possible. Jay had also confirmed in his text that he had no other guests, so they were not expecting to run into anyone else (unless, of course, this man had company in the room, which they had prepared for, as well).

Ted made sure to take an exaggerated angle to the right as they began their trek toward the lodge, in hopes of avoiding the sight of those strange stone structures. Being near them had made Ted uneasy, and trying to figure out how they could have possibly been constructed, as some in the circle towered over six feet, disturbed him more than learning about the dead body had. The cool, cloudy day did not deliver rain, so traversing the short patch of woods proved to be relatively easy for the two (far easier than stumbling around at dusk while dragging a dead body along the night before had proven to be). Soon enough, they were on the old logging trail and then at the Sly Fox Lodge, which comprised four buildings of two town houses each. They were arranged by size, starting at the small, one-bedroom units closest to the trail and going up to two-story, four-bedroom units that were tucked further back into the woods.

Ted pulled out the key ring with the green rubber tag that identified the room as 137 and wondered why the rooms were not instead numbered one through eight. The duo approached the very first one farthest to the right, which the deceased had been staying in. It shared a building with unit 245, and both units combined as part of a modern-looking structure painted in sandy brown, with the door of 137 painted in red, while the neighboring unit's door had been painted in blue. Two owls carved from wood surrounded this unit as if keeping watch, while two wooden eagles that were most likely crafted by the same person flanked the other door. Ted issued three swift but powerful knocks before speaking.

"Waterville Valley chief of police!" Ted said. "Please come to the door and identify yourself!" Ted did this two more times and only received the gentle breeze shuffling through the dead leaves along with the slow but steady gurgling of the nearby Mad River as a response.

Ted and Freddy exchanged one final look before Ted put the key in the front door and opened it. After pushing the door open, Ted put his right hand on his trusted Glock 22 as he unsnapped the latch of its holster. He had only fired his weapon three times in the line of duty in Waterville Valley, and each time had been in order to scare a bear away from civilians in the village. Still, he would draw it now, if duty required.

A subtle staleness washed over Ted, the kind of dead air contained in a room that had not been disturbed for at least a few days. Freddy shut the door behind them before they made their way down the steps of the small hallway and into the living room. Ted drew his gun and made sure that the bedroom and bathroom were both clear before meeting up with Freddy in the living room. The walls of the living room were painted maroon, similar to the dark red of the front door, and were covered with paintings of fish jumping in a river and skiers traversing snowy slopes. Above the fireplace in the corner rested the head of an eight-point buck, whose glassy eyes seemingly kept watch over the room's activities or lack thereof. Freddy took a seat on the light-blue sofa that rested on the beige carpet behind the birch coffee table that had been unevenly carved out of a tree trunk. He stared directly down at the table, and Ted followed his gaze to a black leather wallet sitting right in the open.

"That was easy," Freddy said, allowing Ted to pick it up, trying to keep his fingerprints to a minimum at the scene. Ted flipped it opened and found a license.

"Says his name is Daniel Raggel, and he lives in New York City," Ted reported, "but there's no street address listed."

As he wondered how he could have a license without an address printed on it, Ted kept flipping through the wallet and found something else of great interest. He pulled out a business card and put it on the coffee table for Freddy to investigate. Freddy took off his thick glasses and rubbed his eyes before looking at a card that read: "Talandoor's Exquisite Antiques. Daniel Raggel: Owner. East 40th Street, Midtown Manhattan."

"Well, Detective," Ted asked Freddy, "what are you thinking?"

"I have to be honest," Freddy said as he went into the bedroom and opened the closet door before heading to the kitchen, "even though there isn't a lot of stuff here, this place clearly has the feel that someone else was here. Look at this." Freddy pointed to bottles and cans on the counter. "There are a couple of empty bottles of Seagram's here to go along with several empty 7-Up cans. Either this guy was a very heavy drinker, or else he had help. Another thing: in the bedroom closet, what few clothes Daniel hung up in there are all shoved to one side, as if he had been sharing it with someone." Freddy grabbed a pad of Sly Fox Lodge paper sitting upon the counter. After pulling a pen out from the chest pocket of his shirt, Freddy began shading the first page of the pad as if working in a coloring book. When he finished, Freddy put the pen back in his pocket and smiled before holding the pad of paper up for Ted to examine. Ted saw in between the dark shades of blue were words in a lighter shade imprinted from the previous piece of paper: "You have gone too far, Daniel. I can no longer be a part of this. I hope you find peace before it is too late. Tessa."

"That explains why I haven't seen a car with New York plates just sitting around in the village parking lot," Ted said. "She may have been just mad enough to take their only vehicle and abandon him."

Just as Ted finished speaking, he received a text. "It's from Jay," Ted said to Freddy, "the owner of the lodge. He just confirmed Daniel Raggel as the name. But he also said his name is the only name listed for the room and that Daniel had refused to provide a billing address when he registered." Ted wrote a "thank you" text back to Jay before putting his phone away, wondering why this Daniel Raggel remained so mysterious. Then again, with the cairn stones piled up just down over yonder, Ted admitted that nothing should surprise him at this point.

"So," Freddy said, "we have a confirmed name, a New York City license, and a Midtown Manhattan address from the business card—and most likely, a love interest as well. Now, we have gone far beyond tainting a crime scene. We are undergoing endeavors that could put us both in prison. So, as I did yesterday, let me once again clearly ask: do you want to turn this over to Plymouth before it's too late?"

"Did you ever see the movie *Groundhog Day*?" Ted asked. Freddy nodded. "Remember how Bill Murray's character kept repeating the same day, knowing that he had to figure out what was wrong so he could make the necessary changes in order to set his life back on course again? Well, I know this may sound crazy, but this is my personal *Groundhog Day*. No, I'm not waking up repeating the same literal day, but there is something I am repeating, over and over, that just is not right. I don't know how to explain it, but all I can tell you is that this whole business with Samuel and Shane just feels wrong. With my dad being a minister and all, I went through the motions of church but never fully connected to it. I felt like it was forced down my throat on behalf of my father. Well, something about this makes me feel like it's my personal wake-up call from God. I feel like the angels have given me a job to do, and along with your help, I need to see it through, even at the risk of persecution. So, yes, I accept the risk and dangers, and I am more than happy to relieve you from your deputy duties. So, let me turn the tables and ask you: are you still with me in this?"

Freddy took off his glasses and used his shirt to clean them after thoroughly rubbing his eyes. "Well," he said with a sly smile, "I think there's only one choice for us: let's go home and pack because we're heading for the Big Apple!"

PART II
THE CITY

CHAPTER 12

Ted and Freddy agreed to depart for New York City on Wednesday. That gave Ted a couple of days to keep an eye on local police business in case anyone else surfaced with information on a dead man mysteriously appearing in their woods. Luckily, most locals avoided Black Bear Brook, as its dryness made it useless for fishing and also because no hiking trail existed to connect through to another. Unless there were more nosy kids, Ted did not expect anyone else to stumble upon the mystical cairn stones, which would buy him time to try to solve the mystery. Freddy, in turn, also wanted a couple of days to prepare, stating that he would be stocking up on supplies and getting ready for what he referred to as an "urban undercover mission."

Monday and Tuesday proved to be relatively quiet in regard to police duties, and Ted took advantage of the lull, avoiding Shane as much as possible. After work hours on Tuesday, he went into the station just as he had done a few nights before, but this time, he left a note for Shane, reading: "Out of town for a bit because of a personal emergency. Call Plymouth with any problems. Chief Hannon."

After a restless night's sleep, Ted made his way to Freddy's an hour before dawn. He drove his truck behind the bait and tackle shop and covered it with a camouflage tarp that Freddy had on hand. They had agreed to take Freddy's old truck, although it took some convincing by Freddy to win Ted over on the matter.

"It's got two hundred thousand miles on it and is still going strong," Freddy had texted to Ted. "Also, just got an oil change and tune-up at Tim's last month. She's good to go."

Reluctantly, Ted had agreed. He certainly did not want to drive his vehicle, which had no chance of blending in. Additionally, neither one of them wanted to go to the nearest rental place in Plymouth, where they would not only create a paper trail but also risk running into

Samuel or one of his badge-wearing henchmen. In the end, Freddy's twenty-year-old vehicle made the most sense, and Ted would just have to hope that they would not break down at any point along the way.

Ted and Freddy were on the road by six. Freddy had the back of the Bronco well stocked with beef jerky packs, bottled water, and 5-Hour Energy drinks. If the drive went perfectly, it would take just over five hours. But the two knew that it would be far from that, as they would be running into rush-hour traffic as they crossed through several heavily populated areas. They were both okay with this, as they planned on giving themselves the rest of the week for this undercover operation, with the worst-case scenario putting them in the heart of New York City by Wednesday evening and having them returning home on Sunday. Ted reasoned that if they could not find any additional information within three-plus days, then they would return to New Hampshire and he would consider turning all the information over to Samuel and the Plymouth Police Department. Ted did not allow himself much time to think about that, as turning the case over to Samuel would be the least of his problems under that circumstance; he would most likely lose his job and possibly face prison time for hampering and tampering with a murder case. If it came to this, they would spend the drive back on Sunday formulating an excuse that they could present Samuel with, in hopes of, at the very least, avoiding jail time. Ted decided to focus on the present. He really did believe what he told Freddy before their departure. He had never been quite comfortable with himself regarding his disdain for God and the church based on his father gently but insistently shoving it down his throat as a child. The way this case had begun to unfold made Ted believe he could right this potential wrong with his Maker. As such, he would do everything he could to not return home empty-handed.

The drive through New Hampshire proved to be pretty smooth. They encountered a minor accident in New Hampton, but it did not slow down rural traffic much. After two hours of driving put them into Massachusetts, they hit rush-hour traffic on Route 495. Ted immediately became overwhelmed by memories of his ex-wife, Eleanor, who had returned to her native state after their divorce. Ted began pouring through the scenarios of the affair that she had, wondering if he could have done anything differently to stop her from going down the path that ultimately ended their marriage. Depression overcame him as he thought about how at his current age, he might not find another companion—ever again. Ted needed to stop himself from continuing to spiral down a never-ending hole, so he grabbed an energy drink and some beef jerky and turned up the satellite radio that he had connected to Freddy's ancient stereo system by way of an auxiliary cord and enjoyed some country classics.

As painful as the drive across the Bay State proved to be, entering Connecticut proved to be even worse. More accidents and traffic jams severely slowed their commute, so Ted and Freddy stopped at a rest area on the outskirts of Bridgeport to fill up on gas and relieve themselves. Freddy also grabbed some salted peanuts to complement the beef jerky, and then the two were back on the road again. They were heading for a Holiday Inn on Eighth Street, which would put them just over a mile away from the location of the dead man's antique shop. They planned on stashing Freddy's truck in a parking garage around the corner from the hotel, as they would most likely be spending all their time on foot, in cabs, or, as a last resort, on the subway. After coming to a near stop because of a car fire on Hutchinson River Parkway, they finally reached the parking garage just after three, making their total commute a nine-hour drive. Ted covered the parking fee, and Freddy pulled into a spot before pulling out a yellow steering wheel lock from the backseat to accompany the alarm system. "Pack all the food and water into our bags," Freddy told Ted. "The parking attendant isn't gonna do squat for us, so let's not give any potential thieves lurking about an easy grab. Take your satellite radio too."

Ted did as Freddy advised and packed everything that Freddy did not grab into his large duffel bag, which only had a few different outfits and some body-care necessities. Once they had everything and Freddy had secured his vehicle, they made their way to the Holiday Inn.

Ted checked them into their twelfth-floor two-bed room. The blandness of their room underwhelmed him, which, thanks to the shade of red painted on the walls, looked like a McDonald's dining area with two beds stuck haphazardly in the middle. But Ted quickly got over it and returned his focus to the important reason they had traveled all the way to the big city for.

"Freddy," Ted said to his companion, who rested his thick glasses on the bathroom sink counter as he brushed his teeth, "we have a couple of hours of daylight left. We could probably be there in a half hour, at the latest. I'd like to do some surveillance before daylight ends."

"Let me see what you brought for clothes," Freddy requested.

Ted pulled out his jeans, overalls, flannel shirts, and the one long-sleeve Bass Pro Shop T-shirt that he had packed.

"I suppose the T-shirt is good, but I'm not crazy about the flannel," Freddy said as he studied Ted's clothing. "We have to assume the worst; we have to assume that Tessa, or whoever else we may find, knows that someone is looking for her. So we should buy some of the tacky tourist clothing in the lobby because it would be much better if we looked like dumb tourists instead of really dumb country cops."

Ted agreed with his logic, so after swapping out his flannel shirt for the fishing T-shirt, and with Freddy donning a fresh pair of jeans to go with a yellow John Deere T-shirt, the two made their way to the lobby to go shopping. Ted bought himself a white "I Love NY" T-shirt with a heart symbol in place of the word "Love" to go along with a pair of black ten-dollar sunglasses. He bought Freddy a white-and-black baseball cap with a picture of the Statue of Liberty centered upon it. Ted bought them a few more New York shirts (although he refused to buy any Yankees clothing, being a lifelong Red Sox fan) so that they could rotate their tourist outfits throughout the week. After Freddy put on his baseball cap, covering his salt-and-pepper hair while making his salt-and-pepper mustache stand out even more prominently, the pair made their way out into the Manhattan borough of New York City.

Once outside and on Eighth Street, it took Ted less than a minute to become overwhelmed. Ted had been to Boston twice, once to go to the Boston Museum of Science and again to go to a funeral of an uncle he never knew. Both times were as a teenager, and both times he absolutely hated it, being much more comfortable in his country New Hampshire homeland than among the hectic city chaos. As he walked the crowded street with Freddy, he quickly broke into a sweat. Gone were the fresh smells of Waterville Valley's pine needles gently wafting through the wind, as they had been replaced by the stench of rotten armpit sweat and overpowering car exhausts. People apathetically bounced into him as they stared mindlessly at their cell phones, annoying him further. Cars congested the streets; half were driven by taxi drivers who recklessly cut off other vehicles before yelling, "Fuck you, pal!" while thrusting a middle finger out of their driver's windows. Ted yelled after he stepped in someone's vomit, tainting his brand-new New Balance running shoes that he had purchased just for walking around the city. Although still somewhat built like a football player, having a sturdy body covered in more muscle than fat, his dark-red hair and dark-red handlebar mustache made him look more like a firefighter than a cop, which he hoped would intimidate the average idiot passing him by enough to leave him alone. But that optimistic thought did not stop Ted from beginning to panic. He took off his new sunglasses for a moment and stared up at the sky, silently pleading to anyone who would listen for some peace and quiet.

"Ain't like home, is it?" Freddy asked. "I've only been here a few times. It's a bit angrier than Philly—unless you're at an Eagles game," Freddy said with a wink from behind his thick glasses.

Ted smiled, trying to take comfort in the fact that his detective companion could navigate a large, complicated city with relative ease. After a short journey, they arrived at East Fortieth Street, a claustrophobic one-way road full of cyclists weaving in and out of slow-moving traffic. Freddy held up his arm, silently requesting a pause in their trek. "Should be about a block up on the left," Freddy said. "When we get to a spot I like, I'll stop us again. When I do, pull out your cell phone. We're gonna pretend that you're using the GPS because we're lost. This will buy us some time while I get myself a good look at the area. The street is small, so we'll need to be careful in order to avoid being spotted. If we're lucky, we'll get some good intel we can use for putting a plan into action tomorrow."

Freddy took off his soda-bottle glasses and switched them out for a similar pair. But when Ted took a closer look at the glasses, he noticed two small dials, one on each side. Ted also noticed that the lenses of these glasses were somehow even thicker than his normal pair. "There actually is a benefit to being half-blind," Freddy said, "'cause I can get away with stuff like this. I crafted these. They're homemade binocular glasses. While I pretend to be watching you with your phone, I'll be zooming in to watch what's going on across the street."

Ted smiled, wondering what other tricks Freddy had up his sleeve. After crossing the street and walking half a block to position themselves behind three garbage cans, Freddy gave the signal. Ted stopped, pulled out his cell phone, and pretended to get directions online. In between looking down at his phone, Ted sneaked in a couple of quick glances across the street, where he found two large windows flanking either side of a large glass door. A black sign sat above the door with the word "Talandoor's" written in fancy golden lettering. Satisfied that Freddy had them in the right place, Ted went back to looking at his phone while letting Freddy continue his surveillance with his binocular glasses.

After about a minute, Freddy pointed to Ted's phone and said, "That's it; that's where we need to go. Let's get going."

Ted put his phone away, and the two walked for another block. Then, Freddy stopped them and once again switched out his glasses.

"What did you see?" Ted asked.

"I saw a woman behind the counter," Freddy responded as he took off his Statue of Liberty hat to scratch his head. Ted kept the observation of Freddy beginning to bald on the back of his head to himself. "She's quite an attractive redhead, probably in her late thirties or early forties. She puttered around, but I didn't see any customers. Definitely a chance that she's our Tessa."

"Got any ideas for what to do next?" Ted asked after taking his sunglasses off for a moment. He already had light chaffing above his ears from the arms of the glasses and let out an annoyed sigh.

"Actually, yes," Freddy answered. "The sign on the shop door says they close at five. That's in about a half hour. See the Dunks sign up about two blocks? Let's go up there and grab a coffee and then return this way. We can try to time it to be coming through here around ten past. Maybe we'll get lucky and see her leave after closing shop. If she walks, we can follow her; if she gets picked up, we'll try to get a plate number."

Excited about the prospect of grabbing a black coffee from Dunkin' Donuts, Ted followed Freddy up the street before buying them each a much-needed source of energy. By the time they made their purchase and Freddy had added cream and sugar to his, they reasoned that they should be able to get back in front of Talandoor's just after closing, so they reversed direction and quickly headed back. When they had reached the store just after five o'clock, it did not require any undercover surveillance to notice that now there were bars in front of both the door and windows, as well as a closed sign hanging from the door. Freddy paused momentarily, pretending to make small talk with Ted, just in case they might get lucky and see the woman emerge after closing shop.

When she did not appear after a few minutes, Freddy finished his fake conversation with Ted and walked onward. The two went all the way back to their hotel room, where they finished their coffees. Ted threw the shopping bag full of tourist T-shirts into the corner of the room.

"Could be a door in the back," Ted said.

"Could be," Freddy agreed. "Or they could live in a loft above the shop. Not uncommon in this city. I suggest we do the same thing tomorrow: we casually make a few passes, maybe even trying to get there just before the store opens. We can do the same as we did today and try to pass by at closing to see if we can catch our mysterious woman leaving. I recommend we do this tomorrow and then again Friday if need be. If we can't identify her by Saturday, then I'll come up with a bolder plan, since that'll be our last day here. How does that sound?"

"That works for me," Ted said. "There's a restaurant downstairs. Let's get us some dinner and see if we can come up with additional ideas while we eat." He led the way to the restaurant, where the hostess casually insulted them for eating during what she referred to as the "geriatric dinner hour." As Ted went to town on his double cheeseburger, he reflected on the words of the hostess, wondering if two middle-aged country boys were capable of solving such a mysterious case. He could hardly believe that Shane never called him once, not even to complain about his absence. He began to wonder what value he truly added to the world.

When they returned to their room after dinner to grab a couple of showers and get ready for an early night of watching television before bed, Ted did something he had not done in decades: he prayed.

CHAPTER 13

Ted and Freddy spent Thursday picking up where they had left off late Wednesday afternoon, making casual passes past Talandoor's as Freddy tried to sneak a quick glance inside the store with his binocular glasses. After that, they would hit Dunkin' Donuts for a coffee or doughnut (or both), or if they were not in the mood for either, they would sit at a bus stop and take a rest. The New York fall weather provided them with a warming sun that burned any potential rain clouds away. Ted's shin muscles were already sore from all the walking around. On the positive side, it seemed as though he may have lost a pound or two of flab on his belly and hoped that that side benefit would continue. Ted and Freddy had made four such passes by Talandoor's on Thursday and each time ended with the same result. One time, Freddy noticed that the woman working the store looked somewhat frantic after taking a phone call. But for the most part, Freddy saw her alone and wandering around, seemingly not doing much of anything.

"If she knows that Daniel's dead," Freddy said, "then she's handling it really well."

Ted agreed. Some people might return to work when struck by trauma in order to distract themselves, but one would have to have ice running through one's veins in order to be so nonchalant about murdering someone. And that brought up another question: Daniel's business card only had his name on it as the shop's owner. What did that make Tessa? A lover who also helped out in the store? Something else? Ted and Freddy had chatted about this fact over dinner Wednesday night and reasoned that since she shared his room at the Sly Fox Lodge, they were probably lovers. But they also realized that they should remain open to all possibilities in order not to close doors on any leads, especially since they had not yet identified this redhead as Tessa. But it remained their strongest lead, especially considering they had not yet seen the woman leave the building. This store employee being Tessa and sharing a loft above the building with Daniel became more and more likely.

After an unsuccessful Thursday and Friday morning, in which Ted and Freddy made multiple, careful sweeps in front of the store (twice, Freddy went by himself, just in case they were becoming obvious as a snooping duo), late Friday afternoon finally yielded results. At just after five o'clock, Ted and Freddy paused across the street from Talandoor's, pretending to have a casual conversation about whether the Red Sox would finish the season ahead of the Yankees. After the bars had been secured in front of the door and windows, the main entrance opened, and a woman dressed in jeans, a T-shirt, and a Knicks baseball cap quickly turned around to lock the door before flagging down a passing cab.

"Holy shit!" Freddy said. "Stay here. I'm moving in!"

Before Ted could say anything in response, Freddy bolted into the narrow street, barely missing a ten-speeder that weaved his way in between traffic. It only took Freddy a brief jog on the small and narrow street to get up behind the cab. At this point, Ted realized that Freddy was pretending to try to hail the cab himself in order to get a better look at their suspect. The cab paid him no mind and drove off once his passenger had secured herself inside. Freddy quickly jogged back across the street and up to Ted.

"Did you get anything?" Ted asked.

"Yeah," Freddy said, lightly panting as he removed his glasses and then cleaned the lenses, "she's heading to Central Park. If I didn't know any better, I'd say she does not wanna be noticed. She normally wears nice dresses in the store, but she's dressed really casual now. Maybe she made us. There's only one way to find out: we gotta get a cab and follow her!"

Ted agreed and looked up the one-way street to see if any were coming. Freddy tried to wave the first one down and failed terribly as it blazed by, so when the second one came along, Ted took his large frame into the middle of the street and waved his arms frantically, as though playing chicken with the vehicle. Ted claimed the victory, as the cab stopped about three feet before running him over. Freddy wasted no time before opening the back door and jumping in.

"Central Park, please!" Freddy yelled, and Ted quickly ran around from the front of the cab to join him, climbing in the backseat after Freddy slid over.

"What part?" the driver said with a thick accent as he looked at Ted and Freddy through the rearview mirror. He had dark skin and coarse black hair with a matching beard, appearing to be of some sort of Middle Eastern descent, which Ted confirmed after seeing an ID mounted on the dash reading "Hamded."

"North? South? The zoo?" Hamded asked.

Ted exchanged a brief glance with Freddy after taking off his cheap sunglasses.

"Can you take us to the middle?" Freddy asked.

"I'll take you to Eighty-Sixth Street Transverse," the driver responded after a brief pause. "That will get you near the Met and the Great Lawn. Is this fine?"

"Sounds good," Freddy answered, causing the driver to immediately step on the gas and take off. The driver's rapid pace quickly slowed down as they ran into Friday-afternoon New York City traffic. He stuck his left arm out his window after turning on the radio, tuning into some station that played what sounded like a talk show in a foreign language. His heavy cologne smelled like a type of Polo. Having seen *Taxi Driver,* Ted reasoned that the driver wore that much in order to block any smells created by whatever sinister activities took place with his passengers in the back. Ted and Freddy spent the drive in silence, both of them focusing on the task at hand. The night before, they had come up with their final plan, agreeing that they would spend Friday as their last day conducting surveillance. If they failed again, they would spend Saturday, their last day in the city before returning home on Sunday, giving up their advantage and confronting the woman they suspected to be Tessa inside the store. Ted and Freddy both understood that this course of action could result in many outcomes, one of which would possibly be her closing them off completely (as after all, they were far from where Ted held jurisdiction in Waterville Valley). As such, they both realized that this would be their only real chance to maintain the advantage and discreetly watch her actions, possibly picking up information that she would not voluntarily give them in the store.

Although less than four miles, the congested commute took nearly a half hour. When the driver had pulled his cab to a complete stop, they were between a fairly large body of water on one side and a large field on the other. After Ted used a credit card to pay the driver and tipped him well, the driver "suddenly" found a couple of tourist maps of the park in his glove box. Ted thanked him twice, not caring that the man probably would not have given him the maps if he had not tipped well.

"All right," Freddy said as he adjusted his regular glasses. "We got about an hour of daylight left. If you look at the map, that water should be the Jacqueline Kennedy Onassis Reservoir, and this field over here would be the Great Lawn. I was thinking of a plan on the drive over. She's probably here to meet someone. The question is will they stay, or will they leave to go somewhere else? If they're heading somewhere else, she'll meet whoever it is and go. That doesn't give us much time. If we're lucky, she'll stay for a while, which buys us more time. Either case is about as easy as finding a needle in the Mad River, but it is what it is. Here"—Freddy pulled out his cell phone—"While I was pretending to look at my phone when I tried to hail the cab, I got a partial picture of her. It's from the back, but you can see long, curly red hair under that ball cap. Her T-shirt is red, and she has white sneakers on. And you can't tell from this picture, but she's tall, maybe as tall as I am. Got it?"

"Yeah," Ted answered. For her to be as tall as Freddy would make her stand out among most other women in the park.

"Good," Freddy said. "So here's what I propose: we split up. You go south, and I'll go north. We'll go fast as we head to the opposite ends of the park, just in case she's not sticking around. Surely she beat us here, so we're already behind the eight ball. Then we do slow sweeps back. We can text each other with any leads. I say we do this until about nine. If we don't find her by then, we probably won't at all. How does that sound?"

"Sounds better than anything I came up with," Ted responded. "Good luck."

Freddy nodded and headed north. Ted headed south along a footpath of the Great Lawn, an oval-shaped patch of grass surrounded by clumps of trees that probably were considered a forest by the city folk. Several baseball diamonds were on the outskirts of the lawn, and all of them were filled with what appeared to be after-hours, recreational adult softball teams. And in the center of it all, families had blankets down all over the ground as they enjoyed picnics during the last hours of daylight. Although more peaceful than the rest of the city that Ted had seen so far, the large group of people that crammed themselves into the park made him claustrophobic. The canopy of trees did a good job of eliminating most of the screeching tires and beeping horns of the city's vehicles, but the yelling and screaming of all the people within the park replaced most of that missing noise.

Ted did his best to shake off the strangling sensations that New York City had been raining down upon him all week and scoured every person he saw in hopes of finding the redhead before dark. He passed by several other fields, small bodies of water, and even the outskirts of the zoo before finally making it to the other end of the park. At this point, dusk had arrived, and the lights above the walkways kicked on, immediately becoming blanketed by moths and other insects that preyed upon creatures drawn to the strong artificial light. After using a bathroom at Heckscher Playground at the southern end of the park, Ted texted Freddy, "Nothing yet." Within a minute, Freddy responded that his results thus far had been the same. Ted decided to take a break from walking (as, on this trip, he had walked more in one week than he had walked all year) and grabbed a hot dog and bottled water from a nearby vendor. After finishing his food, Ted took the westernmost route back to meet Freddy, as he had taken a southeastern course to get to this end and wanted to cover different areas on the way back. And just as Ted reached Umpire Rock, the large slab of shale (or so he thought; it had been a long time since high school geology) at the other side of the playground that overlooked the action on the baseball diamonds, he saw her.

Ted had nearly overlooked her at first because of his quick glance; he now saw the red hair and the T-shirt clearly, but she no longer wore the blue baseball cap because she had given it to the man next to her. He had a hard time making out their features from this distance, as he relied solely on the overhead park lights, so he cautiously made his way to what he deemed to be a safe distance. Just as soon as he had spotted them, the two were getting up, taking a light-blue blanket and folding it up before stuffing it into the man's backpack. And just as Ted started to get a good look at them, the two climbed off the rock and started making their way directly toward him. Ted let his police instincts take over and started scooting across the playground toward the other end, with his phone up to his ear pretending to listen to someone. He made his way to a fountain, which offered some cover as it spewed water nearly twenty feet into the air. Ted positioned himself to where he thought he would be far enough out of their direct walking path not to draw much of their attention while also being close enough to get a better look at them. Once they were passing him by, Ted put his other hand up to pretend to rub his forehead so he could turn and get a quick peek while—he hoped—obscuring most of his face.

When the woman they suspected to be Tessa passed by Ted, he nearly dropped his phone into the fountain after getting a better look at her companion. Once they were past him at a safe tailing distance, Ted called Freddy.

"Anything?" Freddy asked.

"Yeah," Ted responded. "I'm down here at Heckscher Playground, and I got her."

"That's amazing!" Freddy said. "I can't believe our luck! Was she with someone? If she was, did you get a good look?"

"I got more than a good look at him. I got a positive ID."

"What? Who is it?"

"It's Marvin, the guy that works for Dave at Grizzly's Bar. I couldn't believe it at first, but I got a better look as they passed by. Hundred percent, it's him."

"What the hell is one of our locals doing down here with a murder suspect?" Freddy asked.

"My thoughts exactly," Ted said. "So get down here as fast as you can, and let's find out." Ted started following the two at a safe distance, wondering what in the world could be going on in his small community of Waterville Valley.

CHAPTER 14

Ted and Freddy kept in contact by text as Freddy made his way south to unite with Ted at the southern end of Central Park. Ted turned his phone on mute, as Tessa and Marvin were not exactly breaking any world records for speed. Ted followed somewhat closely behind in order to keep an eye on them by means of the humming overhead lights illuminating the walkways.

Ted had not had many previous interactions with Marvin. He had been homeless when he strolled into Waterville Valley about two years prior, and after Marvin's hanging out each day at Grizzly's Bar, scrounging for leftover scraps like a lost bear, Dave finally offered him a job as his general handyman and assistant. He performed relatively simple tasks while receiving some of his payment by means of bar food. Ted did not know much about Marvin's history, having no idea where he had come from (as during the few times that Ted had interacted with him, Marvin did not volunteer information about his past), but Ted didn't care simply because Marvin stayed out of trouble. He rented a small studio ski lodge in the village and minded his own business, which made his sudden appearance in New York City quite strange.

After about twenty minutes of tailing Tessa and Marvin at a snail's pace as they continued to traverse the walkway of Heckscher Playground, Freddy emerged through the darkness of the other end of the park and slowly made his way to Ted. "Let me take point," Freddy said quietly. "I've never had an encounter with Marvin. Me on point might increase our chances of not being recognized, so trail just far enough behind where you can still see my hand signals. If you lose me, just text me."

Ted nodded. Neither of them had any idea if the woman had gotten a good look at Freddy earlier when he bolted toward the cab, but, given the circumstances, they did not have many other choices. Before

Freddy took point, Ted commented that he could hear them talking as he followed them but had not been able to make out what they were saying. Ted let everyone get ahead of him, relying on Freddy's leadership to manage the situation.

Less than ten minutes later, Freddy rapidly waved one of his hands behind his back. Ted quickly picked up his pace, trying not to look too obvious as he panted from the slow jog.

"They just veered off into the patch of woods over there," Freddy said. As he waited for Ted to approach him, he began rummaging through the plastic shopping bag that Ted had gotten on their first day. Freddy kept it on them in an attempt to look like tourists who bought useless garbage as they walked mindlessly around the city. But instead of filling it with worthless nonsense, Freddy used it to carry around his special binocular glasses along with some other trinkets. Finally, he pulled out two pairs of large clunky glasses. "These are night vision," Freddy said. "We're going in."

"I don't want to watch them do that!" Ted responded. He didn't mind performing surveillance work, but he had his limits.

"That may not be what they're doing," Freddy said after activating his glasses and strapping them around his head. He turned the second pair on and handed them to Ted. "They may be up to something else, and we can't afford to lose them. Here—look at these knobs. You can zoom in and out with them. Just don't look up at the streetlights when you wear them, or you'll quickly regret it."

"Why do you even have these?" Ted asked, perplexed.

"I'm a survival enthusiast," Freddy answered. "I've been collecting stuff for a while. Look, we can talk about my hobbies another time. Let's move. And watch your step. Try to use the glasses to avoid stepping on fallen branches. Let's go!"

Ted agreed that he and Freddy could talk at a much later time about Freddy's peculiar hobbies, and he also acknowledged the possibility that maybe the two were not in the woods to fool around. There were still too many variables in play, and they did not have enough time to risk being presumptuous. Additionally, the trees would provide good cover for them to hide behind in the shadowy darkness. The warmer New York City temperature meant that although nearly all had turned color, hardly any leaves had fallen off the trees yet. Provided they could move relatively quietly, Ted reasoned that they should be able to get a good look at their suspect and her companion with the assistance of the glasses and then sneak away if they found them "doing it."

Ted took a moment to get used to the night-vision glasses as he stared at the ground. Their heaviness made them a bit awkward, but once Freddy decided that he had had enough time to get used to them, he grabbed Ted by the arm and gently pulled him forward. Although based on the signs that they saw, it looked as though the park would be open until at least one in the morning, the crowd had quickly thinned the later it got. Ted also noticed a few cops here and there as he walked, so he knew that they would need to be mindful not to run into them, as they would most likely look like the ones doing wrong as they followed two potential lovers into the patch of trees. But they absolutely had to act on this lead; for all they knew, Tessa and Marvin would be leaving for somewhere else tomorrow, so they really needed to get somewhere with this case and gather some useful intel.

Freddy's advice of watching the ground closely as Ted walked proved to be on point. Immediately after stepping off the trail, Ted nearly tripped over a large rock that he certainly would have missed without the night-vision glasses. Off the well-maintained walkway, Ted found broken sticks mingled together with small amounts of garbage littered all over the ground, causing both of them to need to tread as carefully as if they were dodging land mines. Finally, after a cautious walk that seemed to last an eternity, Freddy waved his hand in front of Ted's field of vision before making a clenched fist. Once he looked up, he saw that Freddy had halted them in front of a large leafy cherry tree surrounded by shrubbery that ran up to Ted's waist. After raising his field of view fully off the ground and ahead of where they were crouching, Ted saw that they were perched behind the woman and Marvin, who were both sitting on a slope several feet down. Freddy turned around after reaching into his pocket and handed Ted a small device. Then he pulled out a second one and put it in his ear, gesturing for Ted to do the same with his. Ted popped it in his left ear and noticed that it amplified the sounds around him, as he could now quite clearly hear a conversation occurring between the woman they believed to be Tessa and Marvin at the bottom of the small hill below. Freddy gestured once more to Ted by pointing down the slope, instructing him to watch and listen as they squatted down in the shrubbery surrounding the cherry tree. Ted nodded and focused his attention down below. It did not take long for the device to start making out words quite clearly.

"Are you ready?" the woman asked.

"As ready as I'm going to be, Tess," Marvin responded. *Finally, confirmation that this woman is indeed Tessa*, Ted thought. "Don't we need to be near the cairn stones?"

"No," Tessa answered. "The ability is within you now. You can do it at will in the cover of night and with practice and the right conditions, possibly even in daylight as well. I'm going to be here with you for your first time. I promise you will be safe."

"Shouldn't Daniel be a part of this?"

"No. Daniel and I got in a fight. He's still in New Hampshire. Besides, it doesn't matter. He can't do what I can do. He can't help you like I'm going to."

"Sorry. I didn't know that. I didn't go back out to the cairn stones after that night, so I never saw him before I left. I've been so overwhelmed by all of this. Once we talked over the phone and you offered to help, I got out of work and got my ass down here."

So she does not know that Daniel is dead—or is at least selling that as her story, Ted thought.

"Okay," Tessa said. "We're not gonna be alone forever. We need to get started."

Ted watched as Tessa reached into the back pocket of her jeans and pulled out what looked like some sort of wand. She used it to draw something on the ground, but the angle of the slope of the hill along with various patches of shrubbery prohibited Ted from seeing any of those details clearly. But he could easily see when Tessa raised the wand and pointed it at Marvin. She then muttered indecipherable words that may have been Latin. *What in the hell are they doing?* Ted wondered as chills began to run up his spine. He realized that Tessa and Marvin did not appear to have a light source yet were able to see each other in the darkness as they conversed. And what Ted witnessed next caused him to nearly lose his mind.

As Ted watched the strange ritual blanketed by a haze of confusion, he noticed that Marvin became fidgety. And then Marvin's restlessness turned into some sort of transformation. Ted watched with his jaw wide open as Marvin's body began to convulse. Soon after, his body began twisting, turning, and growing. Clothes and all, Marvin's body began to morph into an entirely new entity. His arms and legs grew into limbs that ended in large paws, and his body became four times the size as it sprouted dark fur. Marvin's head distorted, making creaking and cracking sounds until he grew a powerful jaw. After the transformation finally ended, Marvin stood on all fours in front of Tessa, who had risen to her own feet. Marvin's head came nearly up to Tessa's shoulders, and as he looked at her, he roared. Ted could not believe his eyes: Marvin had somehow transformed into a friggin' bear!

Ted stood up and screamed as he ran toward them down the hill. In one moment, all his police training had gone out the window, except for the fact that he habitually reached for the Glock that would normally be strapped to his waist. But it instead sat in the glove box of his truck back in New Hampshire, as he did not have an open carry permit for New York and did not want to risk it. But considering the fact that he had only used his gun to scare off bears when they had wandered too close to Waterville Valley Village, Ted found himself wishing that he had foregone his respect for another state's law and brought his weapon with him. Overwhelmed and overstimulated, Ted made an imaginary gun with his hand and used it to shoot at the creature, as if he were playing cops and robbers with his childhood friends after watching an *Adam-12* episode.

"What are you?" Ted screamed as his survival instincts took over. "What are you!" Ted had unknowingly ripped his night-vision goggles off in the chaos but stood close enough to the two that he could see the Marvin-bear turn toward him.

"Ted?" Marvin seemed to ask in a growly bear voice. "Chief Ted Hannon, is that you?"

Just as Tessa started to turn toward Ted, she quickly whirled around in the other direction.

"My traps!" Tessa yelled as she grabbed Marvin's bear-head gently with each hand. "They've been set off! We have to get out of here!"

A bullet whizzed two inches above Ted's head, and he attempted to fire one back at the invisible target with his imaginary finger-gun.

"We have to go!" Tessa yelled to Marvin, who after taking one last look at Ted's shocked face, immediately lumbered into the woods with his bear-body.

Tessa reached into her pocket and pulled out a set of keys before roughly placing them in Ted's hand. She grabbed him by the face just as she had done with Marvin a moment before. Her hands channeled warmth into his cheeks, and his nerves began to settle.

"Find the lamp!" Tessa yelled at Ted. "Seven zero seven six! The lamp! Seven zero seven six!" As soon as Tessa finished speaking, more shots were fired. She gently caressed Ted's cheeks one last time before following Marvin through the small patch of trees.

Someone grabbed Ted abruptly from behind. He quickly turned around and found Freddy standing behind him. Freddy also had removed his goggles at some point and looked alarmed but not anywhere near the state of chaos that Ted had reached. "We gotta get out of here!" Freddy said with a strained voice. "Now! There are guys coming with guns. And dogs too. We'll make a new plan later, but we need to focus on survival first. Let's go!"

Freddy dragged Ted by the arm and then pulled him down toward the ground, behind the same cherry tree they had been perched behind before. "Let's watch for a moment," Freddy said in a hushed voice. "And make sure you stay quiet!" Ted did not know what he would have said even if he could have talked, so being quiet did not prove to be a challenge for him. He looked along with Freddy toward the same spot where Tessa and Marvin had been conversing moments before. Three men in dark suits emerged with flashlights as they rapidly searched the area. Each held a gun in the other hand, and after briefly murmuring something to each other (Ted had somehow lost the hearing device in the chaos, so he could not make their conversation out), two dogs that looked more like wolves trotted up to them. They each smelled the ground for a moment before transforming into two fully dressed humans.

"Do you have the scent?" one of the men in suits asked the other two.

"Oh yeah," one of the wolf-men answered in a deep voice. "We know exactly which direction they headed."

Ted gently rocked forward and fell into the bushes, having fainted.

CHAPTER 15

"Give me those!" Freddy said to Ted, taking Tessa's keys from him. After stuffing the key ring in his pocket, Freddy gently slapped Ted's face a couple of times, fully returning him to consciousness. "You weren't out that long. We still might be able to catch up to them. Let's go!"

Ted allowed Freddy to assist him back to his feet and gently guide him back toward the lighted trail.

"We don't have time to traipse through the woods anymore," Freddy said. "I'm going to assume that this chase is going to leave the park. If we jump back on the lighted trail, we may be able to cut 'em off. Let's go!"

Ted followed his friend. He still had a lot to process, having watched a fellow Waterville Valley resident transform into an animal right in front of him before watching wolves shift into human forms. But Ted's adrenal glands were working overtime, and the adrenaline coursing through his body forced the seemingly impossible thoughts to take a backseat in his mind as he dealt with his current situation. Ted followed Freddy south through Heckscher Playground until they reached a road that led out of Central Park. Once there, Ted watched an armed man force Tessa and Marvin (once again in human form) into the back of a van before jumping in behind them as the vehicle screeched off into the city. Freddy frantically ran after them after pulling his phone out, trying to snap a picture of the license plate. After a brief pause to catch his breath, he trotted back to Ted.

"Shit," Freddy said, "I didn't get anything." Then, Freddy's face lit up as if he had just remembered something. He reached up and put his arms on Ted's broad shoulders, gently shaking them. "This is really important," Freddy said as he stared at Ted through his thick glasses. "What did she tell you when she gave you the keys?"

Ted tried to recall what had happened just before he fainted. He remembered spying on Tessa and Marvin as they conversed at the bottom of the hill. He remembered Tessa waving a magic wand before Marvin suddenly transformed into a bear. (Ted decided he would try to figure out how this could even be possible at a later time.) And then he remembered "enthusiastically" (the perfect way to define how he temporarily lost his mind) running down the hill. And after Marvin acknowledged him, Tessa approached him before shots were fired and Ted shot back with his imaginary finger-gun. Ted channeled all his attention to the moment that Tessa had spoken to him.

"She came over to me and gave me a set of keys, which you took," Ted said as he rubbed his forehead. "Then she said something about getting a lamp. And then she told me some numbers."

"Good," Freddy said. "Very good. These numbers are important, Ted. What were they?"

Ted thought for a moment before answering, "Four zero seven six. No! Seven zero seven six. That's it."

"Are you sure?" Freddy asked.

"Yes," Ted said, although he did not want to tell Freddy that his recollection may or may not be correct. He believed he recalled the numbers correctly, so he did not want to overthink it and possibly confuse himself in the process.

"Good," Freddy answered. "I didn't get a plate number. I got a good look at the van, but it's a white van with no windows in the back, basically what every creep in New York City drives, so we have nothing to go to the police with. I don't see any witnesses standing nearby in shock, so we're likely the only ones who saw it. That means our strongest lead is to follow Tessa's instructions. These have to be the keys to the store. Let's head there and see if we can find this lamp that most certainly holds an important clue. Let's go!"

Ted once again followed Freddy's lead as they left Central Park and tried to hail a cab. Although getting a cab on their way to the park had been relatively easy, getting one now proved to be much more difficult. There were plenty of cabs out and about, but all of them passing by were already full. In "the city that never sleeps," Ted assumed that people were just getting ready to start their Friday night as they partied well into the wee hours of the morning. Freddy and Ted decided to start walking in the direction of the shop as they kept trying to hail a cab. Finally, after walking nearly a block, they were successful at flagging one down. "East Fortieth Street to Talandoor's, please!" Freddy instructed the driver. The drive went slightly faster than it had to the park because of the lighter nighttime traffic, but the roads were far from empty, as they would have been back in Waterville Valley.

Once in front of the store, Ted paid the driver before he and Freddy jumped out. Security lights authoritatively lit the iron gates in front of both the large picture windows and the front door. Freddy pulled out Tessa's keys and found the one that unlocked the gate before locating the one that opened the front door. The key ring had several keys along with a small blue gemstone, most likely a personal keepsake of Tessa's but nothing of value, as it seemed to be made of plastic. As soon as Freddy opened the front door, a loud, oppressive squealing began sounding off and echoed throughout the store. Freddy immediately ran inside and checked the walls next to the door before once again lighting up as if he had figured everything out.

"The numbers!" Freddy yelled to Ted. "What were the numbers, again?"

"Seven zero seven six," Ted answered after a brief pause.

Ted and Freddy collectively sighed as the alarm shut off after Freddy punched the exact numbers in.

"One problem down," Freddy said, shutting the front door and locking them inside. He did not turn on the main lights, most likely in order to try to avoid attention from passersby on the street outside. "Now, for the lamp."

Ted glanced around the store, which looked to be a mix of collectibles and high-end antiques. Growing up in New England, Ted knew more than a little about antiques, as seemingly people who owned a piece of farm equipment at least fifty years old suddenly believed that they were antique dealers and opened a store to sell their goods out of their own house. Ted had been to at least a dozen such "stores" over the years, but it did not take much surveying of his current surroundings to realize that Talandoor's went far beyond that. Although the same types of items were in the store, such as dressers, chairs, and clocks, the items in Talandoor's seemed to be more urban themed, looking as though they were top of the line in regard to their brand or fashion for their time. Additionally, Talandoor's had a long glass case with the cash register on top of it that housed several gemstones and pieces of jewelry priced at several thousand dollars each. The gentle scent of potpourri drowned out the strange collision of smells that wood, metal, and other incompatible materials often created when they merged together, and not a single thing seemed to be out of place. Ted watched Freddy sitting at a desk while twisting and turning the desk lamp that sat upon it, seemingly looking for a clue in regard to the second part of Tessa's message, when an intuitive thought came to him.

"Freddy," Ted said solemnly to Freddy's back, as he faced away from him while working the lamp on the dark-stained wooden desk, "how can you be so calm? Have you seen that much as a detective that none of this overwhelms you?"

Freddy paused for a moment before placing the lamp sideways on the desk and picking up the chair in order to spin it around. He took off his thick glasses and rubbed his eyes. "I think it's time we talked some truth," Freddy said. "You have displayed a great deal of trust in me with this case, and I'm ready to return the favor. Do you remember what I told you about my second wife, Beth?"

"I believe so," Ted said. "You told me that you separated because of her drug use."

"Well, some of what I told you is true. I do have a second wife named Beth, and technically, we are separated, but there is much, much more to the story than that, none of which involves drugs."

Ted leaned against the glass case next to the cash register as he listened intently.

"Decades ago, I was working a kidnapping case," Freddy said. "And I'll tell ya what, if I didn't see it all for myself, I would have never believed what I'm about to tell you. Our kidnapper was a repeat offender that we suspected of being a serial killer, because the young women he abducted seemed to stay missing. We were trying to be optimistic when we dealt with the public, but there was no doubt among us on the force that things were not ending well for these girls. After working our sources, we had gotten a really good lead that the guy was operating out of a house on a dead-end street in the Badlands, a Philly neighborhood that was ravaged by the crack epidemic. It was also becoming clear to us that our guy was most likely not working alone, and because of that, we got clearance from the judge and went in full-force: police, SWAT, everyone. After the muscle cleared the main floor of the house, my partner, Henry, and I went in. And what we saw was appalling." Freddy paused to remove his glasses and rub his eyes.

"In place of furniture, pictures, and appliances, as a normal house would have, was scattered debris and ritualistic symbols painted and carved into the walls," Freddy said after putting his glasses back on. "After finding nothing of interest on the first floor, SWAT made their way into the basement and cleared it, and while Henry and I were nosing around upstairs, we got called down to take a look. When we made our way downstairs, I instantly became sick to my stomach. As the SWAT team shined their bright flashlights all over the basement, I saw piles and piles of bodies. Worse, the bodies were not even whole; in most cases, I only saw the remains of arms, legs, and torsos torn apart and scattered everywhere. The entire basement floor was covered in blood nearly an inch deep. There were at least twenty times the number of carcasses in the basement than the number of missing women that had been reported. But blood and bodies weren't the only things on the basement floor. The floor also had several coffins sitting on waist-high pedestals. SWAT had already torn them open when they cleared the room; they were all empty."

Ted's body began to lightly convulse with chills as he listened to Freddy's living nightmare.

"Coincidentally, the raid occurred at nighttime," Freddy said. "And as you probably know, there are many weirdoes who pretend to be monsters out there, so it was not unusual for a bunch of maniac killers to sleep in coffins among their victims, thinking they're Dracula or something like that. But there quickly proved to be much more to the case than that. We found three mysterious books after raiding the house for evidence. These books were the largest books I have ever seen—and the oldest too. In fact, they were thousands of years old, forensics estimated, after examining their bindings, which were crafted from human flesh. None of us could read them, as they were written in a strange, ancient language. After bringing in some language experts, we learned that they were written in Tamil, which may be the oldest language known to man. After the experts made their way through the books, they were able to determine that they contained instructions for an ancient cult that worshipped Lucifer, or perhaps an even older bad guy, as the books were written before the Old Testament. According to the experts, the books stated that those worthy of being in the cult, whatever that meant, had to choose between becoming a vampire or a lycanthrope, which are shape-shifters, like werewolves. Once the worshippers had chosen between the two paths, they became immortal and killed in the name of their lord, over and over.

"Things went somewhat back to normal for a while after that night. We continued to work the case but didn't have much to go on, as no perp ever returned to that house, at least based on our constant surveillance of the place. So Henry and I began working other cases. And just when I was getting the horrors of that house out of my mind, something woke me up late one night. After I adjusted my eyes, I saw a man standing at the foot of my bed in the shadows of the nightlight. He said that his name was Nostradamus and that he was very upset that I desecrated his lair. And he wasn't alone. He had Beth next to him and had his hand wrapped around her mouth so she couldn't scream. As I reached for my pistol in the nightstand, I felt an invisible force freeze my body. Even worse, the force made me stare directly at this man, and I watched helplessly as he sank fangs into my wife's neck. When he was done, he told me that this was my price for what I did to his home. And then he vanished, along with Beth. Vanished into thin air, but not before emitting some sort of dark, disgusting negative energy that overwhelmed me so much that it blinded me. I've needed to wear these friggin' thick glasses ever since.

"As soon as I got to my senses, I called Henry, and after he came to my house and listened to me ramble for a while, he woke the chief up, telling him the story as clearly as he understood it. Less than twelve hours later, I was in the chief's office along with everyone. And by everyone, I mean everyone: the DA, the mayor, even friggin' FBI agents were there. At this meeting, I was told that the case had gone far beyond the city's pay grade and that the FBI would be taking over. The FBI agents promised me that they would do everything to find my wife and bring her back to me but also were honest and said that she was most likely dead. And if that little tidbit of news wasn't bad enough, I was 'asked' to retire early, as the DA shoved so much paperwork in front of my face that I could hardly even comprehend it all, asking me to sign this form and that form, one after another. The documents were all stamped "Top Secret," and signing them was the requirement for me getting an early full pension, which, back then, does not adjust well to the cost of living of today. I also had to swear confidentiality, going with the 'my wife was a coke fiend' storyline as the alleged truth, or else I'd risk spending the rest of my days in a federal prison—or worse." Freddy stood up, bracing himself as he wobbled from the overwhelming emotions that now coursed through his body.

"So, when you ask why I'm not so startled by tonight's occurrence," Freddy said, "it's for two reasons. The first is that after watching what this Nostradamus creature did, I have known for a very long time that monsters do indeed exist. But the second is much more important to me. As I mentioned, the translations of the books indicated that vampires were working alongside werewolves. Well, it just so happened that we saw two werewolves tonight, and whatever transformation Marvin underwent, he, too, may also be a type of lycanthrope. Although my first marriage was a disaster, my second was not. Beth and I were truly in love, and the fact that there is even the slightest chance that she may still be alive is the only thing that's kept me from drowning myself in the Mad River. So, as happy as I am to help you, I am now even more motivated to follow the strongest lead I've had in decades that may lead me to Beth. Philly and New York are not that far apart, and I'm now convinced that Nostradamus must be somehow connected to the people we ran into tonight. I need Beth back in my life, Ted. And if she's somehow a full vampire like you see in the movies, I'll be the one to kill her. If she's a monster now, then I'll kill my own wife." With that, Freddy collapsed into the chair and began crying.

CHAPTER 16

Ted gave Freddy a moment before walking over to him and gently placing a supportive hand on his shoulder. "I got you involved because I knew that I could trust you," he said. "I knew you would have great insights, but more importantly, I desperately needed someone to help me deal with the weight that's on my shoulders from taking actions that may end my career or even put me in jail. I am honored that you feel the same way about me. And although I may faint again if we see another friggin' monster, I'm glad that it's you who will be the one to pick me up off the ground if I do."

"Thank you," Freddy responded after wiping the last of his tears. "Without a doubt, you are my one true best friend in the world. Now, let's finish this job so we can get one more fishing trip to Lake Winnipesaukee in before the snow flies." He lifted himself out of the chair and surveyed the store, leaving the plastic shopping bag that now contained his various toys and trinkets sitting on top of the desk. "There's not much for lamps down here. I checked this one here, thinking that maybe she had left a note or something to that effect, but there's nothing. Look in the back, there."

Ted followed Freddy's pointing in the store's dim security light and saw what looked to be some sort of closed metal door.

"Elevator," Freddy said. "The reason we never saw Tessa come and go must be because they do live here. I bet that goes up to a loft. Let's find out."

Ted followed Freddy toward the back of the room.

After making his way over, Freddy pressed the call button, and the elevator dinged before gently sliding its doors open. Once inside, Ted saw a well-lit cube made of all metal, even the flooring. It had an immaculate shine, which surprised Ted, as he had expected more of a roughed-up interior similar to a service elevator's. On the right of the door were two buttons, L and 1. Ted wondered what this building had been used for before, considering the lobby level now served as the store. Once the doors shut, Freddy pressed the 1 button, but the elevator did not move.

"Oh," Freddy said after a quick analysis, "see this here. This is a keyhole. Makes sense; you wouldn't want any old customer to be able to get up to your apartment." He fumbled through the key ring until he found one that looked like it fit. After putting it in and turning it while pressing the 1 button, the elevator began to ascend.

For only going up one floor, the elevator seemed to crawl at a snail's pace. Eventually, it dinged again, and the door slowly slid open before depositing Ted and Freddy into a beautiful loft apartment. The walls were painted off-white and connected to an angled, open ceiling with exotic chandeliers dangling down intermittently (which all illuminated as soon as the elevator opened). High-end couches and chairs were scattered about on marble tiles. Several large windows looked over the neighboring buildings, and directly in front of the elevator, a suit of armor armed with a halberd stood silently at attention as if guarding the residence. Gentle scents of cinnamon and honey either from an air freshener or incense began wafting their way into the open elevator, creating much more of a welcoming environment than that of the ominous suit of armor.

"Well," Freddy said, "I see a couple of lamps up here. Let's take a look."

Ted picked a floor lamp in a corner near a small indoor trickling pool. The strange lamp stood on a tripod while another tripod held up the lampshade. Ted assumed its unique design made it valuable, so he handled it with care while checking every inch of it. The two spent twenty minutes thoroughly examining every lamp they could find before meeting in front of the elevator.

"There's nothing here," Freddy said after sighing. "Maybe we should go back downstairs. There was a locked door behind the cash register. That's probably a small office. There are probably file cabinets in there because I don't see any up here. We can start digging through them for inventory records. Maybe we'll find what her clue about lamps meant in their purchase history logs."

Back in the elevator, Freddy twirled Tessa's key ring around his finger as the numerous keys clanged together. After spinning the key ring two more times, he said, "This is our only lead. I've done my best to be optimistic, but if we can't find anything soon, we have to face the facts that we may not be able to figure out her riddle. We can report the abduction to the police and leave out the details about Marvin and the werewolves. I know that's far from ideal, and I know that means we'd probably have to answer a lot of questions back in New Hampshire regarding the body. Did you hear Tessa and Marvin talking? It didn't sound like she knows that Daniel is dead. I believe her and want to do right by her."

"I agree," Ted answered, trying not to sound defeated. He knew that if two people hadn't just been abducted at gunpoint in front of their very eyes, they could drag this on longer. But this secret case had quickly turned from trying to discover why a corpse and a circle of mysterious cairn stones had suddenly appeared in Waterville Valley to trying to save two people's lives, one even from back home. Ted knew he had to prioritize correctly and do his best to serve God as he continued his personal *Groundhog Day* quest. "Let's tear the office apart and do our best to come up with something. I'm sure there's a computer down there as well. If it's not locked, we can check that too. Let's give a real cop's shot at solving this before turning this whole thing upside down, both here and back home."

Freddy nodded and turned to make his way over to push the call button to return downstairs. Just then, Ted noticed that Freddy's arm that held on to the key ring jerked somewhat violently. Freddy shared a confused look with Ted before dangling the key ring up to the left side of the elevator doors. And as soon as he waved it waist high, the seemingly false blue gemstone attached to Tessa's key ring inserted itself into a hole to the left of the elevator door as if it were the opposite polarization of another nearby magnet. Ted and Freddy shared a shocked look, as the hole was hardly visible without close scrutiny. Before either of them could say anything, a small panel directly above the nearly invisible hole that now housed the gemstone slid open, revealing a B button.

"Well," Freddy said, "are you ready to go down to the basement?"

"Hold on," Ted answered. Freddy waited for Ted to step back into the loft apartment before pressing any buttons. Ted immediately beelined for the suit of armor. Once there, he gently grabbed the halberd that the suit grasped. Surprisingly, the weapon came right out of the metal glove as soon as Ted touched it. "It's not my Glock," Ted said as he returned to the elevator, "but it'll do."

Freddy nodded, and after the two took one last collective breath, he pressed the B button, causing the elevator to descend. The elevator went down slightly faster than it rose, dinging after passing the lobby level.

Ted looked at Freddy nervously when the elevator descended much deeper than it had risen. Beads of sweat began to form on his forehead as the elevator kept going down. Eventually, it stopped, and as the door began to open, the mysterious hole spewed out the blue gemstone attached to Tessa's key ring.

"Take these," Freddy said, handing Tessa's keys to him. "My pockets are full of enough trinkets right now, and we certainly don't want to lose these."

Ted nodded after accepting the keys and angled himself in front of Freddy so that he would be the first one to face whatever awaited them, ready to jab their potential enemy with the spiked tip of the halberd. But when the door finished opening, nothing but a deep silence awaited them. Ted took his first step into the large room, which immediately lit up from overhead as though the lights operated by motion detection. Because of the extremely high ceiling, Ted could not even see the lights and only saw soft shades of aquatic blue fill the room. The floor seemed to be crafted from blue marble in a checkerboard fashion, between light and dark shades, and Ted's running shoes sent echoes of his footsteps into the room as he stepped forward. The room smelled as though a gentle Portsmouth sea foam breeze wafted in from shore, but Ted did not see any water source nearby. Instead, he saw cases that appeared to be made from some form of glass or crystal evenly spaced throughout the room. Some were small, resting on pedestals covered in various tapestries of different colors, while some were large, standing as tall as Ted. From what he could make out, most of the cases were full of various types of objects, while some were completely empty.

"What do you bet that we find our lamp down here?" Freddy said optimistically from behind Ted after patting him on the back. Ted had no idea if they were going to find a lamp in this mystical chamber, but at the very least, he remained hopeful that they would. As valuable as the antique items in the store up above were, Ted reasoned that whatever Daniel and Tessa kept down in this room must be even more important. The hopeful thought gave him the burst of energy he needed to get started.

"Let's divide and conquer," Freddy said. "You go right. I'll go left. And try to be careful."

"No," Ted said after an intuitive thought. "Do you remember how Tessa told Marvin that their captors set off her traps? What if she has traps down here? If so, maybe that blue gem allows safe passage through them. Wouldn't you think a room like this would be armed?"

"That's some very solid police work there," Freddy answered. "All right, we'll go together. If that's true, hopefully, the gem on the key ring will protect us."

Without another word, Ted and Freddy began making their way through the room. The "basement," if it could truly be called that, looked more like a warehouse. Even after making his way a few steps into the room, he could not see all the way across to the other side. As they began walking, Ted glanced at several strange objects that were safely locked away in their cases. On his left, he passed an old wooden spear nearly as tall as the halberd that he nervously clutched. On his right, he saw what looked to be a battered clown suit on a mannequin. Ted and Freddy moved in silence, not paying much attention to the items that did not match what they were searching for, as interesting as some of them appeared to be.

Finally, after walking for nearly ten minutes, they came upon a pedestal that had a glass case housing a small lamp. Ted had nearly missed it at first, as it looked like some sort of teapot, but when Freddy tugged on his shirtsleeve and pointed at it, Ted noticed that it kind of looked like a genie lamp. After thoroughly examining the case for a moment, Freddy said, "How do we open it?"

The key ring in the front pocket of Ted's jeans began to pulsate. He clung to the halberd with one hand and used his free had to pull the ring out. As soon as he did, the blue gemstone shot into a small opening just as it had inside the elevator. In a moment too confusing for Ted to understand, the glass case seemed to fold in on itself, disappearing as it left the lamp exposed.

"I'll do it," Ted said, answering the unasked question of who should pick it up after stuffing Tessa's key ring back into his jeans pocket. Ted still wanted to assume the risk for this case, as Freddy had already done so much for him over the course of the week. After taking a breath and issuing a silent prayer, Ted grabbed it and cradled it in his arms, having leaned the halberd against a nearby case housing what looked like some sort of tree. The unimpressive lamp did not weigh much and seemed to be made of something cheap, like tin. Curiously, he grabbed the lid and pulled it open, and as soon as he did, dark billows of smoke began surrounding Ted and Freddy. Ted dropped the lamp to the floor, causing it to clang loudly as the lamp and the lid tumbled in opposite directions. He immediately reached out and grabbed the halberd with two hands, ready for just about anything. The dark smoke shifted in color to a mix of yellow and red and drifted unnaturally nearly ten feet above Ted's head before taking on a humanoid shape. It looked to be some sort of creature made purely of fire, and two bright-orange eyes took form in its head shape before they stared down at those who had awakened it.

"What do you ask of me?" a fiery voice asked the two men that looked at it with eyes full of wonder.

"Take us to where Tessa and Marvin are located at this very moment," Ted answered confidently, and before he could even turn to look at Freddy, his vision turned to blackness.

CHAPTER 17

When Ted opened his eyes, he found himself standing in a very long, dimly lit hallway full of books. Shelves rose up nearly three times higher than Ted, on each side of him. He could not read the words on the bindings, and the books emitted a dank, musty smell. High above him from a lofty stone ceiling dangled ancient chandeliers that housed lit candles. It reminded Ted of what castle libraries looked like in medieval movies. Ted gave a tight squeeze to the suit of armor's halberd, which he had taken from Daniel's loft. As he continued to adapt to his surroundings, Ted heard a whisper from behind him.

"Hey," Freddy said. "Look at this." Ted could not withhold a gasp when he saw Freddy holding the tin lamp that had summoned the burning beast that had transported them here.

"How is that possible?" Ted asked. "I clearly remember dropping that on the floor after seeing that ... thing. The lamp bounced in one direction while the lid went in another."

"Well," Freddy whispered, "either we are not done with it, or it's not done with us."

Ted nodded, glumly accepting that explanation. The hallway of books seemed to stretch as far back out of his field of view behind them as it did in front of them. "Any idea which direction we should head in?" Ted asked.

"We both were facing that way when we arrived," Freddy said as he pointed in front of them. "So, I'd say that's as good as any direction to head in."

The floors appeared to be stone, just as the ceilings were, and since he could not see over the looming bookshelves, Ted assumed that the walls, wherever they were, were constructed of the same material. A coldness radiated from the floor and up through Ted's running shoes, adding a chill to the stale air that blanketed him.

Finally, after walking for what seemed like a long time, they came to an intersection. Ted cautiously peered down both directions before stepping into the middle of the intersection. Similar rows in between tall bookshelves went on past his field of vision in either direction. As he turned to ask Freddy if he had thoughts on where to go from there, he heard a faint noise from the left passageway. Freddy nodded in that direction. Reluctantly, Ted agreed. On one hand, they were trying to avoid danger, as they had no idea what they were actually up against. But on the other hand, they were there as part of a rescue mission, trying to save the lives of Tessa and Marvin. Ted realized that the noise could be coming from them, so heading in that direction seemed to be the logical choice. After turning around one more time to make sure Freddy had not come up with a better suggestion, Ted turned left and started walking.

Ted and Freddy quietly trudged down the passageway in the ancient library until a man leaped from the top of one of the lofty bookshelves, gracefully landing on his feet as if he had only jumped from a knee-high surface. The skinny man wore a full suit, including well-polished dress shoes, to accompany messy long hair and a scruffy beard that did not match the outfit. After fully reclaiming his balance, he stood tall and smiled.

"I remember that scent," the man said in a deep voice. "You were at the park."

Before either Ted or Freddy could respond, the man began transforming before their eyes, growing hair everywhere as his body changed into that of a wolf.

While operating on nothing but intuition, Ted aimed the pointed end of the halberd at the beast and lunged forward, stabbing the creature. The pointed tip caught the werewolf in the shoulder and wounded him deeply, causing him to yell out something between a scream and a howl.

"That hurt him!" Freddy yelled excitedly from behind Ted. "Do it again!"

Ted wasted no time and jabbed repeatedly at every angle possible, striking multiple hits on the man-animal hybrid. Each hit struck an impactful blow, drawing blood and breaking bones. Finally, the creature's screams stopped, and he fully retransformed back into a human as he bled out on the floor with one last dying breath.

"How … how did I do that?" Ted asked.

Freddy came up behind him and tried to gently pry the halberd out of Ted's death grip. Once he fully believed that the threat had ended, he let his friend examine the halberd. Freddy took a handkerchief out from his pocket and wiped the blood off the halberd's point before twisting and turning the weapon in several directions.

"Look," Freddy said after adjusting his glasses to study the point. "The tip is made from silver. Some myths are true; silver really does kill werewolves. That's how you killed the monster. And see this?" Freddy asked while pointing at the ax blade of the weapon. "This is iron. If we happen to run into any creatures made by Nostradamus, this will hurt them. Somehow, you actually picked the perfect weapon for our mission, Ted."

"God is guiding me," Ted said after reclaiming the halberd from Freddy. "There is no doubt of that in my mind now. I am atoning for turning my back on him in my younger years. I will never make that mistake again." Just as Ted finished speaking, he heard loud creaking noises coming from above them in random directions.

"There's more of them," Freddy said with a sense of urgency. "They're gonna come at us from above. Let's not wait around for it!"

Ted agreed and hastily began running forward. Guttural howls echoed through the large chamber, and Ted realized that the creatures were transforming into wolves, which would most likely make a foot pursuit jumping from one tall library shelf to another much easier. Soon after, one wolf jumped down in front of them, and Ted wasted no time stabbing it, with both of his hands clutching the halberd tightly, nailing a direct hit in one of the werewolf's eyeballs and dropping it immediately. After confirming the beast's death, Ted and Freddy began running forward again, and soon after that, another beast leaped down, this one landing behind Freddy. With swift reflexes that Ted had not possessed since his high school football days, he found himself weaving and twirling with the halberd as if he had been training with it for his entire life, narrowly missing Freddy's head with expert precision before rapidly piercing the werewolf's ribcage three times, killing it. Eventually, after once again resuming their progression down the passageway in between the bookshelves, Ted and Freddy entered another intersection.

"Look!" Ted yelled after looking down the corridor to his right, being the first of the duo to reach it. "The shelves end, and the hallway seems to open into some sort of room. I can see people, and I think I see Tessa. Let's go!" Ted did not wait to see if Freddy followed before frantically running in that direction.

Soon after, they entered a circular portion of the gigantic library. The floor dipped slightly down toward its center, and all the large bookshelves ended abruptly, forming a big circle around it. The room had the appearance of a gigantic drain, in which water could run toward its center from all directions and drain away in a similar manner as a tub or sink. But instead of having a drain in the middle, Ted saw an altar made of some form of metal, and from each passageway in between the bookshelves that ended at this circular portion of the room, small, gutter-like channels were carved into the stone floor that connected to the altar. Each channel had some sort of silvery liquid running through it that seemed to be draining from the books themselves, and all the silvery streams ran directly up to the altar, covering Tessa's body from head to toe as though they were solid chains. Tessa did not move and appeared to be overpowered by the strange silvery material that imprisoned her. A black-haired man wearing sunglasses and dressed in a full black suit menacingly stood over her. As soon as Ted and Freddy entered the top of the circular part of the room, he addressed them.

"I must say, I'm quite impressed that you were able to follow us here," the man said to Ted and Freddy. "There's no way to get here without the aid of magic; maybe our dear friend Tessa is more powerful than I thought, and she somehow guided you here. No matter, as now that I know that she does not have the item, nor did your bear friend who has momentarily escaped us, the only conclusion is that one of you must have it. So please, hand it over."

"What, this?" Ted asked, confused, raising the halberd.

The man let out a wicked laugh. "You know," the man said as he pointed at Ted while looking down at Tessa, "he actually sounds sincere. Are you seriously going to tell me that you left such a valuable artifact in the hands of your dimwitted boyfriend? I have to be honest; I did not see that coming. We've been following you since you met him, and we followed you two all the way to New Hampshire. I've always been convinced that you know far more about the artifact than he ever will, so I had my men pull off him and follow you when you returned to New York. I simply assumed you left New Hampshire because you had a chance to steal it away from him and planned on taking it to your coven, but apparently, I was wrong. My men also said that they had not seen Daniel since you two separated, so I thought maybe he went back to his hometown in Vermont. But I can now see that I made many foolish assumptions. You must have left him in order to draw my attention to you while he stayed behind with it until you and your coven came up with a better plan. I guess we'll have to tear Waterville Valley apart until we find where Daniel is. You," the man said, glaring at Ted from behind his sunglasses, "you must know, Mr. Chief of Police. So tell me: where is Daniel Raggel?"

"Daniel is dead," Ted said flatly, and as soon as he had said it, he let out an anguished groan. He did not want to say that in front of Tessa, yet when the strange man's gaze locked onto his, even through his dark sunglasses, Ted could not resist telling the truth. Ted squirmed when Tessa screamed as she lay trapped upon the altar.

"So it seems," the man said as he stroked his cleanly shaven chin. "Clearly, you are telling the truth. Huh. Another surprise that I did not see coming. Perhaps I should have stayed in closer contact with my associate up there. Ah, you there, Detective," the man said as he pointed over Ted's shoulder. Ted watched Freddy emerge from behind him, who held his glasses as he stared blankly down the slope of the room to where the captor stood. "Tell me, did you find anything out of the ordinary when you examined Daniel's body or his surroundings?"

"Nothing," Freddy responded, "other than some of his innards had been eaten away by animals because he had been dead for a couple of days." Freddy remained in the same trance that Ted had been under when Tessa's subjugator stared directly at him. Tessa gasped again before sobbing. "Did not find any unusual items on his person, or at the surrounding scene, other than those weird stone pillars. Did not find anything in the town house they had rented, either," Freddy blurted out.

"Very well, then," the strange man said before turning his attention back to Tessa. As soon as he turned away, Ted pulled in a deep breath. He heard Freddy sigh and knew that he also experienced the same sense of relief. "You appear to be a more powerful witch than I had originally thought. While I'm not surprised that you have the ability to withstand my gaze of truth, you clearly have other talents that I underestimated. I suppose I'll have to torture you for quite a while to get you to talk. But your two companions up there have told me everything of use already, so I'd say that it's time to conclude my business with them." He then let out a guttural scream as he looked at the ceiling.

Ted heard the pattering sounds of pawed feet running across the tops of the wooden bookshelves. The loud volume indicated that several werewolves were inbound. Ted grasped his halberd nervously as he turned to find Freddy, who had once again resumed his position of standing behind him.

"I don't know if I can fight off that many!" Ted yelled.

"I agree," Freddy said, who stooped down to the floor as they talked and reclaimed the lamp. Ted did not recall that Freddy had let it go and thanked the high heavens that he once again had it in his possession. Freddy cradled it with one arm as he began frantically rubbing it up, down, and sideways with his free hand. Soon after, a familiar fiery smoke emerged from the spout as an entity made of pure flames emerged above their heads.

"How may I assist you?" the beast of fire asked.

"Help us defeat our enemies!" Freddy yelled.

"Very well then," the genie said before disappearing back into the lamp. As soon as his burning essence had disappeared, Ted noticed a man standing on top of a nearby bookshelf as he peered down at them over the edge. Although he had long black hair similar to the other werewolves when they were in human form, he did not seem to be one of them, radiating a different type of energy, noticeable even from that distance.

"Huh," the man said as he stared directly at the lamp that Freddy held on to, "so that's how you did it. I'm not exactly easy to summon, you know. But I was curious, and here we are." He looked familiar to Ted, or at least as much of him as he could make out from this distance looked familiar, as he seemed to peer out through a curtained blackness that surrounded only him. Even his voice sounded familiar, but Ted could not place it. The man turned around to scan the tops of the bookshelves around the room. "I see," he said to Ted and Freddy. "Got yourself a werewolf problem. Let me take care of that for ya. Keep in mind, though, I'm gonna call upon you for a favor one day." The man stood in silence for a few moments before Ted heard violent, beastly sounds as bones were broken and limbs were torn apart. He even saw a werewolf thrown down into the hallway behind them. Or at least, he saw half of one, as only the bottom half of the body violently splattered against the bookshelf, sending books flying as blood spattered everywhere. Ted could not see his new allies; he only heard their success in combat as the wolves' yelps echoed throughout the room. In less than a minute, Ted heard no more pattering of werewolf feet running along the bookshelves toward them, and their helper had mysteriously disappeared.

"Apparently, you two are more resourceful than I thought," the man imprisoning Tessa said as Ted turned around to face him. "I must be getting old; I'm making far too many mistakes with this matter. But let me show you one mistake I did not make." The man began to transform. He did not transform into a wolf as the others had but instead changed into a different-looking man, one wearing old gray robes with long, flowing gray hair and a matching beard. A portal began opening behind him. Ted could not make out much on the other side, as it appeared to be a room shadowed in darkness. After the man finished transforming, he lifted his arms, causing Tessa to rise off the table as the bubbling silvery liquid strands fully wrapped around her body, keeping her imprisoned.

"Does that place look familiar to you, Detective? Do you dare follow me?" He stepped through the portal, and Tessa's levitating body soon followed as she screamed all the while.

A strong tug on his shirtsleeve caused Ted to turn. He noticed Freddy standing beside him with a frantic look on his face.

"That's him!" Freddy said. "That's Nostradamus, the vampire that took my wife!" Freddy turned and bolted toward the portal while still holding the genie lamp as the portal slowly began to close.

Ted wasted no time before following his best friend.

CHAPTER 18

Once Ted's eyes had adjusted after traveling through the magical portal, he found himself standing next to Freddy in a dark, decrepit room. Ted nearly jumped when a soft blue light began to gently waft from the ax blade of the weapon, illuminating the room with enough light to allow them to see clearly. On one hand, Ted appreciated the light, as he had no desire to stumble around in the darkness of his enemy's lair. On the other hand, sheer terror overcame Ted upon seeing what the glow revealed.

Ted and Freddy appeared to have arrived in a living room, as evident by the couch that had been torn in half in the center of the room. The couch faced several windows that most likely would have revealed the neighborhood outside if they had not been boarded up. The old hardwood floors were rotted in several places, with gaping holes that went straight through to the basement ceiling. Globs of material that Ted could only reason used to reside inside of living bodies before being aggressively torn out of them were plastered to what remained of the walls.

"I cannot thank you enough for grabbing that weapon," Freddy told Ted as he studied the glow of the halberd. "It seems like it was made for this adventure. And we're gonna need it. This is the house, Ted. This is Nostradamus's lair that we had raided in Philly all those years ago. He must have returned after we stopped watching the place."

"So that probably means what I think it means?" Ted asked nervously.

"Yes," Freddy answered. "We most likely need to go to the basement. And I have no idea who or what will be waiting for us there. Since you have the light source, I'll let you take point. But I'll be right behind you, every step of the way. Exit the living room and head right. The entrance to the basement should be at the end of the hallway."

Since Freddy had mentioned that all the coffins were in the basement the first time he went there, Ted agreed that the best course of action would be heading directly to their enemy's hideout. He desperately wished that Freddy had a weapon similar to his, but he still sent God a thankful prayer for at least arming them with something. After Ted finished his prayer, he headed for the open doorway of the living room and stepped into the hallway.

The soft blue light of the halberd revealed a heavily reinforced and barricaded door to Ted's left, presumably the front door. He felt a shiver dance up his spine, knowing that that way would not prove to be a way out for them, at least without some serious, time-consuming work involved. With the glowing halberd held out in front of him, Ted turned right and began heading down the hallway, with Freddy close on his heels. Ted had to put the base of the halberd on to the floor and balance himself momentarily upon it to get a good look at the hallway. The ceiling and floor seemed to slope, making it look as though they were walking somewhat sideways. Even the frames of the doorways were uneven or in some cases constructed in odd shapes that would not fit a normal door. "Are you sure we're still in Philly and not in some friggin' alternate reality?" Ted whispered over his shoulder.

"Yes," Freddy responded in a raised whisper of his own. "Believe it or not, this is how the house looked when we raided it. We talked to cult experts about it, and they said that this was normal behavior for those who practiced the dark arts. They said that building things at strange angles was some sort of inversion of sacred geometry, which is very important to them." Ted nodded as if he understood, but he had never heard of sacred geometry before.

The soft blue glow from the halberd revealed much of the same in the hallways as it did in the living room, making it seem as though old, dried-up organs had congealed to the walls and ceiling. On the right, they passed a tilted painting of an old castle in the process of burning to the ground. Ted reasoned that when they were done with this mission, they should consider razing this structure, forever removing its tainted evil from the face of the earth.

Ted appreciated that all the doorways they passed were boarded up, which prevented the duo from being ambushed from the sides and allowed them to keep their focus on reaching the basement door. After a walk that seemed as though it had taken an eternity, Ted reached a normal-looking doorway that rested shut, the passageway that led directly to the basement. Upon sharing a silent "Are you ready?" exchange after glancing at Freddy, Ted reached out and opened the door.

The open doorway revealed a wooden staircase that descended to a small landing before taking a ninety-degree turn and continuing downward from that point. Unlike the rest of what Ted had seen of the house, the stairway remained in excellent condition, to the point that he had no fear of it enduring their combined body weights. The first stair did not even creak when he stepped on it, confirming his belief. For some reason, this small victory gave Ted confidence, so he began his descent with a new sense of vigor he had not had since arriving at this lair.

Upon reaching the bottom of the stairway, Ted could see in the soft glow of the halberd's light that the basement appeared to be one large, open room that matched the size of the first floor above. The stone foundation and earthen ground meant it had probably been built at least a hundred years ago. Before Ted had taken five steps forward into the basement, the entire room lit up in a manner similar to a dimmer switch being turned up. It issued enough light for Ted to be able to see everything, and everyone, in front of him without having to rely on the glow of his weapon.

"I'm going to skip the dramatic speech," Nostradamus said from across the room. He stood on a raised platform that had Tessa chained to an altar behind him with the same silvery liquid that had imprisoned her back in the library. "If you can defeat all my servants, you can have your woman." No sooner did Nostradamus finish speaking than a man with long black hair, dressed in outdated clothing similar to what Nostradamus wore, emerged from Ted's right. His gray skin drooped, and his nails were more like claws of the same color. The man took a swipe at Ted with one of his clawed hands before revealing a mouthful of fangs. Instinctively, Ted whirled around and cut the vampire's arm off, causing it to hiss in pain. Less than a second later, Ted cut the beast's head off. In addition to the iron of the ax portion of the halberd easily slicing through the vampire, the soft blue glow that the weapon emitted also burned the monster upon contact. Before the creature's body and severed head had hit the ground, two more vampires emerged from Ted's right. With three swift motions that seemed to be impossible for a man of Ted's size, he sliced both of them apart.

On and on the assault continued. Vampires dressed in outfits that ranged from those of the modern era to those of several hundred years ago emerged from all directions. But even with Freddy's exposure from behind, Ted used the halberd to spin and thrust with such speed and accuracy that he managed to defend all points of attack. Freddy earned his keep as well; although he did not have a weapon, he aided Ted, yelling, "Two to the right!" and "One from the front!" helping Ted keep his attention on the most imminent threats. Finally, after Ted had killed at least a dozen vampires without receiving a wound of his own, the fight had ended. Or at least, so he thought.

"You know," Nostradamus said, never having moved from the pedestal where he stood guard over Tessa, "when I said you must kill all my servants, I meant all."

A female vampire emerged from the shadows next to the pedestal. She had dirty-blond hair dangling down to her thin frame. She wore the remains of a tattered nightgown that had holes all over, just barely together enough to still qualify as an outfit. "Beth!" Freddy yelled as he began to run forward. Before he could get too far, Ted reached out and grabbed him by the arm.

"No!" Ted yelled. "You know what the truth is. That's not your wife anymore."

"Maybe not," Freddy said before reaching down to the ground and picking up the genie lamp. Ted had not noticed it since they had arrived in the vampire's lair and had nearly forgotten about it. "But I think I can fix that." Freddy began rubbing the lamp just as he had done earlier.

"Wait!" Tessa yelled. She had enough freedom within her restraints to be able to pick her head up and look in their direction. "How many times have you used the lamp tonight?"

"Twice," Ted answered, not waiting for Freddy to respond.

"What you've heard about those lamps is true!" Tessa shouted. "That's a real djinni in there. If you use it three times, you will owe the beast an enormous debt!"

"Totally worth it," Freddy said. Soon after, a now familiar creature of pure fire emerged into the basement, causing the entire room to light up.

"How may I serve you?" the creature asked through its smoky, gravelly voice.

"Free my wife from the curse that plagues her!" Freddy yelled as he pointed at Beth, who now crouched in attack position. Ted became nervous, wondering if this situation would resolve itself before he had to cut the remains of his best friend's wife in half. Just before Beth made a move, Nostradamus boldly stepped forward.

"You can't free her!" Nostradamus said with a wicked laugh. "I am her maker. Her curse is mine and mine alone to break. And I choose not to do so. Instead, you all will join her and become my servants!" But before Nostradamus could take another step toward Ted and Freddy, the genie reached out a burning arm that stretched several feet, grabbing the master vampire by the neck and raising him up toward the ceiling. "This is impossible!" Nostradamus said in a choked voice. "I am ancient! By the laws of Lucifer himself, I command you to release me!"

The djinni moved his entire body over to catch up with the arm that grasped Nostradamus so that he now hovered fully in front of him.

"I was a hundred thousand years old before your mortal sack of flesh had even formed," the genie answered. "Before there were vampires, there was djinni. We are fire, and fire shall always be." As soon as the beast finished speaking, the genie ripped Nostradamus in half. The vampire screamed as the remains of his body burned. When it ended, the genie drifted over to hover in front of Freddy. "I will give you a moment to say farewell."

Tears welled up in Ted's eyes. But before he tried to talk to Freddy, he gave him a moment to run over to his wife, who had collapsed onto the earthen floor. Freddy helped her sit up as he cradled her in his arms. She looked weak and sickly, but the gray skin she had had as a vampire began to slowly transform into a pinkish white color. Freddy whispered in her ear over and over as he helped her to her feet, supporting her bodyweight as they returned to where Ted stood. Once there, Freddy stood in front of Ted and looked at him through his thick glasses.

"No tears for me, old friend," Freddy said to Ted. "It doesn't matter if I'm in there for an eternity. I will be at peace, knowing that she is no longer a monster. Her freedom is my freedom."

Ted ignored Freddy's request and allowed tears to roll down his cheeks as he hugged him. He did this as delicately as possible, as Beth remained in Freddy's arms, so Ted made sure not to endanger her fragile form.

"It is time," the genie said, interrupting their tender moment.

Freddy exchanged one final look with Ted before looking at the genie and nodding. He kissed Beth tenderly before telling her to cling to Ted's shoulder just as she had been doing with his. Beth began shedding her own tears, causing her to clutch Ted tightly in order to avoid falling over. Once Beth had fully removed herself from grasping onto Freddy, the genie put a burning hand onto Freddy's shoulder, and within moments, the genie and Freddy turned into smoke and began drifting into the spout of the genie lamp sitting on the basement floor. And before Ted could react, Beth broke away from him and lunged toward the drifting smoke.

"I'm going with him!" Beth yelled as she jumped for the trailing smoke.

"No!" Ted yelled as he began to lunge forward, but before he could, someone blindsided him and tackled him to the ground. He reached for the halberd, which he had driven straight into the earthen floor so that he could have his arms free to hug Freddy goodbye but stopped when he found a tall redhead on top of him.

"Let her be!" Tessa yelled as she looked at Ted. Ted could hardly believe that she smelled like lavender and honey, even after all she had been through. "This is her choice. Let her go, so you don't get sucked in too!" Ted agreed with Tessa's logic and watched as Beth immediately transformed into smoke upon grabbing the smoldering entrails of her husband. A few moments later, all the smoke went into the lamp without leaving a trace behind.

"I'm Tessa, by the way," Tessa said as she stood and helped Ted up. "Nice to officially meet you. But more importantly, thank you for saving my life." She kissed Ted's cheek.

"I'm Ted," he responded, blushing. It had been a long while since he had been so close to a woman, especially one as attractive as Tessa. The two exchanged a brief energetic sharing of thankful energy for having survived the night before heading for the stairway, but not before Tessa reached down to grab the lamp, and Ted retrieved the halberd along with the last item Freddy had left behind: his glasses.

CHAPTER 19

Ted followed Tessa upstairs and out of the basement.

"I know we have a lot to talk about," Tessa said while gently grabbing Ted's arm, "but it'll have to wait. We gotta get out of this house and get out of Philly. At least I know that we're in Philly now; I could not even tell you where, or when, that library was. Nostradamus was unbelievably powerful, but he was not the top of the food chain. He was a general in someone's very powerful organization. If we linger here, more of his companions will find us." Ted did not question Tessa one bit. It had taken an ancient genie as well as the mortal sacrifice of his best friend to defeat Nostradamus. As such, Ted had no interest in finding out whom the vampire had been working for. Swiftly, Ted followed Tessa up the stairs to the first floor before making their way to the living room.

After a quick surveillance of the first floor, it seemed as though the living room windows were not as heavily reinforced as the front door, so Ted and Tessa decided to break out one in order to create an escape route. "I'm not a very powerful witch," Tessa said as they took turns kicking the plywood that covered up the open window. "But I do have a few tricks that I can use to help us. I can cast a spell to disguise us and allow us to blend in with the locals, and I can disguise that," she said as she pointed at Ted's enormous weapon. "Once we're outside, we'll get ourselves to the train station and head back to New York."

Ted nodded and went back to kicking the plywood and striking it with his halberd. Tessa surprised him with kicks nearly as strong as his. After a short time of diligent work, they broke through and created a hole large enough to crawl outside.

Once outside, Ted found himself standing in knee-high grass in the front yard of a decrepit house on a dead-end street. The overcast sky threatened a storm, a perfect metaphor for the stormy emotions crashing around in his body. But enough light peeked through the clouds for Ted to realize that Friday night had passed into Saturday morning. After not seeing anyone standing nearby, he made the hopeful assumption that no local residents had seen two strangers crawl out of an allegedly abandoned house.

"We're under my spell, changing our appearance now," Tessa said after dusting off her jeans and checking her torso for wounds, which took an extra moment since her red T-shirt would have blended in with any blood she had shed. "And whatever we talk about will be altered to sound like we're neighborhood people talking about neighborhood things. Hopefully, it will be a little bit before we start running into people. This is not the greatest of neighborhoods, and unfortunately, you probably just killed any homeless or drug addicts that hung out on this particular street when you fought Nostradamus's servants."

That was quite a somber note to begin their journey on, so as soon as they started walking up the street, Ted began asking Tessa the long list of questions he had for her.

"Okay," Ted said as he walked next to Tessa while using the halberd like a combination of a walking stick to lean upon and a broom to sweep debris out of their path, "please tell me what the hell is going on."

"I met Daniel in 2013," Tessa said as she walked carefully, stepping over the garbage on the sidewalk that Ted had not previously swept aside. "My backstory was that I needed a dresser for my guest bedroom, and I found his shop during my search. In reality, I was undercover. I am part of a coven, a group of witches that trace our bloodline all the way back to the witches of Salem, and probably even further than that. As I already mentioned, I'm not a very powerful one. The more direct your blood is to the original witches of Salem, the more powerful you are. I'm a few times removed from that pure source, but I do have enough skill to do what my high priestess needed me to do, which was to charm Daniel and gain access to his business. Our coven had been watching Talandoor's since it opened. Our sources learned that Daniel was working with some very powerful people, some of them you have now met. It did not take me long to fall in favor with Daniel. He was a great salesman but did not have any supernatural powers, so it was kinda easy to charm him."

These powerful people must have helped Daniel keep his address off his license and most likely other important public records as well, Ted thought.

"Soon after I met Daniel, we started dating, and soon after that, we became business partners," Tessa said. "As I know that you know from finding the djinni lamp, Talandoor's deals in much more than valuable antiques. The real part of the business was to buy and sell magical items in a black market for those types of things. My job was to watch the traffic for that part of the business and hopefully find the top dog that Daniel worked with and then take that information back to my high priestess. I'm sure that you can see now that many of the 'people' in this industry are evil and pose a threat to humanity. Identifying Daniel's employers proved to be very difficult, as Daniel had taken an oath of secrecy and risked his life just letting me know about his line of work, which, admittedly, I coaxed out of him with some magical charm. So we came up with a story of Daniel hiring me to work upstairs with the antiques, and if anyone asked, I would play dumb about any other part of the business, all while I continued to gather as much information about Daniel's employers as I could. But even Daniel did not know much about them. Many of them operated in secrecy, disguising their identities and so on, so it wasn't like I could pry his brain for the information.

"As the years went on, an unexpected side effect occurred with my pretend relationship with Daniel: it became very real. Daniel proved to be smart, kind, and sweet, and I fell in love with him. In fact, we got engaged and planned on marrying at some point next year."

Tessa started fidgeting with the ring on her ring finger. It did not look like a traditional engagement ring and in fact looked fairly cheap, with a gold band that may not have been real gold and an onyx stone that may have been a fake as well. But considering all the "cheap-looking" items he had seen in the last twenty-four hours that had proven to be much more powerful than he ever could have imagined, Ted had already become wise enough to reserve those types of judgment.

"Daniel was a master of buying and selling," Tessa said as she continued her story. "And the best part about it was that he did not become overly attached to the items. This would have been easy for anyone to do; after all, the items were crafted by magic, and they all have their own special powers. But outside of a rare few, Daniel was more excited to wheel and deal the items than he was to hold on to them. The exception was the item that brought us to New Hampshire a couple of weeks ago."

"Why exactly did you go to New Hampshire?" Ted asked.

"We could have easily ended up in Vermont," Tessa responded. "Daniel grew up there, and it certainly has the right kind of landscape for what we wanted to do. But I told Daniel that he should not mix magic and family and convinced him to go to a place I knew about, which was Waterville Valley. I told him another half truth, telling him that I knew about the area because a coven member was from there. But the real truth of that story is that my coven believes there is currently an undiscovered witch living in your town, one who doesn't know her powers or her heritage. That was one of the reasons I didn't check in at the town house as a guest. I don't know who she is, but I couldn't for sure say the same about her. If by chance our information was wrong, and she had started to awaken to her powers, then she may have done research on our coven and learned who I was. We don't advertise, but we aren't impossible to find either; look at how Daniel's employers found me. And that was the other reason. Daniel and I were not publicly advertising our relationship. He did not want his bosses to start connecting dots and assume that I knew more than I was supposed to. So we each pretended to leave on separate vacations to visit our own relatives, which was my excuse for not staying behind and working the shop while he went to New Hampshire."

"A witch in Waterville Valley?" Ted asked. "I would think I would've seen someone like you up there. I've been there for several years, and before you and Daniel came along, there was never anything out of the ordinary going on."

"She probably has no idea that she's a witch, then," Tessa answered. "Because of that, she probably won't be showing any signs, and she most certainly would not be able to cast any spells yet. The signs she would be showing at this point are so subtle that they probably just look like personality traits."

"Okay," Ted said while nodding. "I know what I'd be looking for now, so I can take a look around when I get back there. But tell me, how in the world did Marvin get sucked into this?"

"That really is a great question," Tessa said. "The short answer is that Daniel and I were at Grizzly's Bar one night and had a bit too much to drink. Daniel accidentally dropped the magic item on the floor, and Marvin picked it up. I believe that initiated his change. Marvin is a werebear, a special kind of lycanthrope that changes into a bear instead of a wolf. He has a bloodline that he is not aware of. Based on how he explained it, he went through most of his childhood in foster homes before becoming a homeless drifter as an adult. Perhaps his real parents hoped that if they got rid of him, then maybe somehow their curse would not pass down to their son. And it's not really a curse, as only society and its relentless need for judgment and labels make it seem so. There are plenty of lycanthropes that are productive members of society, and Marvin certainly seems like a great guy. I think that because he touched the item, and because there is something special about the woods of your homeland, it awakened him to his true heritage. After all, Marvin visited Daniel at the cairn stones the following day, and I'm sure that being there sped up his awakening.

"And this is when things got difficult. After we met Marvin, Daniel started to change. In all the years I had known him, he had never acted like he started to act in the middle of that week. He suddenly became short-tempered and nervous, constantly looking over his shoulder. At first, he thought that we may have been followed to New Hampshire. Then he became convinced that his employer already had agents there, which seemed ridiculous at the time, but based on how everything turned out, I'm starting to think that he was right. In hindsight, it's clear that something must have happened to Daniel, and I don't know what it is. It wasn't Marvin; I've spent enough time with him to see that he's okay. Something else must've happened. Daniel must have encountered something, or someone, when I was not with him. He had fallen asleep in the woods the night that we met Marvin, by himself. Maybe something happened then."

Ted contemplated Tessa's words. First, she claimed that a witch lived in Waterville Valley. On top of that, she insinuated that allies of Nostradamus were likely running around in his woods. Nausea began to knock around in his stomach as he wondered how he could have missed all of this. *Am I any kind of good cop at all?* he asked himself. He could not answer at that moment.

"Before the week was over, Daniel had turned against me," Tessa said. "He began looking at me like I was his enemy. Perhaps he had somehow uncovered the fact that I was indeed sent to spy on him in the beginning. If he did, he would certainly have a right to be upset with me. But we could've talked about that. He slapped me, something he had never done before, and that was it for me. I wondered if it was the artifact, but based on the little bit of research I had done on it before we went to New Hampshire, that just did not seem like the answer. At that time, I gave up trying to make up excuses for him and decided that I would leave him alone for the rest of the vacation. I hoped that time alone in the woods would help him come back to his senses. So I left him a note that said I was leaving and took the car back to New York. I figured that if he called me and apologized, I'd come back and pick him up. But that call never came. Instead, I received a frantic call from Marvin, who had become aware of his werebear bloodline. I felt that the initiation of his change was our fault and arranged for him to come to New York, where I could teach him about what he truly was and be there for his first transformation as I held his hand through the whole thing.

"That's when you found us, and unfortunately, so did my enemy. They either followed Marvin down from New Hampshire or followed me after I left. Either way, they were on to me, somehow knowing that I was a witch who had found a way into Daniel's business. I felt like someone more powerful than me had followed us into the park, which is why I did not have a disguise spell activated. It may have worked on you and other regular people, but it would not have worked on them, so I didn't bother, hoping that I could instead turn Marvin loose on them after his transformation, which would have hopefully given us a fighting chance. And finding Marvin was a huge bonus for them, as their cult involves forcing vampirism or lycanthrope upon their initiates, and they do not take too kindly to ones that exist outside their organization. However, they mostly deal with werewolves and were not ready for the brute strength that Marvin has when he's in bear form. He changed in the back of the van after they had taken us and crashed through the back doors before taking off into the city streets. I really hope he's okay, wherever he is. And I feel so foolish for not sensing that something was happening outside of Daniel's control. I was devastated when I heard you say that he's dead. I am at least partially to blame, and I'll have to live with that."

"Based on what I've seen this weekend, none of us could have foreseen all of this, not even you," Ted said, trying to offer some condolences and support. "Look at me. I never knew that my own best friend had a vampire as an archenemy. This entire week has been nothing but surprises for all of us, including you, and most likely even Daniel, so give yourself a break on that."

Tessa nodded, and the two walked in silence as they began to pass people out and about in the neighborhood. Ted noticed that just like the neighborhood of the vampire house, each block seemed like a poor area that continued to be ravaged by drugs. As such, Ted could not help but pity the people of the Badlands. In a much different way, New Hampshire had a similar problem, as many illegal and quite lethal drugs were slowly penetrating through its woods, resulting in several addictions that, in turn, led to multiple fatalities. Ted vowed that he would do better within the larger community of New Hampshire, coming up with volunteer programs to help out his neighbors after returning to his job—if he still had a job to return to.

"Now it's time for me to ask you a question," Tessa said. "I've been dreading asking you this since we defeated Nostradamus, but I can't hide from it any longer: how exactly did Daniel die?"

Ted tried not to let out as big of a sigh as he did. "He was in the woods," he said, leaving out the details of a bunch of teenagers finding the body. Ted grumbled to himself, still not knowing what to do about the damned kids. But he realized he needed to table that thought for a later time. "He was lying down in the circle of cairn stones. Did you make those?"

"No," Tessa said with a small laugh, "those were already there. Daniel roamed your trails for a bit, looking for a good place to start using his item, and that's when we found it. I thought that was something that had been there for a while, maybe your town's version of Stonehenge."

"No," Ted said, confused by the fact that Tessa had not made the cairn stones. Although one could not see Black Bear Brook from either the road or the village, it did not exactly take miles to walk to either. It added even more confusion to the entire situation, but Ted decided to set aside that thought and get back to the important conversation. "On a much smaller scale, I suppose that I could say I sensed some unexplainable danger as well. I'm sure you can imagine that we don't get many dead bodies up my way. So I went rogue. My department reports to a larger unit in a nearby town. Proper protocol would have had me calling it in to my superior and letting him take over the investigation. But some strange feelings tugging at my intuition were encouraging me to go in a different direction. So in a maneuver that will most likely cost me my job and my career and may even put me in prison, I took matters into my own hands. Freddy, who you briefly met, was a former detective. He was my best friend, and I knew that he could keep a secret, so I deputized him and enlisted his help. His preliminary investigation did not reveal anything, but when we checked your town house and found the imprint of your name etched into the pad of paper along with a business card in Daniel's wallet, that was a good enough lead to follow down to New York. Today was scheduled to be our last day in the city, and I promised Freddy that I would tell my superior everything if we returned home empty-handed, which is clearly now far from the case." Ted paused a moment. "We have his body secured," he said uncomfortably. "It'd probably make sense to take you back to New Hampshire and have you ID him, just to be sure."

"This is all my fault," Tessa said as tears welled up in her eyes. Even through the tears, Ted found their sharp blue gaze to be stunning. "Daniel took a blood oath when he began working for those people. I can attest to the fact that he was not a bad guy. I know for certain now that our enemy did something to turn him violent in his last days, and I'll get to the bottom of that. But his blood oath was a life oath. I made him break that bond, and it cost him his life. And now you may lose your job over all of this or, worse, go to jail. I cannot believe how much I screwed everything up." Tessa abruptly dropped to the dirty sidewalk in an eruption of tears.

Ted had no idea what to say to her, so he said nothing, holding the halberd in one hand while putting his other hand on her shoulder as she sat in the middle of Philadelphia's Badlands on a dreary Saturday morning.

CHAPTER 20

After Tessa collected herself, Ted helped her up off the sidewalk. "I'm going to pop in that convenience store across the street and see if they will let me use their bathroom," Tessa said.

Ted waited for her outside, nervously clutching the halberd in hopes that Tessa's spell continued to work even when she did not stand directly beside him. The longer they had walked, the more that people began to accompany them on the sidewalks as they began their Saturday morning. Ted grasped the weapon extra tightly when two young teenagers approached him, but he sucked in a large breath of relief when they trotted up the steps and entered the convenience store without giving him a second glance. Just as Ted began to wonder what Tessa's spell must be making him look like to strangers, Tessa popped out of the store, counting bills in her hands.

"All set," she said. "I also grabbed a public transportation map. It looks like we need to take two different buses to get to the train station. On Saturday hours, it may take over an hour, so let's get going. Oh, and don't worry about that," Tessa said as she pointed at the halberd. "It's going to look like a large backpack or an overstuffed briefcase, depending on who looks at it. I've changed our appearance to look pretty tough for this neighborhood. As we enter the business district, I'll make us look like corporate employees putting in extra weekend hours."

Ted nodded, taking Tessa's word that her disguises were as good as she claimed them to be.

Ted and Tessa walked for two blocks to get to the first bus stop. Just as Tessa had predicted, it took two different buses to get to where they were going, and also as she had predicted, the buses had less frequent routes because of it being a weekend. Still, the trip did not take too long, and the two found themselves in the Thirtieth Street Station to catch a train departing for New York City just before eleven thirty. Tessa had paid for their bus passage, and after using the restroom at the train station, she bought their train tickets as well. Ted still had his wallet on him since departing his hotel room the day before and offered to help with the expense, but Tessa refused.

"This is my mess," she told him while putting a comforting hand on his shoulder, sending waves of relief running through his body. "It's the least I can do."

Ted could not help but notice that Tessa kept playing with her wedding finger ring before going to the bathroom and then came out counting cash just as she did at the convenience store, but he kept that detail to himself.

Ted took the aisle seat after boarding the train, needing to stand the tall halberd up at the edge of the aisle. Although it might have looked different to strangers, it did not change its shape in reality, so Ted had to deal with the awkwardness of carrying it around in cramped places. After taking two different bus rides, he became more proficient at it, leaning it in as boarding passengers passed him by. Tessa took the inside seat and fell asleep on Ted's shoulder as soon as the train departed. Her soothing touch kept him awake and gave him the focus to continue to navigate the halberd around passersby. Ted could not stop himself from smelling her hair, which radiated scents of vanilla and mint. He had no idea how she could smell so good after the night she had endured but assumed it had something to do with her magical abilities. After about an hour and a half, they arrived at Penn Station. Tessa awoke with a gentle yawn and patted Ted gently on the chest, sending more butterflies fluttering through his stomach.

"I need to check out of the hotel," Ted said. "Freddy's keys to his truck are back there. I can grab the truck and take you back to Talandoor's from there."

"Sounds good," Tessa responded before patting Ted's chest one more time.

Once they were off the train, they navigated their way through the crowded train station. Philadelphia dwarfed Waterville Valley or even Plymouth with its large population, but it seemed to Ted that New York did the same to Philly. Once on street level, they sought a cab, and Ted left the duties of hailing one down to Tessa. With one of her long legs, which seemed to stretch forever playfully dancing over the edge of the sidewalk, Tessa's beauty made her stand out from all the competition trying to flag down a ride. Sure enough, Tessa won the unofficial contest and secured a ride. Ted did not hesitate to rush after her and climb in the back of the cab after angling the halberd inside first.

After twenty minutes, they were in front of the hotel on Eighth Street, and Tessa paid, again reaching into the pockets of her jeans and pulling out what seemed to be a never-ending supply of money. Once inside, they took the elevator to the room, where Ted silently vowed that he would do a thorough job packing. He and Freddy had not brought much stuff, but he wanted to make sure he grabbed everything that Freddy had left in the room, even trivial things like socks and a toothbrush. At some point, when the dust had settled, Ted planned on tracking down Freddy's next of kin, informing them of his death and passing on his belongings to them. As he went methodically around the room, Tessa sat on the bed seemingly studying him.

Once Ted had gotten the last of Freddy's possessions from the hotel room, he went downstairs and checked out. He apologized for only having one keycard, stating that his friend had a family emergency and had to leave town suddenly. (*Not too far from the truth*, Ted morbidly thought.) The attendant understood and waved the fee, smiling at Tessa as he did so. Once they made their way to the garage, Ted stashed the halberd in the back of Freddy's Bronco before they drove off, relieved to get a break from holding it.

Ted gleamed with a small sense of pride for how he handled driving through the insanity of New York's traffic, which, for some reason, seemed harder than killing werewolves and vampires. After making their way to East Fortieth Street, Tessa pointed at a small alleyway that preceded the store. "Go down there," Tessa said. Ted cautiously turned down the narrow passageway before Tessa indicated that he should take the first left. After they had driven about halfway down the alleyway, Tessa stopped Ted and jumped out of the passenger seat before touching something on the building's wall that he could not see. A small garage door previously camouflaged as part of the wall opened up. Ted took the sharp turn after Tessa had climbed back in and then drove down the slope into the private garage as the door closed behind them.

After Ted parked in a narrow parking space, Tessa gently grabbed him by the forearm. "Will you come up?"

"At the very least, I should return the halberd to the suit," Ted said, "and we should still arrange a time in the very near future for you to provide a positive ID for Daniel."

"Leave the halberd here," Tessa said. "Each magical item has a partner. When it finds its partner, it seems to fit with them just like a comfortable shirt. I don't know what it is yet, but you and that halberd have a history. I could not have blended that in with you while we were in public so easily if you did not. So the halberd stays with you, and the suit of armor is going with you as well. I have a strange feeling that it would somehow fit you perfectly."

"Okay," Ted said, not knowing how to interpret her comments or what else he should say at the moment. "Thank you. I think Freddy may have left a bag of his gadgets in the store while we were looking for the lamp, so I'll grab that as well."

"Great," Tessa said as she exited the truck. "Follow me."

Ted did, joining her as she walked across the parking lot.

"I hope you still have my keys," Tessa said with a smile after they reached the elevator.

"Yes," Ted said, nearly forgetting that he did.

After he handed the key ring to Tessa, she took the blue gemstone and waved it in front of an invisible sensor, causing the elevator door to open. Upon walking into the elevator, Tessa made a similar movement, opening up a secret panel that had call buttons for the store and the loft (but noticeably not for the basement).

Once up in the loft, Tessa threw the keys on the counter and began walking toward the bathroom. "I'm in desperate need of a shower," she said. "There's beer in the fridge. Grab one. Relax. There will be plenty of time to deal with the armor and anything you left in the store later."

Although Ted still had a sense of urgency to make some sort of good out of Freddy's death, he immediately succumbed to fatigue upon reaching the loft. He took Tessa's offer as an order and grabbed a beer from the fridge before plopping down on the couch. He took two sips before putting it on the coffee table. He must have nodded off, because the next moment he awoke, he saw Tessa standing in front of him, wearing nothing but a purple nightgown as her wet hair clung to its shoulder straps. Her piercing blue eyes seemed to stare right through him.

"Do you believe in fate?" Tessa asked.

"I believe in God," Ted answered. This journey had gotten him back in touch with God, and he believed that God—and God alone—provided him with what he needed to survive the night.

Tessa smiled at his answer. "I'm going to let you in on a little secret," she said. "All of us who serve higher forces believe in God. The only difference is 'God' is not what the church says. Unfortunately, the church became a business a long time ago. And when it did, it lost its true vision. But a universal being certainly exists, and as such, we all serve it one way or another."

A wave of relief washed over Ted. He finally had an answer as to why he did not fully connect with his father's preaching during his younger years. Clearly, his father had meant well with his sermons, but he had been operating in a broken, corrupt system far above his pay grade. Ted had lost touch with his father over the years, and at this moment, he decided to make amends. Upon returning to New Hampshire, he would visit him and make peace with him. At long last, Ted's personal *Groundhog Day* had an end in sight.

"Even in servitude of God, we all live under the guidance of fate," Tessa said. "We all have free will, but our fate is the most optimal path, creating the easiest life for us to live if we choose to follow it. Look at us. I said two things to you when I got captured: the code to shut off the alarm, and the description of the one magical item in the basement that could deliver you to me. Look at all the dots you had to connect in between hearing me say those things and finding me again: finding the gem in my key ring, finding the halberd, getting to the basement, and locating the lamp. Do you think just anyone could have done that? I loved Daniel, and I am devastated that he is dead. But our fate has intertwined, and it is clear that our destiny lies together."

Tessa slipped out of her nightgown, revealing her supple skin and perfect body as she sat on Ted's lap and began kissing him. Her warm kisses caused Ted to moan. But he did need to stop, at least for a moment, so he gently pushed her away.

"I need to know one thing," Ted said. "I need to know if you have me under a spell right now, like when you first met Daniel."

Tessa smiled and let out a soft laugh before kissing Ted on the cheek. "I promise you, you are not," Tessa responded. "And that is how I know this is real. For the first time in my life, I know real love. I knew it from the first moment I saw you in the park, and I know it even more now by touching you."

Ted accepted her answer and fully embraced her, making love to Tessa for the remainder of Saturday afternoon.

CHAPTER 21

Ted took a shower and climbed into bed with Tessa, letting her convince him to spend the night before departing for New Hampshire on Sunday. They made love several more times throughout the night, sending sensations of pure bliss throughout Ted's body every moment that Tessa remained in his arms. Even though he had been married to Eleanor in his earlier years, lovemaking had never been such moments of ecstasy with her, nor were they ever with any other woman he had been with before. Ted had started to accept Tessa's explanation of their destinies belonging together.

Ted playfully ran one hand through Tessa's luscious red curls as they lay in bed watching the sunrise begin gently poking rays of light through the eastern windows across the other end of the loft. "So now that things are finally settling down and coming into order," Tessa said as she rested her head on one of his broad shoulders, "where is the artifact?"

"The lamp?" Ted asked, confused. "I thought you held on to it. I'm sorry if I was supposed to be paying attention to that."

"No," Tessa said with a smile as she sat up, wrapping the silk sheet around her. "You were right; I did grab that in Philly and made sure it got back here. I'm talking about Daniel's item."

"I'm still not sure what you mean," Ted said as he sat up alongside Tessa, looking at her with confusion. His heart began to drop when he noticed Tessa's smile rapidly fade away, only to get replaced by a look of concern.

"The whole reason Daniel went to New Hampshire in the first place," Tessa said seriously. "The magic item I mentioned when I was catching you up on my backstory in Philly."

"I remember," Ted said nervously. "I thought you were talkin' about the ring you were wearing on your wedding band finger. I noticed you playin' with it ever since we left the vampire house." Ted just now noticed that Tessa must have removed the ring at some point the previous night, as for the first time, he did not see it on her. Pangs of fear began gnawing at his stomach as he wondered what other magical item Tessa could be referring to.

"Are you seriously telling me that you and Freddy did not find the mask on Daniel's body?"

"We didn't find anything but the town house room key," Ted said, and then in a moment of clarity, he sprang to his feet, standing naked inside the loft. "Dammit!" he yelled. "Those little shits!" Before he could say anything else, Tessa had gotten out of bed and started getting dressed.

"Grab the suit of armor," Tessa said as she frantically grasped any clothes within reach. "You can explain what you mean in the truck. We're going to Waterville Valley—now. But we're gonna take a quick detour through Springfield on the way."

"Why?" Ted asked. "That's a bit outta the way. It'll slow us down."

"It will be worth it," Tessa said frantically. "We're going to talk to someone who can help. Daniel never knew that I did some research on the mask before we left for New Hampshire. In the wrong hands, that item can be dangerous beyond words, and I only know a little about it. We're going to talk to someone who knows much more than I do about what we may be up against."

Ted finished getting dressed as fast as he could, silently cursing himself for being fooled by a group of fourteen-year-olds.

Devin made his way back home after striking out trying to find Chief Hannon with Corey and Matthew. He wondered where the hell the chief could be and hoped that his absence had nothing to do with the dead body. Once home, he found his dad still sitting his lazy ass on the couch, drinking beer and watching the Patriots game while his mother had her Kiss the Cook apron on as she prepared all the scraps that were going to be deposited in the slow cooker for tonight's venison stew dinner. His sister, Mandy, did her normal Sunday routine, running around doing who-knows-what. Devin made his way up to his room and took a quick glance at the unfinished Lego *Millennium Falcon* and opted for his bass instead, practicing acoustically.

After about ten minutes, he had a bold idea and texted Li, asking her if he could come by and start working on one of the Symphony X songs that she wanted him to learn as "payment" for joining the band. Plus, he added to his text, he missed Frank and wanted to see him. (*I can't believe it, but it's true,* Devin thought.)

Surprisingly, Li texted him back within five minutes and invited him over, even telling Devin that she had an acoustic bass on hand for him to use. Devin did not need to hear anything else, so after grabbing his fleece jacket and stuffing his magical item securely into the pocket before zipping it up, he bolted downstairs, telling his mother of his plan. "Just be home by six for dinner," she said, which gave him a few hours to spend with Li.

Devin rapidly pedaled his mountain bike to Li's house, walking it up her steep driveway instead of trying to be a champion and ride it up. After he made it inside her house and exchanged pleasantries with her father and her younger brother, Li told Devin to wait for her out back in the Zen garden. Soon, she made her way there with a guitar case in each arm as Frank followed closely behind. Upon grabbing a seat on the bench, Li popped opened each case, gesturing for Devin to pick up the acoustic bass, while she grabbed the acoustic guitar.

Once comfortable, Li pulled out an iPad from an inner jacket pocket and opened a web browser with guitar tabs. "I'll show you one of their newer songs, 'Without You,'" Li said. "It's a simple song—for them, at least. It will be a good place for us to start."

Devin had no clue how to read guitar tablature but embraced the moment of sitting next to Li, especially since she engaged with him instead of burying her face in her phone. She looked sexy in her simple outfit of a hot-pink jacket and matching running pants, and every time she shook her head, her hair waved around, leaving a scent of honey and cinnamon floating gently under Devin's nose, sending his heart racing.

"Listen," Devin said. "I really wanna thank you. Not just for helping out the band but for helping me. I've never had so much creativity and focus before."

"No problem," Li said. "And to be honest, you're kinda doing the same for me. I'm not sure the Waterville Valley white girls know what to do with me yet. Sometimes they look at me like I'm an exotic animal sitting behind a cage in the zoo. Even Mandy is kind of like that with me. It's nice to hang out with you guys. You just don't seem to see me like that."

"I think your ethnicity is one of the things that makes you interesting," Devin said. "And don't worry; Mandy doesn't like me either."

Li let out a small laugh before running her fingers through her hair, leaving Devin to wonder which of his comments struck gold with her.

"Look at you, making a move," Frank said inside Devin's head as he began to rub against his legs. Devin reached down and scratched his head, causing Frank to softly purr.

"It's nice to see you too, Frank," Devin responded. In truth, he did have more confidence around Li today. He reasoned that maybe Li opening up a bit to him gave him a much-needed morale boost.

"I wish my mother felt that way," Li said. "She's still back in San Fran dealing with my grandmother. There's some stuff going on with her that would make your head spin."

"Oh, you'd be surprised," Devin said, now taking his turn to chuckle.

Li remained silent for a moment, reading the guitar tab. The wind rustling through the dead leaves on the ground created the only sound.

"We're here because my parents want to protect me," Li abruptly said. "My grandmother is a *wu*, which is a type of female shaman. Apparently, she's got herself tied up in a magical feud with someone, and now the family is in danger. To be honest, I have a hard time believing in that kind of shit. But the danger is real because the people are real, and they don't need magic to hurt us with a gun, knife, or just plain brute force. She used to live with us back there, so my dad insisted on getting me and my brother far away while my mother figures out what to do with her. Crazy family drama, right?"

"No," Devin said, and with a clear burst of consciousness that he had never had before, he unzipped his fleece pocket. "A couple of weeks ago, I would have been right there with you, not believing in anything like that. And then I found this." For the first time since he had taken it, Devin pulled out the strange leathery item in front of another person.

"So that's why you're always playing with your jacket pocket,"

Li said, which caused Devin to momentarily panic, as he hoped that nobody else had been so perceptive. "What is it?"

"Honesty, I don't know," Devin responded. "I wonder if it was some sort of sack that decayed with age. See, there are a couple of holes there. But I'll be even more honest with you: it has special powers, and I can talk to animals with it. I've been using it to talk to Frank since I found him."

"You mean since I found you," Frank said as he sat in front of the reflecting pool, beaming with pride.

"Come on!" Li said while laughing. "I'm new here, so you think I'm gullible, right?"

"Tell her that she has a yellow fidget spinner on her bedroom nightstand that she uses to relieve stress," Frank said.

Devin repeated Frank's words verbatim to Li.

"So what!" Li said, now putting her guitar back in its case and almost falling off the bench laughing. "You snooped around my bedroom when you went to the bathroom one time—right, perv?"

Devin reached out his hand. "Take it," he said evenly. "Take it and see for yourself."

Cautiously, Li did, handling it as though it might burn at the touch. She held it for a moment and dropped it as she screamed and jumped up from the bench.

"No way!" Li yelled excitedly. "Frank said hi to me in my head! I actually heard him! It was like a thought but stronger and clearer." She sat down and picked the item back up, grabbing the leather cord and examining it carefully. "No," Li said. "No. It wasn't a sack. Look at these holes. They're evenly spaced apart. This wasn't a sack; this was a mask."

Embarrassment came over Devin for never having made that connection after spending so much time handling the item over the last week. "Well?" Li asked.

"Well, what?" Devin asked.

"Put it on, silly."

Now even more embarrassed, Devin grabbed the mask and looked at Frank. If a cat could shrug its shoulders in an "I don't know what to tell you" fashion, Devin believed that Frank had done just that. After taking a deep breath, Devin stretched the cord over the back of his head and put the leathery mask over his face. An overwhelming energy surge throughout his entire body caused him to quickly take it off, careful not to tear it in the process.

"This is amazing!" Devin yelled. "Try it!"

Li did not hesitate and immediately put it on. Devin could tell by the large smile that nearly dropped her jaw into her lap that Li experienced the same sensation, somehow even feeding an acorn to a squirrel that had jumped in her lap! After taking the mask off, Li yelled out in joy before kissing Devin's cheek. Riding high on his newfound courage, he gently grabbed Li by the base of her neck and shared a deep kiss with her.

Devin began riding home with a huge smile on his face: he had kissed Li! He beamed with pride for having the courage, which only grew stronger when he thought of the fact that she had kissed him back. Even Frank had gotten in on it, saying, *"See? Looks like you two share a destiny together. If it wasn't for me coming into your life, you would never know that."* Devin had thanked him and petted him an extra amount of time, agreeing with the feline. Giving Frank to Li seemed to be the first step of opening the door to her heart. And on top of all that, Li helped Devin identify the magical item as a mask, and wearing it did amazing things that were beyond comprehension.

Devin and Li agreed to meet privately after school on Monday to explore its powers further, as the powers from wearing the mask went far beyond the ones they received just from holding it. Additionally, Devin took a cautious approach with how he talked about his own history with the item with Li, telling her that he had found it in the woods on a rock, not wanting to involve her in Chief Hannon's secret about a dead body. He also told her that neither Corey nor Matthew knew, and he wanted it to remain their secret, at least for the time being. Li thanked him for trusting her enough to include her on his little adventure of magical discovery, sending butterflies crashing and banging around Devin's stomach.

In the meantime, Devin took the mask home with him, securing it in his jacket pocket. The two agreed that since he had the routine of hiding it from his family down so well, he would be the one to possess it for now. Additionally, Devin's week to take care of Hank the hamster would be starting the next day, and he wanted to use the mask to talk to him more. So far, the hamster had not proven to be as interesting as a cat (talking of nothing save for pellets), but he also wondered if Hank would open up more if he made a concentrated effort to communicate with him.

Devin pedaled his mountain bike along Route 49, smiling and yelling out whatever Youzed Panteez lyrics came to him, hoping that at the very least, the nearby trees were entertained with his expression of joy. In between belting out song lyrics, Devin heard a car approaching from behind. He paid it no mind, as he rode far enough off the side of the road to be well out of the vehicle's way. Regardless, that did not stop the car from slamming into him. Devin screamed as he unexpectedly went flying over the handlebars before landing on the rough gravel of the ditch. He yelled out in pain and panicked, feeling around his body in order to survey the damage. He found rough scrapes under his running pants and fleece jacket and knew that blood had started running from more than one wound. Groaning, Devin turned his head to see a familiar blue Honda Accord on the side of the road.

"Well, well, well," a familiar voice said. "Look at you, you little fucking twatbag. What an idiot I am. I've been watching the adults in this town like a hawk, but it's one of you little fucksticks that had it all along. Now, no more screwing around. Hand it over."

"What are you talking about, Shane?" Devin said, wondering if Chief Hannon's assistant could truly know about the existence of the mask. After glancing at both sides of the street for potential witnesses, Shane pulled the hunting knife he normally kept on his desk from his belt and pointed it directly at Devin's head.

"Your hair is looking a little unruly," Shane said. "Perhaps I ought to give you a haircut." Although he wore a leather jacket and trucker cap to at least attempt to hide his appearance, the maniacal look from behind his dark-brown eyes showed Devin that Shane meant business. "I'll make sure you'll have a closed-casket funeral because I cut your fucking face off. But your family won't be able to go, because I'll kill them too. Your pretty little sister, your hot mom, your idiot dad ... I'll kill them all."

Devin clearly understood the severity of the situation, so he unzipped his jacket pocket and threw the mask at Shane as best as he could while lying on the ground in pain.

"Enjoy it, dickhole," Devin said.

"Oh, I will," Shane replied in a crazed tone. "I will." Shane stashed the knife under his belt before doing the same with the mask and then climbed into his car and sped off down the road as Devin continued to groan in agony.

PART III
THE SHOWDOWN

CHAPTER 22

When Devin opened his eyes next, the eggshell-white walls that complemented the stiff bed he lay on confirmed that he had been transported to Speare Memorial Hospital in Plymouth. His mother and father crowded in front of the drawn curtain that divided the room in half, looking at him as they anxiously waited for him to awaken. Devin had not been in this hospital for four years, when he had a tonsillectomy. He did not have many fond memories of being in the hospital then and certainly hoped that his stay would be short for this particular trip. The back of his head hurt, and he started to remember how he had gotten there in the first place: he had gone flying over the handlebars of his mountain bike and landed headfirst on a pile of hard gravel because of Shane. As anger began to boil Devin's blood, his mother gently held his hand and encouraged him to remain lying down.

"You've been in and out," she told him, "but Dr. Jenkks thinks it's mostly been sleep. He said your neck is okay, and the wounds on the back of your head will heal in a couple of weeks. He's going to consider issuing a CT scan to check for a concussion; otherwise, he'll turn you over to us, and we'll make sure you take it very easy for the next few days. Tell me, baby, do you remember what happened?"

"I'm not sure how everything went down," Devin answered as a half truth. For some reason, he did not want to tell the story in front of his father. Devin did not know why, but he certainly had no desire to try to reason it out while still dealing with jolts of electrical-like pain crashing around inside of his head. "All I know is that I went flying over the handlebars. The next thing I remember, I woke up here."

"Harold, the guy that has the farm on the outskirts of Campton, just happened to be passing by," Devin's father said as he looked nervously at his son. Even from this distance, Devin could smell the beer on his breath and remembered that he had been drinking while watching the football game when he had left the house. "He called the police because he thought your back tire was kind of mangled. He was worried that someone may have hit you from behind; honestly, so are we. Of course, nobody answered, so the call came here to Plymouth. Chief Hannon never seems to work anymore, and who knows what his idiot assistant, Shane, is up to?"

Devin shifted uncomfortably hearing his father tell the story. He clearly remembered that Shane hit him and began to wonder if Shane had something to do with Chief Hannon's mysterious disappearance.

"I'm gonna go grab a coffee," Devin's father said. "Anybody want a coffee or a soda?"

Devin's mother shook her head. Devin had no interest in having sugar and caffeine send more jolts of electricity through his traumatized brain, so he also declined by way of a pained, grumbled murmur. He watched as his father kissed his mother on the cheek and, after a brief struggle, finally found a part in the curtain that divided the room. Once he had finally left, Devin's mother wiped his scruffy hair away from his forehead and gently cradled the back of his head. He began to relax from her warm and soothing touch.

"I may have to make a special pie run for Harold," Devin's mother said as she used her free hand to stroke Devin's hair. "It was really nice of him to make sure you got help. Believe it or not, he actually recognized you and made sure the EMT called us when they got you."

Devin started becoming lost in his mother's nurturing touch. It revived him, and that made him want to talk.

"Mom, I need to tell you something," Devin said. "I need you to listen, and I need you to trust me."

"Of course," she responded.

After looking at her purple turtleneck and earrings, Devin wondered if she had taken time to dress up a bit before leaving for the hospital.

"Mom, Waterville Valley is in trouble," Devin said after letting go of the fact that his mother may have delayed her visit to see her son in the hospital in order to put makeup on. "There's a conspiracy that goes all the way up to Chief Hannon, and he may actually be in trouble. There are some very bad things happening right now in this town."

Devin's mother gently removed her caressing hands and rose to her feet. Some of his rejuvenation drained away as she did so.

"Oh boy," she answered as she began looking for a call button. "I guess I need to see if Dr. Jenkks can do a CT scan, after all. Maybe you do have a concussion."

"No, Mom," Devin said as forcefully as he could with the amount of energy he currently had. He surprised himself by reaching out to grab his mother's arm with more strength than he expected to have. "I told you that I needed you to trust me. Shane ran me over, just to try to steal something from me. And Chief Hannon is missing for the same reason, I think. Mom, someone died in our town. Someone died out in the woods behind the village just over a week ago. I know, because I saw the body. Me, Corey, and Matthew all saw it."

"You're not kidding about this?"

"No, I'm not. I'll tell you everything." And Devin did. His father had still not come back from his beverage run, which gave Devin a chance to tell his mother the full story. He started at the beginning: seeing the dead body and the strange cairn stones with his friends at the dried-up Black Bear Brook and reporting what they saw to Chief Hannon, who ordered the boys to keep the matter a secret while he took some time to investigate. He even told his mother about the special item he had found, which allowed him to talk to animals, even Frank, the stray cat that had followed him home a few days before. Devin ended his story with how he had told Li about the magical item and how she identified it as a mask that could do even more amazing things when worn. He finished up the tale with Shane running him over and stealing the mask from him.

Devin's mother stood as motionless as a statue as she listened to Devin's story. For the first time ever, he noticed a bead of sweat form on the perfect skin of her forehead. It began running down one of her cheeks, flawing her immaculate makeup. She closed her eyes, and soon after that, he found himself looking around nervously as his bed began to softly shake. Devin at first thought that she had started rocking it but then noticed that her hands were placed firmly at her sides as her eyes remained closed. The bed started shaking violently, as did the small table next to him where a cup of water stood. The shaking grew more intense to the point that Devin became concerned that they were having one of their rare New England earthquakes. But something about his mother standing with her eyes closed as she began to sweat made Devin think otherwise. The shaking turned into

141

a full-on bouncing, and Devin clung to the rails of his bed as it began to jump up and down like a rubber ball bouncing against the pavement. All the items in the room began doing the same, and all the electronics monitoring Devin's health status began beeping. Even the dividing curtain ripped in half and came down. *At least nobody is in the bed next to me to see this crazy shit*, Devin frantically thought.

"Mom!" Devin yelled, knowing that her anger somehow caused the chaos.

Two weeks earlier, he never would have believed anything like that to be possible. But based on all that had transpired since that time, Devin now found himself quite open to believing many unusual things. "Mom!" Devin screamed again, and finally, he caught his mother's attention.

She opened her eyes, and as soon as she did, everything in the room abruptly came to rest. After surveying her surroundings and catching her breath (she panted like she had just sprinted all the way up Mount Washington), Devin's mother looked at him with eyes full of rage clearly intended for someone else.

"I'm going to check you out of here," she said calmly but quite disturbingly. "I'm going to check you out, and I'm going to take you to Shane. I'm going to make him confess in front of you, and then I'm going to kill him."

Devin did not know what to say to his mother as he sat up. He could hardly comprehend that her touch seemingly healed him, nor could he understand how his mother had nearly destroyed the hospital room with some unknown powers. Before he could think of anything to say, his father emerged from the open doorway as he sipped a coffee.

"Umm, what exactly did I miss here?" Devin's father asked with a look of terror on his face.

"A mother's wrath," Devin's mother responded as she began gathering Devin's clothes. For a very brief moment, Devin actually pitied Shane, as he had no idea what would be coming for him.

CHAPTER 23

Shane could not believe his fortune. He had been on his way to Plymouth in order to give a status report to Samuel, or as Shane called him, "Father," regarding his ongoing investigation of Chief Hannon and Waterville Valley. As he passed the rich Asian dentist's driveway on his way, he saw that little fuckstick Devin riding his bike down the hill. Shane had been watching nearly every adult in Waterville Valley closely for the last couple of months, and unbeknownst to his father (as Shane lied to him regularly), Shane actually knew quite a bit as to the happenings in the quaint little valley town. It all started with that greasy fuck, Marvin. Marvin had been in Waterville Valley for about two years by this point, and Shane mostly stayed away from him, simply because he thought he smelled like a sack of beaten shit. But his opinion of the fool changed back in August when "Teddy" (Shane's unflattering nickname for Chief Hannon) dragged him out to the village one day when Dave had called in a report of a bear snooping around their dumpster behind the bar. Sure enough, a big ol' black bear sat there lazily dipping its snout into a pile of leftover ribs and fries that it had dragged out of the dumpster, and there stood the dipshit Marvin, actually talking to the fucking bear. Teddy thought that Marvin attempted to calm the bear to keep him from going on a rampage, but Shane thought that, with this issue as well as most others, Teddy thought like a fucking idiot.

Something about the way that Marvin talked to the bear had caught Shane's attention. So, that night after his shift had ended, Shane summoned "Mr. Wellington," a very old vampire and, most important, his true boss. Mr. Wellington had first appeared one night in Shane's bedroom in the Snowy Owl complex town house rental, scaring him so much that he nearly pissed his bed. The vampire introduced himself to Shane and claimed to be second in command to an entire sect of humans and monsters that Shane's father worked with. "You're getting a promotion, kiddo," Mr. Wellington told Shane with a raspy voice as he stood in his bedroom wearing an outdated suit and top hat. "I'm afraid that your father may be slipping, still stuck in his towny roots, as you modern-day folk say. So, do the spying that your father asks of you, but before you report back to him, bring what you learn to me, and I'll tell you what to say to him."

Shane had no problem with that arrangement. He held no fear of Mr. Wellington; he had known for years that creatures that most people thought were only from fairy tales actually existed, thanks to his extensive training. In truth, he actually agreed with the old vampire, recognizing that his father's pettiness with Teddy, because of old high school bullshit that meant nothing then and meant even less now, clouded his head. Shane gladly accepted his promotion, as he had no qualms about stepping over his father since he did not care much about him in the first place. When Shane had summoned Mr. Wellington the night after Marvin had talked to the bear, the master vampire simply responded: "Good work, kiddo. That's exactly why you're here. Keep watching."

Unlike Shane's biological father, Shane did not have a childhood experience that could be considered normal under any circumstances. As far as Shane knew (or, to put it more accurately, as far as he had been told), Shane had been born in a secret underground complex in the defense district of El Segundo, California. Shane only knew that Samuel fathered him because that, too, had been told to him. Shane had met him at age ten while on a break from one of his "tests." But he did not know his biological mother, as the group of women that he called Mommy were paid to do only a handful of motherly things to the children in the program called Operation Metamorphosis, a top-secret government initiative aptly named for the transformation of innocent children into biological machines. All the children that were born in the El Segundo complex had been sold off from one or two of their biological parents, based on the strong genetics of the parents or simply because the government had potentially slanderous information and used it to blackmail them into selling their sperm and eggs. Once born, the children were tested in oh-so-loving ways, such as going three days without sleep, being blasted with a high-powered water hose, and so on, and these sessions accompanied exhausting mental testing procedures that were almost harder to deal with than the physical ones. This went on regularly between the ages of three and seven, and by age eight, the child had clearly defined proficiencies and a career in place. However, children who did not possess enough skills disappeared from the complex overnight, leaving Shane and the other children to guess as to what had happened to them. At age eight, Shane became a Lynx, a member of the group dedicated to stalking and spying on their prey before reporting their findings back to their superiors.

Shane had been put in the field at age ten. He first worked in Brussels, where he attended a dinner party held in honor of the prime minister. On the surface, he appeared to be an errand boy, fetching clean silverware to replace a dropped utensil, providing additional napkins for the enthusiastic eaters, and so on. In reality, Shane spied on an American envoy using the dinner as a rendezvous point to meet with a former Russian KGB member. The two were planning on selling intelligence information to an unknown third party, and Shane had orders to intercept their coded conversation and relay that information back to his handler. Already an expert at such tasks and able to recite verbatim things of this nature, Shane successfully completed this mission with relative ease.

Shane completed successful missions all over the world as a teenager before being assigned to New Hampshire. "You're going to work for me now, son," Shane's father said to him after Shane had relocated from California to New Hampshire. "I'm going to assign you to watch someone for me. Nobody here knows that you're my son, and we are going to keep it that way."

Soon after, Shane moved to the quaint little town of Waterville Valley, where he began working for Chief Ted Hannon as an assistant when the police department and the selectmen were dismantled and absorbed by Plymouth, the town that Shane's father secretly ran. Shane would later learn that his employers believed there to be some sort of sacredness to the valley that had not yet been discovered, and as such, they wanted to secure the land in order to study and control it, and they would use Shane to "see what you see," as their expression went. Shane could not have cared less about the assignment, as his handlers and guardians rarely told him the why and instead always focused on the what. Shane had no relationship with his father and did not care to begin one at this time, having only known the loveless life of a spy. His managers always ensured he had food and shelter and whatever money needed to complete the task at hand, and that proved to be far more than he could say about anything his father had ever done for him.

Shane played his character of "police assistant" well, pretending to be a whiny brat mad about not getting sponsored to go to the police academy, being forced instead to settle for a desk job where he performed meaningless administrative work. Shane further committed to the role by pretending to channel all this animosity toward Chief Hannon, as though his life's shortcomings had been entirely his fault. Even though Shane often thought that Teddy acted like a redneck idiot, he actually respected the chief on a certain level, believing that he did a lot while only having a little to work with and he had much more passion for being a cop than his father had.

Everything changed a couple of weeks ago when Shane had dinner at Grizzly's Bar one night after work. As he sat mindlessly eating buffalo wings and drinking a beer, a tourist dropped something that looked like a large chunk of old, dried-up beef jerky. The item looked meaningless, but the strange reaction that Marvin had when he picked it up and handed it back to the stranger, combined with the nervousness that both the tourist and his cute redhead companion had upon the item being accidentally exposed, sent bells ringing through Shane's head. When he finished his dinner and two more beers, Shane returned to his town house and tried to summon Mr. Wellington. Soon after, a deathly chill filled the room. Shane opened his eyes and saw the outline of Mr. Wellington's top hat and outdated suit standing in the shadowy darkness in front of him.

"You seem like you have something important to tell me," Mr. Wellington said in an eerie tone. Shane recited the events that had occurred earlier in the evening, making sure he covered every important detail, as he always did. "You have done well to bring this to my attention," Mr. Wellington said after pausing to have his own conversation with unknown beings in the silent ethers of beyond. "The tourist you saw is also one of ours and lives in New York City. He is a dealer of magical items. But the item you saw was an unsanctioned purchase. And if that isn't bad enough, he broke his blood oath to us. He was not supposed to tell anyone about his business, and we have since confirmed that he broke that promise. Because of that, we are going to kill him. I'm going to secretly visit him in the night. Then, he will slowly begin to die. He will have no idea what's happening to him; his temperament will begin to change over the next day or two, and then suddenly and somewhat unexpectedly, he will drop dead.

"This is where things will get very important for you," Mr. Wellington had continued on. "Since the purchase of that item was unsanctioned, we do not yet know exactly what it is. So we need you to steal it from him and bring it to me. This may prove challenging; I do not know exactly where he will croak. That means he could be anywhere in your town, or possibly even on his way back to New York when it happens, see? Wherever he goes, follow him and choose your moment to get that thing. And this assignment outranks your father, so do not mention any of this to him. Got it?"

Shane received his instructions loud and clear and did his best to keep his eyes on the New Yorker while also still pretending to be doing his job for Teddy, while also still pretending to be working for his father. Shane had been in training for such tasks since age three and believed he could handle this complex matter without issue. Shane did some digging locally and learned that the man and his redheaded companion were staying at the Sly Fox Lodge, a group of town houses about a half mile from where Shane lived. He also learned that they had driven a dark-blue 2018 Jaguar XJ from New York. But just when he began to put some serious effort into spying on his targets, he could not find them.

Shane first confirmed that the Jag had disappeared from the parking lot and could only assume that they had returned to New York. But since they did not check out of their town house room, Shane wondered if he had made an error in his initial inquiries, somehow revealing himself and then spooking them out of town. He did not want to bring that news back to Mr. Wellington, so he vowed to do his own private investigation before reporting his failure to his undead boss. However, he also remembered that Mr. Wellington made it clear that Daniel would quite literally drop dead within a few days after visiting him in the night. So, Shane came up with as good of a plan as any. On this Sunday afternoon, Shane had been on his way to meet with his father in a secluded area outside of Plymouth to report anything unusual about Teddy's activities. Somewhat surprisingly, this time Shane actually did have something interesting to report to his father, something that Mr. Wellington probably already knew because everyone in town seemed to: Chief Hannon had fucking disappeared. Shane's reaction to the stupid teenagers that came into the office earlier in the day had been quite authentic, as he could not believe that Teddy would take time off without telling him something about it. Instead, his boss had just left a short, pathetic note, indicating that he'd be away for a while.

But as Shane drove to meet with his father and passed the Asian's driveway and saw Devin pedaling his bike down the hill, he slammed on the brakes and turned his car around. Something about seeing Devin later in the afternoon after seeing him and his idiot friends in the office, after already having seen them hold a closed-door meeting with the chief a week earlier, reminded him of his childhood training in the secret El Segundo complex. "Just because you do not yet see how to connect points A and B does not mean that the connecting line is not already right in front of your face," one of his trainers had told him. Shane rolled that important line over and over in his head as he turned his car around and headed toward Devin. Why did three fourteen-year-olds want to talk to a police chief in private? Why the fuck did the chief run off? And come to think of it, why had Teddy's dipshit fisherman friend, Freddy, also been invisible all week? Even Marvin had been gone a couple of days, as Shane learned when he stopped in at Grizzly's Bar for dinner Friday night and did not see him working his usual shift. Shane smiled as he now saw a previously invisible line connecting all the points. And his connecting of the dots all lined up after running the shithead down on his bike. He bluffed the kid when he asked Devin to give him the item he hid, not certain that he possessed it. But somehow, Shane intuitively sensed that he had now connected points A and B and that the little turd and his friends were somehow involved with everything going on.

After leaving the scene of the crime, Shane made his way toward Waterville Valley Village, ditching the leather jacket and trucker hat that he had worn as a disguise in the backseat. It had been an instinctual move, one that came to him after touching the mysterious item. He texted his father as he drove, telling him that he needed to follow an important lead on Chief Hannon (which, in a way, had actually been true) and that he would need to postpone his meeting with him until the following day so he could gather some intel. He also added a line telling his father not to send any cops if someone called a bike accident in, saying, "I'm taking care of it," as he did not want any of his father's idiot Plymouth cops bumbling around and screwing things up for him. He then turned his phone off, not giving a shit as to what his father's response might be. After arriving in the parking lot of the village, Shane made his way straight to the gazebo in the village center. During summer tourist times, there would often be several people sitting in there, eating lunch or simply enjoying the breeze that came off Corcoran Pond. But the summer tourists were gone, and Shane found himself able to claim the gazebo all for himself. At first, at least.

"It's a mask," Mr. Wellington said, suddenly standing beside Shane after he had grabbed a seat in a plastic lawn chair at a circular plastic table. Shane wondered how he could be standing in sunlight. But in the end, it did not matter, as they both had more important business to discuss in the present moment.

"I was able to do some research on our mystery item since we last talked," Mr. Wellington said. "It's an old Native American mask. One of my colleagues had attempted to get it from Daniel's buffoons but ran into … unexpected problems. No matter. You and I got it, now. Go ahead, put it on. We've got some work to do."

Shane stood up and donned the mask. He let out a wicked laugh and turned to Mr. Wellington, who, just like the rest of his surroundings, now looked quite different.

"I'm ready," Shane said as he smiled. After adjusting to the strong energy that now coursed through his body, he began using the powers granted to him by the mask as Mr. Wellington eagerly watched everything unfold.

CHAPTER 24

Ted and Tessa got off I-95 and made their way to a two-story gray colonial with white trim on the outskirts of Springfield. They had wasted no time packing the suit of armor into Freddy's truck and heading out immediately after Tessa confirmed that Ted did not have Daniel's prized item in his possession. Ted confessed everything to Tessa, telling her that three teenagers had first discovered the body and that he had asked them to keep it quiet while he had a chance to poke around and see if he could learn anything for himself. Additionally, Ted admitted that one of them must have found the mask and taken it without telling him.

Tessa offered support, telling him, "You were trying to do the right thing for your community. That was very noble. Besides, you did not screw anything up half as bad as I have. There's still time for us to fix this."

Ted gently caressed Tessa's thigh while keeping one hand on the wheel.

Even with a stop for gas, they made decent time, arriving at the home in just over two and a half hours.

"She's expecting us," Tessa said. "I texted her and told her I had an emergency and needed her help. I've never done that before, so she knows it's for real. I also texted her some details about the mask so she can get a head start on helping us out."

Ted hoped that seeing the leader of Tessa's coven would be worth it. They had to slightly divert their route in order to stop in Springfield, and each moment not on the road delayed their return to Waterville Valley, where Tessa had Ted convinced that bad things were imminent as a result of the magical item potentially making its way into the wrong hands.

As soon as Ted stopped in the brick driveway, Tessa bolted from the passenger seat toward the house, and after shutting off the engine, he quickly followed behind. But before Tessa could trot up the front two steps in order to ring the doorbell, the front door opened, revealing a very attractive middle-aged African American woman with long dreadlocks running down to the waistline of her jeans.

"It's great to see you again," the woman said as she smiled and hugged Tessa. "I'm so sorry to hear about Daniel."

Tessa kissed her cheek before turning and pointing at Ted.

"This is Ted," she said. "And, Ted, this is Zalna, my high priestess."

The woman introduced as Zalna cautiously glanced in the direction of her neighbors' houses.

"Come inside," Zalna said after putting a hand on Ted's shoulders. Her warm touch comforted Ted nearly as much as Tessa's did. "We'll talk in my living room."

Tessa grabbed Ted by the arm and led him through the front door and into the living room, where he found a matching couch and chair, a flat-screen television, and a painting of a lighthouse mounted over the fireplace. The inviting room smelled as if a vanilla candle burned somewhere.

"Not exactly the lair you'd expect for a powerful witch, is it?" Zalna asked Ted with a smile.

"With everything I've seen over the last forty-eight hours, nothing surprises me anymore," Ted responded.

"I wish we were meeting under more optimistic circumstances," Zalna said as her smile began to fade, "but I know that we have some very serious matters to attend to. So let's not waste any time and get right into it. I've been doing some research since Tessa started texting me, and I've learned a little bit about the item you seek to reclaim. Please, sit." Zalna made a sweeping gesture with her arm, and Ted and Tessa took a seat on the couch before helping themselves to some green tea that Zalna had set out for them. She sat in the recliner chair and continued. "I understand that Daniel had purchased the item on the dark web. I have some people who are proficient with that, so I called one of them and had him trace down the sales transaction. He was not able to determine who the seller was, but that doesn't matter. He gave me enough information on the item itself for me to begin to paint a clear picture as to what we're up against. There's a bit of a history lesson here, but I know that time is of the essence, so I'll give you the condensed version.

"A long time ago, a very small clan of a particular tribe came to be, which I'll call the Bear Clan. The men of this clan had the ability to telepathically communicate with animals. I'm sure that you can imagine how valuable this would be to humans who are constantly living in survival mode; the natives could have the animals help them find the best places to get food, seek shelter, and secure just about any resources they needed. Everything was going great for the clan, and they were thriving—until the white man made their way onto the continent. As the whites came and quite literally scorched the earth, they forced the natives to flee west, not only stealing their resources but also crowding them into lands with other native tribes who did not openly welcome them. And the white man's constant defiling of the land tainted the animals that grazed upon the resources that the lands provided. As the animals became tainted, so did the natives of the clan that bonded with them. And if this wasn't bad enough for the clan, one day they found themselves with another matter that they never had to deal with before: a woman had been born with the men's ability to telepathically communicate with animals.

"The men of the Bear Clan found this to be very insulting. They believed that this gift belonged to them, and even with the gift, all of them had to receive training for long periods of time in order to use it. But this woman, who went by many names over the years—I'll call her Mama Bear—quickly came into her own, becoming the most powerful person possessing the gift in all the clan. And after she endured many trials and tribulations that included an attempt on her life, the clan eventually grew to trust her and followed her as a leader. She went on to take a mate, and together, they had a child. This child, who we'll call Shadow Man for reasons I will explain later, had the clan's gift of speaking with animals but not nearly as strongly as Mama Bear did, or perhaps he did and he just did not care to develop it. Either way, Shadow Man grew up alongside the ever-intrusive white man, and somehow, he found himself really connecting with them and vice versa. It did not take long for Shadow Man to start to dismiss the ways of his very old clan as outdated garbage and start taking on the modern ways of the whites. As you can imagine, this created a rift between him and his mother, and once he had grown into a young man, he decided

152

that he wanted to rule the clan for himself. So, after making a deal with Lucifer, or whoever the Native American equivalent for that is, Shadow Man had his mother killed and claimed her spot as the ruler of the Bear Clan, where he lived out the rest of the days ruling the clan until he too was killed.

"Now, this is where the story gets a little weird. I did not have enough time to delve too deeply into this specific part of it, but this is what I was able to learn. Someone, either surviving clan members or the whites, had the idea that Mama Bear, even though she was dead, still possessed the power to communicate with animals, so they cut her face off and made a mask from it. Clearly, they were right. It would take me a lot more digging to learn its full potential, but a logical guess is that it has something to do with speaking with animals."

"This is all very interesting," Ted said, "but Tessa is convinced that this is a very dangerous item. Were you able to figure out why?"

"Actually, yes," Zalna answered. "There is something else very interesting about the mask. I called this the Bear Clan because rumors say it started when a native chief who slipped and fell on a hunt was saved by a bear that he was able to mind-link with, and through the link, the bear was able to nurture him back to health. The chief then returned to his clan with the bear, and the two were able to teach the men how to speak with animals. This skill was then passed down to each generation. It just so happens that the encounter between the chief and the bear occurred in what is now your very own Waterville Valley. Oftentimes, these items have a strange way of finding their way home. Maybe it's got some sort of universal karmic resolution to undergo; I don't know. Regardless, when a magical item is home, so to speak, its power is often magnified, so whatever the mask actually does will be much more powerful in your woods. And if the item makes its way into the wrong hands, whether the intent is bad or the user is just plain ignorant, this can lead to a very dangerous outcome. Not to mention, Tessa told me that Daniel made this purchase behind his employer's back. This could mean that they are going to seek retribution and hunt it down, if they know about it. And from what I know about my lifelong enemy, assuming so would be very safe. That means you've probably got some bad dudes running around your woods right now. In fact, I hate to come out and say this, Tessa, but they may be the reason Daniel's dead. They may have killed him while looking for the mask."

"Your thoughts about it returning home make a lot of sense," Tessa said. "The area where Daniel had been trying to use the mask is surrounded by cairn stones. Some are six feet tall, at least. I certainly don't have the kind of power to make them and thought that they must have been there for eons. But Ted told me that's just not possible."

"That's right," Ted said. "With all the hiking tourists we get in the summer, there's just no way they could've been there a month ago. Where they are located is not too far from the village or the road on the opposite side. Someone would have seen them, and someone would most likely have heard them getting built as well."

"Well," Zalna said, "I have a theory for that. I told you how some magic items try to return home. Sometimes, if they are organic in nature, Mother Gaia steps in and helps this process along. Based on what I've learned, it seems more and more likely that there's some very bad karma that needs to be resolved. As soon as she sensed that the mask was back where it truly belongs, Gaia may have stepped in and created a platform for it to return home to. Gaia controls nature, and it would be quite easy for her to manipulate sights and sounds in order to create such a grand structure that you would never know was there, even if it was quite literally in front of your face. She could have raised an entire mountain overnight just out of sight of your town, and none would be the wiser. I'm guessing that where these cairn stones are centered is where the mask is supposed to get to, kind of like Mother Nature built her own type of runway to guide it home."

"But Daniel was there with it," Tessa responded. "If Mother Gaia was supposed to reclaim the mask in order to heal the trauma, then why didn't it happen with Daniel?"

"That is a very good question," Zalna answered. "And as of right now, I really cannot answer it. Perhaps it is a bloodline matter. Perhaps a descendant of the Bear Clan must be the one to deliver it to the sacred spot, and Daniel was not of this lineage."

"Speaking of bloodlines," Tessa said as she put a comforting hand on Ted's forearm, "Ted saved my life by using a magical halberd that seemed to be designed to kill vampires and werewolves. He used the weapon as though he had been training with it for his entire life. And what really surprised me about all this is that the halberd was sitting in a suit of armor in our loft. I never told you this, Ted, but Daniel and I had no idea that the armor or halberd was magical. We just bought it as a decorative item for the loft! You discovered this fact all on your own."

Ted shifted uncomfortably on the couch, surprised by Tessa's comments.

"Hmm," Zalna said as she stroked her chin. "Do you know anything about the Dark Ages, Ted?"

"A little," Ted answered as he desperately tried to remember Mrs. Kent's high school history class. "Something about a time several hundred years ago when many historical records were somehow lost."

"That's exactly right," Zalna responded. "At least, that's how current history teaches it. But as stupid as humans can be, we typically aren't that stupid. History is never lost if one mouth can still pass it down to another set of listening ears. But history can be hidden. We don't have time for a full history lesson now, but I will tell you something that may be quite relevant to where you find yourself today. One of the reasons historical documents from the Dark Ages are missing is because quite a lot of things were going on during that period that the powers that be do not want the dumbed down, uneducated public to know about. You now know that monsters exist; now imagine the panic this would cause if everyone knew. It is rumored that during the Dark Ages, evil was doing quite well, and the number of monsters that roamed the earth then was a hundred times today's numbers. In order to combat the evil, a small sect calling themselves the Light of Heaven formed, a group of holy knights that served God by fighting lycanthropes, vampires, and all other forms of undead that were ravaging the earth at the time. Basically, the exact thing you just did this weekend. So maybe you are of that bloodline, and maybe your bloodline plays an essential part of this quest. Regardless, I think that we have talked enough and that you should get to where you are going. Tessa, please check in with me daily and keep me posted. I will send help if needed."

Ted and Tessa arose from the couch. Tessa hugged Zalna one more time and kissed her on the cheek before Zalna made her way over to Ted, hugging him with her warm embrace. Once they were back in Freddy's truck and returning to the highway, Ted did his best to sort through the immense amount of information he had just been provided. Regardless of how much new data swam through his head, one point had been made very clear: if the mask made its way into the hands of Daniel's former employers, then Waterville Valley would be in grave danger. He stepped on the gas to pick up the pace and get back to New Hampshire as quickly as possible.

Devin sat in the back of his mother's Subaru Outback after she and his father had dressed him and pushed him out of the Plymouth hospital in a wheelchair. He would have been concerned about leaving behind medical attention after such a bad accident, but admittedly (and surprisingly), his mother had somehow healed his injury. He had no idea how in the fuck that could be possible; he could barely come to terms with knowing about the powers of the mask and did not have the bandwidth to think about other crazy shit. And for the first time in a week, the mask no longer remained in his possession, instead now residing in the worst possible hands of all: Shane's. His mother's newfound powers, whatever they actually were and wherever they actually came from, had arrived at the most appropriate time.

As they drove to the police station, Devin's mother said, "Chief Hannon better be in. He'd better be back from wherever the hell he ran off to and be hard at work chasing down his criminal of an assistant. And if he's not there, we'll come back to Plymouth and talk to that chief. I'll make sure Shane hangs for this!" Just as his mother paused to catch her breath in the middle of her tirade, her cell phone rang.

Devin looked at the Bluetooth device and identified the caller as his sister, Mandy. After taking a deep breath, Devin's mother pressed the answer button on her steering wheel.

"This better be important," Devin's mother said. "We're in Plymouth because your brother is just getting out of the hospital. He was just hit on his bike by that smug little police assistant, Shane. Devin's okay, but I can't say the same about Shane because when I find him, I'm gonna kill him!"

"He's here, Mom," Mandy answered through the stereo speakers of the car.

Devin's mother and father exchanged a confused glance.

"What do you mean, here?" Devin's mother asked. "Where are you?"

"I'm at Mary's Market with Terry and Denise," Mandy answered.

"We came by to grab a milkshake before the store closed. We're still in the store, and we can't get out. Shane is up in the clock tower with some old weirdo, and they have us trapped in the store. I'm freaking out!"

"How are you trapped, baby?" Devin's father asked nervously.

"There are animals all over the place," Mandy responded. "But there's something wrong with them. They look dead. And there's a lot of them!"

Devin's mother did not wait to hear another word before stepping harder on the gas pedal and driving dangerously fast toward Waterville Valley Village.

CHAPTER 25

Shane marveled as he looked around Waterville Valley Village with the mask on. He saw everything as it normally would look on that late autumn afternoon and yet saw more, as if two different dimensions, or perhaps two different times, had somehow merged together. Even the outdated, raggedy suit and top hat Mr. Wellington always wore were now pristine, and his normally dull, withered gray skin now looked healthy and vibrant. His face even had life in it, as Shane saw closely cropped black hair sticking out from his top hat over his forehead as well as a long mustache of the same color waxed up into curls on each end. "Amazing!" Shane said to Mr. Wellington as they stood side by side in the gazebo. "You look so ..."

"Human?" Mr. Wellington responded. "Time for some honesty. Although it is true that I put you in charge here to watch your dumb-dumb father, there was much more to my reasoning than that. In the Roaring Twenties, I was a business mogul from Nebraska who was very much alive. I was wealthy, and I bought up properties all over the place as I made my way east. After making my way here, I fell in love with the place. I wanted to buy up some land here—in particular, the golf course, which had been created a while before then. Waterville Valley was a mix of loggers and farmers back then, and they did not take too kindly to out-of-towners coming in and gobbling up their precious homeland. Over and over, I tried to reason with them, but let me tell you, townies don't do reasoning very well. On one such occasion, an argument turned into a fight, and I was killed. But before too much time had passed, my maker found me, and you can guess what happened next. Today, as we watch the sun begin to set on this chilly afternoon in this quaint little town, I'm here for revenge, and together, we are going to destroy this place!"

"I'm with you," Shane said triumphantly. "I'm with you all the way. But tell me, how does this mask fit into everything?"

"Before there were loggers and farmers, there were Indians," Mr. Wellington replied. "Now, normally, we have a strong understanding of most of the magic items that come to and fro, but Daniel snuck behind our backs to buy it. I'm learning as we go about it, but it appears to be made from the flesh of an Indian whose clan formed here in these woods. It has got to do with animals; the mask is meant to allow its wearer to connect with animals in some way. But the earth is alive, you see, and she's not too keen on this item ever having been created, 'cause the Indians were her friends. So, she's going to try to get it back and put it in its proper resting place, so to speak. That spot is somewhere out there behind the river, and she's going to send some people to try to take it from us and make sure it gets there. We'll get it there, all right, but not to return it home. It's time to get our own help in place and take control of this situation. Here, grab my arm."

Shane gently grabbed it. As soon as he did, they floated up nearly four stories high to the top of the clock tower next to the bike store.

"While we've been chatting, I've learned that your mask is meant to talk to animals," Mr. Wellington said. "Living ones. But I'm not alive, see? So we're gonna go with a different plan." Mr. Wellington pulled his arm free from Shane's grasp after their feet were securely planted on the top floor of the clock tower and then grabbed onto the side of the mask. "There's a whole lotta woods here," Mr. Wellington said. "That means there's a whole lotta dead animals out there. I want you to concentrate on that. Imagine every dead animal that must be out there. Every single one that has ever died, even the ones that died long before Waterville Valley was even settled. It doesn't matter how long ago they croaked; if there's any kind of remains, even a teeny, tiny bone, we can bring 'em back. Envision that, now."

Shane did, thinking of every squirrel, opossum, owl, bear— everything. Within a few minutes, Shane felt an animalistic perception began developing within him.

"You can feel it, can't you?" Mr. Wellington asked, and Shane nodded. "That's right. Your army is on the way. I suppose I should thank Daniel. Even though he broke the rules and got himself killed because of it, he did bring this mask to its most potent place. And you know what? That gives me an idea." Mr. Wellington let go of the side of the mask and abruptly vanished. By the time the cosmic dust trail created by his teleportation disappeared, Shane looked down from the clock tower and saw that his undead army of animals had arrived.

Mandy moved the Waterville Valley T-shirt hanging in the display window of Mary's Market and stared out at the horror that awaited her in the village center. She steamed over the fact that fate had put her in this situation. She had only been trying to spend a relaxing Sunday afternoon with her two best friends, Terry and Denise. Like Mandy, Terry had a lean, athletic, and tall build. As an all-star cross-country skier, she possibly even had the Olympics in her future. She and Mandy had bonded three years prior when the girls' physical fitness class at the academy went on an all-day field trip to ski some of the flatter hiking trails in the area. The two lined up next to each other and skied side by side for the afternoon, gabbing away and forming the beginning of their friendship. Mandy had most of her mother's good looks, having similar blond hair with a light hint of red in it. Terry, equally as attractive, had long, curly dirty-blond hair. The two went out with boys whenever they pleased, having the freedom to pick and choose.

Denise, in contrast, did not fit this profile. She had a short and chunky body to go along with her somewhat out-of-style short brown hair. But her witty personality oftentimes allowed her to keep up with Mandy and Terry when getting dates with the boys.

"God bless her, she finds a way," Mandy had told Terry through a laugh one time at a party as she watched Denise make out with a boy in the back of her old Dodge Ram pickup truck. And admittedly, having a vehicle made Denise even cooler to both Mandy and Terry, as she would take them wherever they all decided to go. Since they were all the same age, they all attended the same grade of the academy, giving them all day to cause trouble together in addition to the trouble they got up to at nights and on weekends.

And here they were in the market, after screwing around all afternoon, facing an unspeakable terror. Mary's Market combined several stores: a grocery store, an ice-cream shop, an outdoor clothing store, and even a bookstore, as Mary, the owner, had bought out the neighboring bookstore the previous year and absorbed the collection. It essentially served as a Walmart for the locals and tourists who did not want to go to Plymouth if they only needed a few things that did not justify the gas money to do so. And that was what pissed Mandy off even more at this moment, as they had been in Plymouth, driving around in Denise's truck, looking for high school boys to have fun with (as the private academy had limited options for young men that they had pretty much already burned through). But Denise wanted a milkshake and insisted that they go all the way back to the valley to get it from Mary's. "Their shakes are better than everyone else's," Denise had said. "They put a dash of cinnamon in it, just the way I like it."

Mandy and Terry exchanged a brief grumbling but knew better than to argue, as Denise remained stubborn when she wanted her way (and not to mention, she could choose to go wherever she wanted in her truck). So they went to Mary's, Denise promising that they would go screw around somewhere else after she got her shake. But they lost their ability to do so when the dead animals arrived.

Mandy got off the phone with her mother, trying not to be overwhelmed as she began to shift from panicked thoughts into survival mode. Still, she could not help trying to connect all the dots that had formed in front of her. *First Shane tries to run over my brother,* Mandy thought, *and now he's here with an army of dead animals ready to do who knows what? Who the fuck is this guy? And how is any of this possible?* Mandy issued a sigh of relief when her mother said that Devin did not have any serious injuries. She hated the dorky little shit but also loved him, him being her only brother and all. And that brought her attention to her other thought: *Who the fuck is Shane?* Nobody in Waterville Valley knew much about the guy. It seemed like one day several years ago, he just showed up, replacing Chief Hannon's police force by working as his glorified secretary. Shane did not seem to have any friends or family nearby and came across as a complete weirdo.

Mandy had had only one interaction with Shane, last fall when she hand-delivered one of her mother's homemade apple pies to Chief Hannon. Before Mandy could get into Chief Hannon's office, Shane stood up from his paperwork-covered desk and blocked her path. "He's busy!" he had yelled at her. "And so am I. Just leave it with me and get out of here!" Mandy did not want to argue with him and abruptly tossed the pie on his desk. But when she got next to Shane, she picked up on something strange about him. His tough-guy, angry image seemed to be a facade. Mandy had no idea why she thought this, but she really believed that Shane faked being angry all the time in order to hide his darker, more sinister side. She imagined that if Shane had a house, he would probably have a half-dozen bodies buried in the basement, wanting to go on killing and yet wanting to get caught just to brag about it. As she stared out the window, Mandy believed her original assessment of Shane to be spot on.

Before Mandy could spend any more time lost in thought, trying to figure out what Shane planned on doing next, Tony, the only kid currently working in Mary's Market, ran up behind her. "I don't know what the fuck is going on," Tony said as he jangled a large set of keys in front of him, "but I'm locking us in until we can figure it out."

Mandy agreed and issued a silent prayer to anyone listening for Tony standing next to her. A tall redhead who had just graduated in the spring and would be starting basic training in the army in November, Tony would be a great ally to help her get out of the situation. Unfortunately, Terry and Denise probably would not be.

Terry busied herself trying to pick Denise up, as she had collapsed on the floor, dropping her milkshake and splattering it everywhere. Tony ran back over and tried to drag both of them behind the counter. Eventually, Terry managed to get Denise off the floor as she continued to scream, "What the fuck is happening!"

Mandy saw a wet spot on her jeans and wondered if she had spilled her milkshake or if she had peed herself.

Once he had them secured in the safest spot possible, Tony reemerged, clinging to a baseball bat he probably kept on hand just in case a summer flatlander got out of line. He pointed toward the counter and encouraged Mandy to go join her friends huddled together on the floor behind it. Mandy had no intention of doing that and shook her head.

After a brief visual exchange, Tony gave her a nod of respect and pointed at the door. "Only way in, only way out," he said. "If we can keep them bottlenecked, we have a chance."

Mandy nodded and then saw the remains of three birds, probably hawks, flying and slamming themselves into the window. One of them had feathers on one wing and none on the other, leaving bones exposed just like its skull with two empty eye sockets. However, its solid beak began to take good chunks out of the window with strong, repeated pecks. This particular dead bird focused on pecking while the two others repeatedly dive-bombed the window, somehow avoiding damage to their half-dead forms in the process. Their approach worked quite well, as the window slowly began to crack.

Tony pointed at a wall in the corner that had gardening tools mounted on it. "Grab a shovel!" he yelled. "Grab a shovel and guard the window. I'll guard the door!"

Mandy ran over to grab a shovel from the wall before resuming her guard position by the window, staying within arm's reach of where Tony stood by the door. She grimaced when the skeleton of a deer with a large antler began ramming the glass door with powerful bursts. She tried not to look defeated, knowing that it would not be long before the dead animals made their way inside.

A loud crash jolted her attention back to the window, as the dead hawks had broken through and started flapping around inside the store. They screeched as living hawks normally would, but the tone of their noises sounded far darker and more evil to Mandy than those of living hawks ever could. And as soon as all three of them were inside the store, she almost keeled over and gagged from the smell of rotting tissue and old dirt. Mandy swung her shovel and landed a solid thwack on one of them, sending it straight to the floor. Without hesitation, she slammed one of her fury UGG boots onto its body and used the point from the spade shovel to sever its skeleton head from its skeleton body. Before she could focus her attention on the other two birds flapping around the store's ceiling, another louder crash drew her attention back to the door, where the skeleton deer had finally broken through. Tony wasted no time before bashing its ribcage (which only had half of its ribs intact in the first place) with the baseball bat. But he screamed as a dead bear ran both him and the remains of the deer through.

Mandy screamed as the beast broke through the door frame in order to fully fit its carcass inside the store. It looked the most alive out of all the animals she had seen so far, with most of its skin and fur dangling over its back, as though someone had killed it, skinned it, and made a bear rug out of it before draping the rug back over its own body. But the worst of its nauseating presence came from when the beast opened its mouth, as the breath that it spewed forth smelled like a dozen cans of week-old tuna left out in the sun. The charge of the bear had knocked Tony off balance. It placed what remained of its jaws around his neck and clamped down, causing Tony to issue a blood-filled gurgle.

"Fuck you!" Mandy yelled as she threw her shovel like a spear, landing a direct hit into the hindquarters of the dead bear. After biting through Tony's neck with enough force to take his head clean off, splattering blood all over the floor and the nearby shelf full of books, the animal turned its attention to Mandy and charged. With reflexes quicker than she knew she possessed, Mandy dove out of the way, crashing into a shelf stocked full of paper towels and toilet paper. The bear continued its charge and ran straight for the counter Terry and Denise hid behind. With one lunge, the bear smashed through, sending the cash register along with pieces of counter wood flying. Mandy heard her friends scream and assumed the worst as she saw the bear standing over where they had been cowering. Mandy's blood began to boil. The anger quickly turned into rage, and the rage turned into power.

Mandy watched in wonder as all of the store's contents slowly rose into the air. To her left, two cans of dog food floated past her face. To the right, an upside-down bottle of laundry detergent drifted toward the ceiling. With one swift, intuitive motion, Mandy pointed at the bear while issuing what sounded like a primal war cry. Each floating item shot into the creature with such force that it exploded, sending the remaining fur and bones flying around the store, some of its bone fragments even burying themselves into the wall. Mandy presumed that the last two hawks did not survive the blast, as she no longer saw or heard them flying around. But before she could check to see if her two best friends had survived the bear attack, she heard a loud bell sounding from outside. She recognized it as the bell in the clock tower and therefore knew that Shane had rung it.

Mandy stepped through the gigantic hole in the wall that used to be the door to Mary's Market and saw monstrous versions of all the animals she had ever seen growing up in Waterville Valley. Rotting animals as small as mice and as large as moose stood in the village center, far too many to count. But none of them were attacking. Instead, they all stood perfectly still as if they had died yet again. A path straight in front of the market leading to the clock tower remained the only part of the village center not occupied by a dead animal. Mandy looked up and saw Shane, wearing a strange mask that covered the top half of his face, leaning over the rail of the tower.

"Oh, it's you, apple pie girl," Shane said. "I was wondering who had the strength to play with my friends. I'll get right to the point: you've got potential. I don't know what it is yet, but you survived, so you certainly have some talent. I've got something pretty cool going on here, and I could use an ally. So join me. Or die instead. Your choice."

Before Mandy could answer, she heard a crashing sound coming from her left toward the ice rink and parking lot. As if everything that had happened in the last ten minutes did not baffle her enough, Mandy saw a man in a full suit of armor with an ax-type weapon as tall as the man. The weapon radiated a strange blue glow as the man crashed through the dead animal army, stepping on, pushing away, or slicing everything in his way. A woman with curly red hair wearing a gray cloak followed closely behind, suspiciously eyeing Shane.

"Who in the fuck are you?" Shane asked.

The man opened the visor of his helmet, revealing a familiar face.

"It's me, you friggin' idiot," the man responded. "It's Chief Hannon, your superior. I'm here to arrest you. Come on down and surrender peacefully, or I'll take you by force."

"Nope!" Shane responded. And then chaos ensued once again.

CHAPTER 26

Before standing below Shane in front of the Waterville Valley Village clock tower, Ted and Tessa had endured quite an ordeal upon returning to New Hampshire. After exiting the highway and arriving at the outskirts of town, Ted had returned to Freddy's bait and tackle shop. He came up with a plan to switch out the vehicles, as he could increase their arsenal with the weapons he had in his truck. This would also give Tessa some time to positively identify Daniel's body, which Freddy had stowed away in his private freezer in the employee section of his store. While Ted took his time switching out the trucks, he could let Tessa take hers to say goodbye to the remains of her former lover. Ted liked this plan, given the circumstances. But within mere moments, his plan fell to hell.

Ted dug out Freddy's keys from the armrest compartment before leaning over and kissing Tessa on the cheek. He found himself having a hard time prying away from her, getting lost in the soft scents of her hair and perfume, wanting to take her into the backseat and make love to her all over again. After catching his breath, Ted summoned enough will to break himself away from her lusciousness and opened the door of the truck.

"Let me make sure things are in good order," Ted said to Tessa as he climbed out of the truck and grabbed her hand lovingly. "I'll get things set up and then call you in."

Tessa nodded.

After shutting the truck door and fumbling through Freddy's key ring, Ted found the keys that unlocked both the screen door and then the back door to Freddy's store. He exchanged one more loving glance with Tessa before making his way inside.

Ted fumbled for the light switch and turned on the lights in the employee section of Freddy's store. Smells of dug-up dirt and slithering earthworms assaulted his nostrils as soon as he walked in, reminding him of his own office. The small room had a door in the wall straight in front of Ted that led to the counter in the store. To each side of the room were desks covered in worm cups, fishing lures, and loose papers, and a large freezer sat in the corner of the room to Ted's left. Normally, Freddy used this freezer to store herring, shrimp, and any other frozen bait he would be selling. Additionally, Freddy usually stashed a bottle or two of Smirnoff in there, as Ted knew from occasionally stopping by during off-duty hours.

But Ted knew that Daniel's body now occupied the freezer. Standing in front of it, Ted began fumbling through Freddy's keys after seeing a Master padlock fastened securely onto its door. After finding the right key, he took a breath and then unlocked and slid open the freezer door.

"What the hell?" Ted said after looking down at an empty freezer.

"I'm afraid there's no jag juice in there for ya, sonny boy," a voice said from behind him.

Ted whirled around, instinctively reaching for the Glock that still remained tucked away in the glove compartment of his police truck. A man with black hair and a matching waxed mustache stood before him in an outdated suit and top hat that made him look like he had just come from an audition of a period-piece play at the Flying Monkey Theater in Plymouth.

"You won't find my friend in there either," the strange man said. "I knew this would all work out to be the bee's knees. Well, you killing my colleague in Philly was not exactly to be expected, but that may end up leading to a promotion for me, so maybe I should thank you."

Before Ted could respond, he heard a scream from outside. He wasted no time, risking turning his back on the creature that he assumed to be a vampire in order to get to Tessa's side. After getting back outside in three long, quick strides, Ted saw Tessa standing outside of the truck, held captive in the arms of a tall, good-looking man with brown hair. He wore sweatpants and no shirt, exposing a large discolored scar around his abs where it had previously been gnawed to shreds. It did not take long for Ted to identify the undead man.

"Daniel," Ted said flatly.

"That's right," the vampire said after abruptly teleporting next to Daniel, causing Tessa to scream once again. "I wasn't planning on this, but it is kinda neat how it all worked out. At first, I was very mad at you, Daniel. You betrayed us, and it cost you your life. But I guess things have a way of working themselves out. I gotta scram so I can get back to the real reason I'm here, see? I'm gonna let all of you get acquainted, all over again. Daniel, come and find me when it's over. I'm gonna give you a chance to redeem yourself." Just as quickly as the creature had appeared, he disappeared, leaving a small trail of cosmic dust behind.

"I'm sorry, Ted," Tessa said while remaining restricted in Daniel's arms. "I should have sensed it as soon as I rolled down the window. The animals are all silent, and the air is still. I should have known that we were walking into a trap."

"So your name is Ted, huh?" Daniel asked Ted, and much to his surprise, Daniel released his death grip on Tessa.

The truck is unlocked, Ted thought. *If I'm quick, I can get to the hatchback and pull out the halberd and end this.* But again, Daniel surprised Ted when his mannerisms began to change once the other man-creature had disappeared. Daniel ran an undead hand down Tessa's cheek as she began to cry. "I'm so sorry I got you into all of this," he told her.

"What happened?" Tessa asked Daniel as she turned around and looked up at him. "What the hell happened?"

Ted watched closely as he slowly made his way over to the back of Freddy's vehicle. If anything changed and Daniel became a threat to Tessa again, Ted planned on running him through without any hesitation.

"It wasn't me," Daniel responded. "At least, it wasn't the real me that hit you. But I do take responsibility for letting myself get to that point. The name of that thing that just left is Mr. Wellington. He's a very powerful vampire and is one of the high-ranking officers of my employer. I tried to keep you in the dark as to who they were, which now in hindsight does not seem to matter. I made you a part of all this by letting you in and telling you just about everything, and that cost me my life—and almost yours. You know that the mask was an unauthorized purchase; I should have never done that. I actually had them fooled about you for a while, but I screwed that up when I bought the mask. Once they learned about it, they watched my every move, and then they eventually learned about you. They have an agent up here, and he helped Mr. Wellington arrange my demise. The night that I fell asleep in the woods by myself while I was trying to bond with the mask, Mr. Wellington force-fed me some of his blood. The way it played out was so surreal that I thought I had dreamed the whole experience. But he had poisoned me for real, and that caused me to deteriorate from within at a rapid pace. That's why I hit you; my mind was long gone by that point. Within a couple of days of you leaving, the undead poison had fully taken over. I tried to use the mask to save myself, but I never really learned how to use it, and after my stomach exploded from the poison, I dropped dead in the middle of the cairn stones in the woods. My last memory is watching rats eating my exposed intestines, as pleasant as that sounds."

"Who is Mr. Wellington's agent up here?" Ted could not help but interject.

"Now that I'm dead, I can learn quite a bit by looking into the ethers," Daniel responded in a tone that suggested surprise. "It's your employee, Shane."

Rage burned inside of Ted. *I was right all along about that little shit,* Ted thought. *That probably means that Samuel is a part of all this as well.* Ted became lost in several scenarios playing through his mind, wondering to what extent Samuel, by means of Shane, had spied on him over the years, and what they possibly could have done with any information that they had gathered.

"You are not the only one at fault here," Tessa said to Daniel as she placed her hand on his cheek, snapping Ted out of his angry thoughts. "If you can now see the truth of things, you probably know now that I was not who I said I was when we first met. I was sent from my witch's coven to spy on your employer by spying on you. I did fall for you over time; those feelings were real. But my intent at first was not pure, and as such, I feel just as responsible for your death as you do."

"I am beginning to see the truth of this mask," Daniel said to both of them. "The mask belongs here in these woods, and because of that, perhaps more powerful forces are at work here. Maybe there was a scenario that involved us all needing to play our parts in order to get it here. And I know that my part has now come to an end."

"You said that you are dead," Ted said. "Does that mean what I think it means?"

"I imagine so," Daniel responded with an empty tone. "Mr.

Wellington is a vampire, and either by means of his poison or whatever he may have done to me today, he turned me into one as well. And if we were to still be talking an hour from now, my vampiric lust would kick in, and the results would not be pretty. I need you to take care of this, Ted." He shifted his gaze to the back of Freddy's truck as if he already knew that it contained the vampire-slaying halberd. Once certain that Ted had understood the message, Daniel looked at Tessa a final time.

"Our love did become real," Daniel said to Tessa as he wiped tears from her eyes. "And your love goes on, with him. With the living. Play your part and help bring peace to the mask and this land, just as Ted will now bring peace to me." By this point, Daniel had pried himself away from Tessa and approached Ted, who held the halberd.

"Turn away," Daniel said as he looked over his shoulder at Tessa. She did not challenge him and did so immediately.

Daniel walked within swinging reach of the glowing-blue blade of the halberd before looking at Ted and smiling. "You will be good for her, Ted," he said to him.

Ted nodded in some uncomfortable form of approval before making one last glance toward Tessa. After pulling in a deep breath and saying a silent prayer to God, Ted swung the glowing blade at Daniel. Daniel died for the second time in New Hampshire.

Ted allowed a moment for Tessa to collect herself as he loaded the halberd and suit of armor into his vehicle. After finishing, he walked over to Tessa, as she wiped tears away and stared at where Daniel's body had just been before his death caused him to dissipate into thin air. She turned and hugged Ted strongly, kissing his cheek. "I'm sorry you had to see that," Tessa said. "But honestly, I needed that closure to make peace with him. I'm back in the present now. I'm here, with you."

"There's no need to explain anything," Ted said, and he meant it. Now more than ever, he believed that the last week or so he had lived under the guidance of God, a bond that he had been offered in his youth by means of his father but had arrogantly and foolishly turned down. Ted now understood that God did indeed work in mysterious ways. He fully accepted how everything unfolded before him and no longer sought out answers to questions that did not need to be asked. "Daniel was right," he said. "Your destiny is not done. And neither is mine. We need to find which one of the kids took the mask. Once we get it back, we'll go to the cairn stones and end this."

Tessa nodded and climbed into the passenger seat of Ted's Trailblazer police vehicle. The truck fired right up after having sat for a few days, and after revving the engine twice, Ted put it in drive and jumped on Route 49. He believed Devin to be the leader of the three boys, so he decided they would start with him and either claim the mask from him or get him to tell him which of the other two had it, hoping beyond hope that the kids had never tried to use it.

Ted began barreling toward Devin's house in North Sandwich. After a few minutes, he almost slammed on the brakes as he looked out of the driver-side window. "Did you see that?" he asked Tessa. "There's a bobcat runnin' behind the trees over there. But most of its ribcage is exposed. It doesn't make sense; it should be dead with that kinda injury."

"Kind of like this?" Tessa asked, and after Ted followed her gaze, he did slam on the brakes before nearly running over a fox. But it in no way looked like a normal, living fox, as besides having a body mostly rotted down to exposed organs, its head dangled from its neck like a swinging yo-yo.

"Look over here!" Ted yelled as he pointed out several dead-looking animals he could see in between the trees. Everything from owls to otters flapped or crawled around in a state of existence that seemed like something in the middle of life and death.

"Oh shit," Tessa said from the passenger seat, reclaiming Ted's full attention. "I think I know what must be happening. If the mask is connected to animals as strongly as Zalna had stated, and we're seeing half-dead animals everywhere, that must mean ..."

"Mr. Wellington or one of his associates has the mask and is raising the dead animals straight outta the ground," Ted responded.

Tessa nodded, and Ted shuddered at the thought of just how many animal remains must have been within a ten-square-mile radius of that area alone.

"And they're all heading in that direction. They're all heading toward the village. Let's go!"

He floored it, getting to the Waterville Valley Village parking lot about four minutes later. The nightmare journey included them running over a half-dead rabbit and a family of undead geese as they tried to hobble across the road.

Once in the parking lot, Ted had Tessa help him strap the breastplate of the suit of armor on before she put the helmet on his head. Ted would have been surprised that it fit perfectly, even with him having a bit of a flabby belly, but he now believed that God Himself had crafted this suit just for him. Once fully suited, Ted grabbed the halberd, already emitting its bluish glow, and walked toward the village center alongside Tessa.

Ted tried to keep calm; there were undead animals everywhere! He even saw fish bones flailing about in Corcoran Pond, unable to leave the water yet trying to announce their presence nonetheless.

After hearing a voice that he thought may have belonged to Devin's sister, Ted heard a familiar voice coming from the top of the clock tower, and through the closed visor of his helmet (which had a magical enhancement that allowed him to view his surroundings in a full field of view similar to unrestrictive, glare-protecting sunglasses), he saw his now hated enemy, Shane. As Ted and Tessa cautiously made their way through the dead animals that all mysteriously stood still around them, weaving between them and shoving them out of the way when necessary, Ted opened the visor of his helmet and addressed his adversary. For the first time in his entire life, Ted looked forward to killing another human being.

CHAPTER 27

Devin sat nervously in the backseat of his mother's car as she raced toward the village to get to Mandy. Luckily, he had been able to convince his mother to stop and pick up Li along the way.

"She put the mask on and had an even stronger connection to it than I did," Devin told his mother. "She can help us." He thanked the high heavens that his mother still had enough clarity to listen to reason, and she agreed to pick her up on the way by. Devin had texted Li frantically, telling her that Shane had tried to run him down before stealing the mask and that somehow the powers of the mask may have rubbed off on his mother (although he did not elaborate on the craziness that occurred with her in his hospital room). He begged Li to help him, both with tracking down Shane to reclaim the mask and with reclaiming his mother's fleeting sanity. Li immediately agreed and made her way down the hill of her steep driveway. She waited for them street-side in the same hot-pink tracksuit she had been wearing earlier. And just as Li had climbed into the backseat to sit next to Devin, they all witnessed the horror of undead animals stumbling around everywhere.

Devin's mother made her way toward Waterville Valley Village, as all were even more concerned about Mandy's well-being. Li wisely stated that the mask might somehow be connected to half-dead animals in some sort of warped way, which meant that Shane had most likely found a way to use the mask in a tainted manner. By the time they had reached the village parking lot, the rotted animals surrounded them. Already, they had run over two squirrels and a limping deer missing one of its rear legs. Devin's mother stopped for nothing, plowing into the animals and sending fractured bones and rotting flesh flying in all directions.

"First, we're going to save your sister," Devin's mother said as she pulled into the parking lot at such a high speed that Devin went flying across the backseat into Li's lap. "Then, you are all going to watch me kill Shane."

Li exchanged a concerned glance with Devin as she helped him sit up, but before his mother could plow through enough dead animals to claim a parking spot, all four of them looked in horror as the ground began to shake hard enough for the car to start bouncing a few inches off the ground. Soon after, the large ice rink at the edge of the village exploded. Everyone watched in a state of shock as wood, ice, and other debris went flying in all directions, and a skeletal animal four stories tall shook its bony head and flopped a half-covered furry trunk around, letting out a roar loud enough to rattle the car windows.

"No way!" Li yelled. "That's a wooly mammoth!"

The great beast began using its one remaining tusk to smash everything in sight, starting with Mary's Market before turning toward the parking lot and ramming the cars.

"My dad's dentist office!" Li yelled as Devin remembered that he had an office directly above the market. "Thank God nobody's there today."

"But Mandy was in the market when she called!" Devin's mother screamed as she bolted out of the car. "Let's go!"

Devin and Li immediately followed, but before his father could climb out, the wooly mammoth rammed a nearby Toyota Tundra, causing it to fly across the parking lot and slam into the passenger side of his mother's vehicle. Devin reached safety by jumping in the opposite direction of the collision, and as soon as he regained his senses, he saw that both his mother and Li had also evaded any serious damage. But a male scream confirmed that his father had not been so lucky, as the flying pickup truck had pinned the car against a Dodge van on the other side.

"Hold on, Tim!" Devin's mother screamed. "I'm getting you out of there!"

"No!" Devin's father answered. "Get Mandy!"

She opened her mouth to argue the point, but his father cut her off. "Emily, I'm fine. I'll be okay. Go save our daughter!"

Devin's mother eventually nodded before she pulled on Devin's jacket sleeve and encouraged him to follow. Devin made sure that Li also followed along before glancing through the driver's window of his mother's car. He grimaced as he saw his father crunched against the dashboard, but his father gave him a "go with your mother" kind of look, so Devin obliged. Luckily the wooly fucking mammoth had busied itself splashing around in Corcoran Pond, causing the ground to tremble with each step that it took. Devin desperately hoped that it would stay there and keep away from his father.

"Look!" Devin's mother shouted. "The clock tower! Shane is up there!"

"And he's wearing the mask!" Devin shouted more to Li than to his mother. Devin and Li followed his mother, kicking, stepping on, and pushing the rotting remains of animals that got in their way. As they made their way toward the gazebo, Devin saw the last remaining sunlight glimmer off metal. He could not believe his eyes when he saw a knight in shining armor swing a tall weapon with a blue glow around, cutting into the dead animals, while a woman wearing a gray cloak stood near him waving her arms, which somehow resulted in bones flying in all directions as they exploded. Devin could not identify them from this distance, but he knew, based on their actions, that they were on his side. Another woman doing the same type of thing with her arms stood nearby the duo, and Devin had no problem recognizing her after seeing her reddish-blonde hair.

"Look, Mom!" Devin shouted. "It's Mandy!"

Devin's mother seemed to notice her at the same time and began running through the half-dead animals as fast as she could.

After catching up with the group of warriors in the center of the village, Mandy locked eyes with their mother and hugged her. Devin's mother examined his sister closely for injuries, and surprisingly, she looked to Devin as though she had somehow avoided being hurt.

"Terry and Denise are dead!" Mandy screamed. "Mom, I have strange abilities now. And I'm using them. This woman is helping me."

The woman in the gray cloak turned toward Devin and his mother, taking a break while the knight kept fighting beside her, sending blue light dazzling in all directions. She took a few moments to study Devin's mother. Devin saw through the hood of her cloak that she had curly red hair and looked very attractive for someone who might be a little older than his parents.

"I knew there was one of you up here," the redhead said to Devin's mother, "but I did not expect there to be two of you. Certainly makes sense, considering how much stronger my own abilities have become while I'm near you two."

"Two of what?" Devin's mother asked, confused.

"Never mind that now," the woman responded. "We don't have time. I promise I'll tell you everything if we survive this. Let's help Ted. He's fighting by himself as we talk."

"That's Chief Hannon?" Devin asked.

Before anyone else could chime in, a voice bellowed from overhead. "Well, look at you all!" Shane said as he looked down from the clock tower.

Devin shuddered, as the dried, leathery mask made Shane look somewhat like a zombie.

"Do you like the friends I've invited to the party?" As soon as Shane said that, each and every half-dead animal froze in place, even the wooly mammoth, which had made its way back to the parking lot in order to return to its car-smashing frenzy. Devin could not see if his mother's car sat in its path and silently pleaded to anyone listening that it did not. "If you've ever wondered how many animals have died over thousands of years in these woods, I guess you're getting a good sense now. And would you ever have guessed that a mastodon died right under the village, eons ago? Pretty cool, huh?"

"Why are you doing this, Shane?" Chief Hannon asked.

Devin noticed he had lifted the visor of his knight's helmet in order to be heard. Devin looked at his cold stare and could not believe how well the image of knighthood fit the chief. "And where is Samuel? I know he's behind all this."

"Sometimes, Teddy, you are just so fucking stupid," Shane said as he glared at Chief Hannon. "As far as the second part of your question, I don't know where my father is. Like you, he's a fucking idiot, and this little thing I've got going here completely outranks him."

Devin did his best to process the new information. *Isn't Samuel the chief of police in Plymouth?* he thought. *He's Shane's father?*

"And as far as why I am doing this, that information is far above your rank. So say goodbye to your precious little town before I destroy it!"

Devin reached out and held on to Li as the ground began to shake again. He looked at Shane, who stared directly at the wooly mammoth.

"We don't have much time!" the cloak-wearing redhead said to

Devin's mother and sister. "Lock hands with me! Each of you, grab my hand and follow my lead. The rest of you, get out of the way!"

Li tugged Devin's arm aggressively to pull him out of the way. His mother and sister took the woman by the hands without question. The rest of the animal carcasses went back into attack mode, and Devin watched as Sir Hannon began swinging his large weapon around, cleaving the remains of deer, bears, and other animals that Devin could not identify. As the chief focused on them, the women faced the wooly mammoth, which had begun to charge.

"Holy shit!" Devin screamed as the charging mastodon caused the foundation of the gazebo to crack open.

"Come over here!" Li said as she pulled Devin past the gazebo and into the debris of the ice rink. "Give the women a clear path."

"Do you know what they're doing?" Devin asked as they cautiously made their way through nail-covered boards and large shards of ice.

"Yes," Li responded. "Remember what I told you about my grandmother? Looks like your mother and sister are some of the same kind. They're witches."

Devin shook his head, facing far too much danger to even think about that statement, let along argue it.

Once Li believed that they had reached a safe distance, she stopped, ducking down behind a large chunk of what remained of Mary's Market. Devin followed suit and watched the struggle. He looked up at the clock tower and saw that Shane continued to stare at the wooly mammoth through the mask, which most likely directed its charge. The women, in turn, chanted something indecipherable in unison as they faced the beast. The ground shook harder and harder, until a beam of golden light the size of a bus burst forth from the woman wearing the gray cloak, striking the wooly mammoth in what remained of its skeletal head. The ray seemed to either blind or confuse the beast, making it alter its course and crash directly into the clock tower, causing a huge *gong* as the large metal bell went toppling into the Mad River and shards of wood went flying in every direction.

"Shit!" Shane yelled as he found himself upended by the destruction of the tower. But before he could fall four stories to the ground below, Devin watched as three large half-feathered birds that probably used to be eagles swooped in, grabbed him by the arms and legs, stopping his fall, and carried him into the woods.

"He's going to the cairn stones!" the redhead yelled to Chief Hannon. "He's going to try to destroy the mask!"

"But why would he do that?" Devin's mother asked. "Why would he do that to something that gives him so much power?"

"Because he's running out of that power," the redhead answered. "The mask is not meant to do these types of things and will start to rebel against him. One of the ways it has done that already is by pitting us against him. The mask is now in its homeland, and it will augment its efforts to try to stop Shane from destroying it. But if Shane is somehow successful, he'll gain power far beyond what the mask is giving him now. We don't have time to talk anymore; let's follow him!"

Devin exchanged a worried look with Li, wondering what the fuck that could possibly mean before they all began heading for the woods.

CHAPTER 28

Devin and Li followed as fast as they could, weaving through the skeletal animals trailing their master into the woods by limping and crawling with whatever limbs they had left to utilize. As they passed behind Waterville Valley Village and reached the small, sloping hill that led down to the Mad River, the woman that had just identified herself as Tessa grabbed Devin's mother and sister by the arm, pausing their running. "Let's make a bridge!" Tessa said to the other two women. "It will be the quickest way to get Ted across." Devin watched in wonder as the three women channeled their energy in the same manner as they did to defeat the wooly mammoth (which had dramatically fallen over into the bike shop after crashing into the clock tower). They created a similar large beam of golden light that formed a solid pathway between the small hills on each side of the river.

Tessa encouraged Chief Hannon to go across first. He walked quite nimbly in his suit of armor as he meandered across the solid beam of light. After making his way across, everyone else followed suit, Devin and Li picking up the rear. Devin had prepared to argue with his mother about joining them. He had made a firm decision that he would not let his mother and sister go on without him, especially since both he and Li probably knew more about the powers of the mask than the rest of the group combined. He was thankful the challenge did not come, and his mother and Mandy remained at Tessa's side.

"Black Bear Brook!" Chief Hannon shouted once they all had crossed the light bridge. "Black Bear Brook is where all the cairn stones are. That's where Shane's going!"

"And I know where that is," Devin chimed in, happy to add some value, as he figured that neither his mother nor his sister knew. Even though Chief Hannon did, he could not move fast enough to take point in his cumbersome armor. "I'll lead the way!" Devin led, along with Li after his mother exchanged a "be careful" glance with him. Half-dead animals stumbled around all over the place, just not quite as many because they had to navigate through the trees and shrubbery.

Before he got too far, Devin stuck his hand in the air, asking everyone to pause as he saw a glimmer further down the trail. He quickly identified the source. "No fucking way," Devin said. "What are you fools doing here? This is a very dangerous situation. Get out of here!"

"Not a chance!" Corey yelled as he and Matthew rode their mountain bikes toward them, from farther down the trail. Corey's red Angry Birds hat would have been recognizable to Devin a mile away. "We were screwing around outside and saw a fox that kinda looked alive and dead at the same time. We followed it, and here we are. Holy shit, what's going on here? Does it have to do with that dead guy we found?"

"Look, boys," Chief Hannon said after lifting his visor, "I appreciate all that you've done for me, and I promise I will come up with some sort of reward for you all. But the danger here is too great, and you should leave. And that goes for you, too, Devin. I know how to get to the brook from here. I can lead everyone."

"No way," Devin responded evenly. "Li and I have worn the mask, and we know far more about it than any of you. And I'm not leaving my mother and sister." Devin almost fell over when Mandy hugged him tightly, not being able to remember a single other time that she had done so.

"And we're not leaving our friend either," Matthew shouted from ahead on the trail. "We all started this together, Chief, so we're ending it together."

"There's no time to argue!" Tessa yelled to Chief Hannon. "Let them come along. Kids, just do your best to stay out of harm's way and don't distract us with questions. We'll all talk later, if we survive."

Chief Hannon closed his visor, seemingly accepting Tessa's reasoning. Devin wasted no time leading the group forward again. After Corey and Matthew got over the novelty of the situation (and Corey saying, "Whoa, Chief, cool armor!" after he pinged it with his knuckles twice, causing Chief Hannon to roar in frustration), Devin persuaded the two to take the rear. As they made their way down the trail (where Tessa once again used magic to help Ted up the

Skyrim-like stone stairway after he crossed the small wooden bridge), they began encountering sporadic cairn stones, so Devin knew that they did not have much farther to go. Soon after, they reached the base of Black Bear Brook, and Devin looked up the gentle slope of the dried-up brook as he saw the cairn stones become more frequent and larger, some standing as tall as Chief Hannon. Soon after taking a short journey from there, everyone could see and hear Shane, who stood within the center of the cairn circle at the top of the brook bed. He had a skeletal bear with him, and the two attempted to push over the tall stone structures.

"Give it up, Shane!" Chief Hannon shouted through his helmet. "Stop embarrassing yourself. It's over!"

Shane turned to respond, but before he could, a real bear came crashing through the trees from behind him, ramming into the bone-bear and sending what remained of its body parts flying. As soon as he had finished off that creature, the living bear turned to Shane and pounced. The two began rolling around on the ground as they attempted to destroy each other.

"That's him!" Tessa yelled to Chief Hannon as she grabbed his armored arm. "That's Marvin! I have no idea how he got back here. And now he can transform in the daylight!"

Marvin, the guy that works at the bar? Devin wondered. *He's a fucking bear?*

Ted and Tessa began running up the hill to join the battle, passing Devin and Li. From what Devin could see by means of his limited vision, the Marvin-bear had Shane pinned on the ground as it bit into his shoulder, causing Shane to scream in agony. Once Shane had been secured on the ground, Devin's jaw dropped as the bear transformed into Marvin. By this time, the entire group had made it most of the way up the hill and into the cairn circle. Devin saw Marvin look at Tessa and smile. But just as he opened his mouth to speak, his smile turned red as an all-too-familiar hunting knife sliced his neck open from behind. Shane had struck, and, based on the amount of blood spewing forth from Marvin's neck, it most likely would serve as a fatal blow. Marvin's body slumped to the ground as Tessa screamed, and Shane panted heavily as he resecured the mask, which had loosened during the combat. Chief Hannon charged as he raised his large weapon overhead. But before he could cut Shane's head off as he lay defenseless

181

on the ground, a mysterious man teleported in front of the chief, somehow freezing his swing in midair.

"Well, whaddayaknow?" the man said to the chief and Tessa. "Looks like ol' Danny boy didn't come through for me, so I guess I gotta step in. This has gone on long enough, don't ya think?"

Devin looked at the man closely. He wore an outdated suit and hat and had black hair and a waxed mustache of the same color. He talked funny and seemed as though he had just stepped out of an old gangster movie. Devin watched in horror as Chief Hannon's weapon started shining bright blue but also began bending backward toward his helmeted head. Somehow, the women seemed unable to use their powers to fight against the strange man. A hopeless dread washed over Devin, and he wondered if he could do anything to help. But before he got too lost in these thoughts, a voice he had not heard for a few days chimed in from outside the cairn circle.

"I agree; this has gone long enough." Everyone turned around, and Devin saw just about the last person he would have expected to see: Dale, his supervisor at the bike shop. He wore his trusted Slayer baseball cap, which held his long black hair in check as it draped over a black T-shirt with a band name that Devin could not read, as usual. Dale walked into the cairn circle, his hands tucked into the pockets of his blue jeans.

"Is there anyone in town not involved in whatever's going on here?" Corey shouted from the back, and Devin had to agree with him, wondering what in the fuck Dale could possibly be doing here. Chief Hannon stated something about the fact that he recognized Dale from the "night in the library," the last place Devin would ever imagine Dale hanging out in.

"Ah, nice to see you again," the mustache-man said to Dale as he looked him over. Devin picked up on both sarcasm and astonishment, as like everyone else, the man seemed surprised to see Dale. "But this is my operation, see? You know that I've been put in charge up here, and I'm gonna see this through. I'm—"

"That's enough," Dale said as he raised one hand into the air, cutting the man's conversation off. "I know what your orders are. I outrank you. Remember? Y'all are done here. I'll let you take your boy with you, but you need to leave the mask behind. You know full well that the boss wants to let it be retired."

"That's not gonna work for me, sonny boy," mustache-man responded. "We can go to the boss-man and talk about who answers to who later. But this is my little ditty, and I'm seeing it all the way through. Look how healthy I look now! I look like a man again. You think I'm gonna let anyone take that away from me, even the boss?" The strange man put his focus back on Chief Hannon, continuing to channel his magical energy to try to cut Chief Hannon down with his own weapon. But before he could, Chief Hannon's weapon abruptly flew out of his hands, and the blue ax-like blade cut mustache-man's head clean off in one stroke, sending his top hat tumbling down the hill.

"Holy shit, that was cool!" Corey shouted.

"Well, that ends that," Dale said as he began leaving the cairn circle. But before he could, Devin stepped in his path.

"What the fuck is this?" Devin screamed at Dale. "You 'outrank' him? So, you're a bad guy? Who the fuck are you?"

Dale looked at Devin and smiled as he turned his baseball cap around and put it on backward.

"Listen to me, buddy," Dale said. "I just saved all your lives. Would I have done that if I was a bad guy? If there's one thing you should take away from this little ordeal, it's that good and evil are very outdated terms. Life is far more complicated than that."

"Your name isn't even Dale, is it?" Devin asked. "And you probably didn't even have a dock installation business in Alabama with your brother, did you?"

"Sometimes, to tell the best lie, you sneak in a little truth," the man calling himself Dale said, still smiling. "What I told you was not too far from the truth. Just know that you and I really are buds, no matter how you feel today. I like your town, and I like you. I had to come here to make sure things stayed on a certain path. If I didn't, you wouldn't have a town left. That reminds me, we need to hold the rest of this little chat for a later time so I can finish up." Dale went over and examined Shane. "For all of you wanting revenge, you'll be happy to know that Shane is dead. He must have bled out from his shoulder wound."

Devin's mother let out a loud sigh of relief.

Dale (Devin had no idea what else to call him) bent over and gently took the mask off Shane's head.

"If you are in charge of whatever this operation was," Tessa said to

Dale, as everyone tried to crowd into the cramped space of the cairn circle, "then what are you planning on doing next?"

"We need to get the mask to the right person," Dale responded. "I'm gonna tell you a story, and I promise to keep it short, as I know you've all been through a lot today. This here is a magic item. For reasons I'll skip over, it needs to be retired, so to speak, and Waterville Valley is the place it needs to be retired in. The mask is made from a female Native American's face. The skin of her face was peeled off after her son betrayed her and got her killed. Whether you believe it or not, reincarnation is real, and 'cause of that, the ideal way to retire this item would be to have either the reincarnated mother or son wear the mask, right here, in this circle. However, I know for a fact that both of them have been really busy doing … something else in their current reincarnations. That means we need to give it to the next closest person in the bloodline."

"Do you know who that would be?" Tessa asked.

"I didn't at first," Dale responded, "but I do now." Dale walked over and handed the mask to Li. "This charming little lady, here."

Everyone began to murmur among themselves. Devin did not understand how it could be someone else other than him, given the fact that he talked to two different animals with it and seemed to bond with it really well. But he decided he would save that question for another time, still being angry with Dale and overwhelmed by everything else.

"It's true," Li said to Devin, seeming to know his question while also providing an answer for it. "I know it is. What did you see when you put on the mask?"

"I saw places," Devin said. "Almost like a merging of places from different periods of time."

"Well, I saw more than that," Li said as she grabbed Devin by the hands. "I saw her. I saw the beautiful woman this mask truly belongs to. I don't know this guy, but I can tell you that whoever he is, he's telling the truth: I'm somehow connected to this mask, and I can do what needs to be done." Before giving Devin a chance to respond, Li kissed him deeply on the lips. The kiss reinvigorated him, and he enjoyed it even more because of the fact that Corey actually kept his mouth shut while they shared their moment.

After pulling away, Li turned to face Dale and allowed him to tie the leathery mask around her face. Immediately, Li grabbed Devin's hand so strongly that he wondered if she would break his wrist. "I see her!" Li shouted. "I'm there! I'm where I need to be!" Devin nervously watched her and began to wonder what she saw. He soon got his answer. "Oh my God! It's not just her! Quan Yin is here too!"

Devin used his free hand to caress Li's arm as he wondered who that could be. Li's body began to pulsate, and the cairn stones violently shook.

"Everyone else but these two kids, get away from the stones!" Dale yelled. "Now!"

Devin had no idea if they did or not, as Li and the shaking rocks claimed all his attention.

"I forgive you!" Li yelled over and over.

Devin began losing sight of Li and the cairn stones as his vision became swallowed by white light before he saw nothing but black.

EPILOGUE

(One Month Later)

Devin smiled as he sat in the back of the limo next to Li. It had been quite a month since the showdown at Black Bear Brook. He remembered looking at Dale when he could first open his eyes again. Dale then helped him off the ground.

"It's all over," Dale had said with a smile. "She did it!"

Devin looked around anxiously to find Li waiting behind Dale. Devin politely shoved Dale out of the way and practically jumped into Li's arms before she kissed him repeatedly. After their embracing moment had gone on long enough, Li broke them apart so they could get out of the woods. Each cairn stone, along with the mask itself, had disappeared, leaving no trace behind. Thankfully, Devin's family and friends survived the ordeal and stood by with tired smiles.

"Mother Nature got what she wanted," Dale had told him, seemingly reading his thoughts. "Waterville Valley is at peace now."

Devin could tell by the position of the setting sun that he must not have been out very long. Holding hands, he and Li led the gang toward the village. Li had never told Devin exactly what had happened upon her putting on the mask for the final time, only that, "Quan Yin was there, and she guided me every step of the way. She helped me reunite mother and son."

Later, Devin would go on the Internet and look up the name, learning that Quan Yin was a Chinese goddess of compassionate love. Since he had the mask longer than anyone else, it hurt Devin slightly that Li did not tell him the specific details of her experience. It also hurt him that he had not been the "chosen one" to complete the epic task, after all he had done with the mask. But more important, he realized he loved Li, and because of that, he let it all go.

Once back in Waterville Valley Village, everyone shared a big sigh of relief when they found all of the undead animals had been destroyed upon the mask receiving its resolution. Unfortunately, nearly the entire village center had also been destroyed, looking as though a bulldozer had come through and leveled the area. Devin's mother quickly made her way to her car and found his father pinned against the dashboard with a broken back, in tremendous pain, but alive.

Devin's father spent two weeks in Speare Memorial and left wearing a brace. He grumbled about his auto body shop being closed and not earning money, but Devin and the rest of the family laughed at that, as money probably would not be an issue for them ever again.

After everyone's adrenaline came back down to earth, Dale and Chief Hannon had gone to the far edge of the parking lot alone and talked for ten minutes before returning to the rest of the group.

"Let me tell you how things are going to go from here," Dale had said to them all. "Some federal agents are on the way and should arrive within the hour. They are going to interview you extensively, along with any other locals who may have seen what went down today. The agents will come up with a backstory and then tell you what it is. I'm not gonna lie: you'll have to sign a confidentiality agreement. If you don't, the government will find ways to make your lives miserable. So, make it easy on yourself. And if you do, they'll do the same. I'll make sure you are all well compensated for everything you lost."

Dale then walked over to Devin and put a hand on his shoulder. "I'm going to arrange something very cool for you. You'll know what it is in about a month."

Devin asked if he would ever see Dale again, to which he responded, "I'd love to, but it would be best for both of us if you did not."

Based on everything he had just witnessed over the last several days, Devin did not doubt that statement in the slightest.

Sure enough, the FBI had arrived just as Dale said his final goodbyes. Everyone involved in what they referred to as "The Showdown" had been relocated to the police station and interviewed at great length, questioned all night and well into the following morning. Just as Dale had stated, each had to sign a confidentiality agreement, stating that a fucking once-in-a-hundred-years tornado (of all things) had gathered momentum over the golf course and further strengthened over Corcoran Pond before obliterating the village. Devin later learned that eight casualties would be blamed on the tornado: Daniel, Shane, Marvin, Tony, Terry, Denise, Freddy, and Dave, who tragically did not survive a cave-in while working in the bar's office at the time of the destruction.

Similar to when Chief Hannon requested their silence when they first discovered the dead body at Black Bear Brook, Devin and his friends played dumb about what had happened. Corey had no problems playing it up. "I held on to the rail of the gazebo for dear life, praying that I would survive the raging tornado!" he told their classmate Jacob one day. Devin had to laugh, as Corey had pulled off far more than just tall tales of that day. Somehow, he had even convinced the government to fund a soundproofing initiative in his garage, building the band a home practice space while getting Corey a brand-new, black Pearl Masterworks drum set and agreeing to pay for drum lessons for life. The feds also got his mother a ninety-five-inch flat-screen Samsung television for the two of them to watch their crime shows together on, all in addition to their cash settlement. Devin never learned the full settlement amount that the adults had received, but his mother said that they'd be able to do whatever they wanted with their lives going forward. This answer satisfied him.

But the biggest change for Devin and Li had been losing their ability to talk to animals. Both Frank the cat and Hank the hamster now acted like normal animals around them, no longer responding to any mental communications. Devin did not care at all and even hoped that he never heard an animal's voice again. The Waterville Valley area and its residents had once again found peace, and Devin wanted to go back to being a normal teenager, leaving anything involving the supernatural for his mother and sister to handle from then on.

Regarding Devin's mother and sister, he learned that, just like Li had a bloodline that somehow traced back to the mask, the maternal bloodline of his family traced all the way back to the witches of Salem. Devin's mother asked him to keep this a secret from his friends, as she believed that they had not seen either of them use magic after they joined up with the group on the Mad River Trail during the Showdown. Devin had no problem respecting his mother's wishes. Tessa, a powerful witch in her own right, would be relocating to Waterville Valley to live with Chief Hannon, which would allow her to train the women in his family as they became a part of her coven.

Devin smiled when he thought about his mother having these abilities. *Now I know why she was always so fucking immaculate,* Devin thought with a laugh. Somehow, the knowledge of their abilities brought him closer to his sister, Mandy, as the two of them began slowly forming a friendship over the last month. Additionally, Devin hated that her two best friends had been killed during Shane's reign of terror and wanted to do everything he could to help her through the difficult time, which she seemed to appreciate a great deal.

Li's smile in the backseat of the limo returned Devin to the present, where, along with Corey and Matthew, they took a luxurious ride to Portland, Maine. Three days prior, Chief Hannon had come by the house and hand-delivered an envelope to Devin. "This is for you," he had said with a smile before getting back in his police truck and driving away.

Devin opened it and found a letter that went along with an outline of specific instructions, the letter reading, "Don't say I never did anything for you," signed, "the guy you know as Dale."

Devin called the gang and followed the instructions precisely. First, he needed to have them all at his house at three on this Saturday afternoon in order to wait for the limo. All of them dressed comfortably, either in tracksuits or sweatpants and sweatshirts, per the instructions. He smiled back at Li, who wore a dark-pink Hello Kitty sweatshirt over blue jeans and black boots. Corey surprised him by opting not to wear his trusted red Angry Birds hat, instead slicking back his curly tufts.

"Gotta be lit tonight!" Corey said with the largest smile Devin had ever seen him display.

Devin understood, as Dale's gift went far beyond anything he could have imagined.

After a comfortable two-hour drive while the gang ate dark-chocolate M&Ms and pounded Cokes, they had finally arrived at their destination, the Expo. Upon arriving, someone escorted them inside to a private waiting room, where more soda and candy awaited them. As they ate and drank and laughed and had fun, an overweight bearded man wearing an ID card around his neck popped his head inside the room. He identified himself as the tour manager and said that he would be back to get them soon. He asked them if they were prepared, as he had been told that they would be, and they all emphatically answered yes. After about an hour, the manager returned, leading the gang down a dark hallway as he guided them with a flashlight to a different man who handed Devin his Jackson bass, fully tuned and ready to go. He leaned over and yelled, "Good luck!" as he gently shoved Devin toward the stage. Excitement stopped Devin from noticing that his legs quivered. He squinted when he suddenly went from the shadowy darkness of backstage to the bright stage lights.

"Hey, turns out we got a teenage cover band out of New Hampshire!" Jamee Jaxx, the lead singer of Youzed Panteez said to the crowd. "Their name is Straight Gucci! Give them a hand!"

Devin looked out and saw several hundred people yelling and screaming as they obeyed their leader, which gave Devin newfound courage. In truth, he hated their band name, but when they had been surprised by Dale's offer just three days before, they had to come up with something quickly, and all reluctantly agreed to take on Corey's name. As Devin walked over to the front of stage right, he found the bass player, Billy Baybee, waiting for him.

"Don't worry," Billy said with a smile. "I'll be out of your way. This song is all you."

Devin laughed as his favorite bass player turned away and walked to a red couch set up on the side of the stage, where two groupies began kissing and caressing him. He looked around and saw that Matthew had grabbed a mic and claimed the front of the stage, along with Jamee. Li had her guitar plugged in next to Randee, while Dayzed Dean, the drummer (who wore nothing but a purple thong), had given up his drum throne, allowing Corey to take over. He said that he would be going backstage to take a nap, as he knew that the audience would be in good hands. With a huge smile, Corey counted them off before everyone onstage (with the exception of Billy, who smiled as one of the girls started braiding his hair) started playing "Hangin' 'n' Bangin'" together.

A new rush of energy surged through Devin, who no longer had stage fright as he watched Matthew and Jamee trade off singing verses. He looked back at Corey, who mouthed, "Straight Gucci!" to him in his personal moment of triumph.

Devin agreed, realizing that their band sounded better than it ever had before. He made his way over to Li and managed to sneak in a kiss as they played, causing Randee to give an "awww" groan of approval. Devin smiled so hard that his cheeks nearly cracked.

Thank you, Dale, Devin thought as he enjoyed the best moment of his entire life. *Thank you, wherever and whoever you are.*

The man who had been calling himself Dale for the last several months stood anxiously on the black-and-white-checkerboard floor in the flickering torchlight of the secret underground lair in Queens. Admittedly, he had some pride in calling himself that name. He had hated the real Dale very much, all the way up until he killed him. He wanted to test himself, knowing full well that while one grudge had ended, another still remained. But dealing with his other enemy could wait. He believed that he did very well with this little New Hampshire quest and could not wait to get home. He had already returned his hair to its natural red color, happy to shed his false persona. Just one last task awaited him before he could go to his real home and reclaim his real name, forever leaving the Dale identity behind. He had to laugh, thankful that he had been in Plymouth taking care of impending business while an undead wooly mammoth had destroyed his home above the bike shop. After taking a breath, he stepped forward, holding his prisoner tightly by the arm as he prepared to address the one and only person who outranked him in the largest secret society in the entire world.

"Here he is, Houdini," Dale said as he shoved his captive into the center of the room.

Houdini leaned forward as he sat on a throne made of gold, studying their prisoner. It appeared that the three of them were alone in the room, but Dale knew that several invisible entities floated around, keeping guard with more powerful spells than anything the small town in New Hampshire had been witness to the month before. Except, of course, for the magic Quan Yin had used to claim the mask and deliver it to Mother Gaia. Dale was the only one not blinded by her power and watched the goddess take the artifact from the young girl. Admittedly, he was in awe of her might and gladly stood out of her way to let her complete her task.

"Well, well, well," Houdini said as he leaned forward on a silver cane that ended in a wolf's head adorned with red gems for eyes. He wore his very sharp but very outdated black suit, as usual. "Samuel. I held such promise for you. That's why we recruited you out of college and made you one of us. We gave you a better life than you ever could have asked for, including a lovely wife and a lovely son. But sadly, your results are making me doubt my ability to evaluate talent."

Dale watched Samuel as he rested on one knee on the floor, falling over after Dale's rough shove from behind. He still had his Plymouth police uniform on, as Dale and some of his own invisible friends had abducted him while the Showdown had been going on. He smiled as he thought of that. It had been a bit of a bumpy ride, but it ended as well as it could have. Reconstruction had begun, and the village would be rebuilt, better than ever. In addition to a new ice rink, they would also be getting an indoor racetrack built directly behind it. And each and every damaged building would be fully repaired and then some. All the residents involved had been issued huge chunks of money essentially to buy their silence. Dale appreciated that Houdini had ordered the mask to be returned to Mother Gaia at all costs, telling him, "She wins this round; I'm not gonna fight Mama Earth on this one."

That gave permission for Dale to do anything necessary, including cutting down the very powerful vampire, Mr. Wellington, in order to complete his mission. Dale had no problem doing that, preferring the company of demons over undead. Houdini, however, found himself out two generals, having lost both Mr. Wellington and Nostradamus during the ordeal.

But Dale cared nothing for two dead vampires, regardless of how old and important they were supposed to be. He only remained a member of this organization because they promised to help him defeat his last remaining enemy. He did not completely understand why; it created a bit of a conflict of interest since they all reported up to the same "master" in the end. *But that's their fuckin' problem*, Dale thought, not having feared anyone (or anything) for a long time.

Dale found himself really impressed by Chief Hannon, admiring how he transformed into a knight after he donned the armor and wielded the halberd. Dale had promised him that he would now have full authority in Waterville Valley, telling him that Plymouth's reign over his small town had come to an end and that he would be allowed to hire his own police force. The community would even get their own selectmen and mayor, allowing them to be self-sufficient. Dale also made the chief keep the promise that he had enforced upon him for helping him get out of the secret library underneath the pyramids in Giza, Egypt, alive, as he sent him the arrangements for Devin and his friends to play with Youzed Panteez. He even requested that the chief ensure that each of their parents gave them permission to go to the show, no exceptions.

Two days before, Chief Hannon confirmed with Dale that everything had been taken care of. Dale smiled, knowing that the show had been the night before his little stop in Queens. *I hope they all had fun*, he thought.

"And you smell terrible!" Houdini told Samuel, jerking Dale out of his thoughts and back into the present. Houdini had not lied; after they abducted Samuel, they had kept him locked away for a month as they continued to assess everything that had happened in New Hampshire, not allowing him to bathe or change clothes. "What did it, Samuel? What caused you to spit in our faces and reject all that we'd done for you? Was it because we took your son away at such a young age so we could train him in our Los Angeles facility? We allowed you to see him regularly, so that should not be it. Or was it because you never got over the fact that you had to look at Ted, your childhood rival, on a regular basis and it reminded you of how his sister never accepted your advances? Could you truly be that childish? Kinda funny how Mr. Knight is a descendent of the Light of Heaven crusaders and could've kicked the crap out of you anytime he wanted to. You sure know how to pick 'em, Sammy boy."

Finally, after letting out a long sigh while Samuel remained silent as he rested on one knee and stared at the floor, Houdini motioned for Dale to drag him forward. "But none of this matters anymore," Houdini said as he leaned over, peering with eyes that magically glowed. "I gave you one simple task: rule over the Waterville Valley area from your crystal tower in Plymouth, and report anything out of the ordinary. Clearly, even though you are from the area, you never had a clue about the powers humming through those wooded mountains. You didn't even notice that not one but two witches were right in front of your face the entire time! Instead of being diligent and paying attention, you let petty jealousy left over from a meaningless high school matter blind you. And that led not only to you being too dumb to see what was really going on in your own backyard, but it also left your son all alone to pick up your slack and do your job for you—your son, who was a far better, more talented employee than you; your son, who is now dead because of your insolence. Not to mention, I'm out two generals now. It may take me years to replace them! This entire matter could have been handled quickly and quietly if you had just been paying attention. But alas, you were not, and here we all are as a result."

Houdini raised his free hand, which caused a rippled dagger to rise in midair next to the throne. Dale had learned a lot about the history of this dagger as of late, much more than the fact that it had been Daniel's first magical possession. The real Dale had possessed it for a time and used it to do something unforgivable. Dale had no interest in seeing the weapon again and quickly turned away.

"Do you know this dagger?" Houdini asked Samuel.

"No," Samuel responded in a tone of defiant anger.

"Too bad," Houdini replied, "because the dagger knows you."

Dale heard a whisper in the air and knew even without looking that under Houdini's guidance the dagger magically flung itself across the room and plunged into Samuel's chest, killing him instantly. Satisfied that it had ended, Dale turned around and looked at the throne.

"See you soon," Houdini said casually before vanishing.

Dale did not see Samuel's body or the dagger anywhere.

"I really hope not," Dale said to the empty throne. He listened to the echoing *clip-clop* of his sneakers as he began walking toward the elevator.

"Are you sure you don't wanna take over Daniel's operation?" a different voice bellowed from behind.

Dale quickly spun around to see a tall man with long black hair and a black goatee waxed to a point. He wore a heavy trench coat and now stood in the middle of the room. Dale tried not to smile. *What is he calling himself now? Ben?* Dale thought. *He lies more about his real name than I do.*

"You could have anything you want. In time, you could even replace Houdini and run the entire operation. Just start with Talandoor's, and we'll go from there."

"Nah," Dale answered. "I'm good. I only want one thing, and you know what that is."

"Ah yes," Ben said as his eyes shimmered a silvery color. "The tired old tale of revenge, where one chases an old enemy because of past occurrences when they should instead just get over it and focus on the present."

"That's right," Dale responded. "Call me a stubborn southerner, if you'd like. He's gonna pay for what he did to me. Unless you're willing to drag him out of his little hiding hole, wherever in the friggin' universe that is, and force him to face me like a man, then I really don't have anything to say to you."

"Well," Ben said with a wicked smile, "can't do that just yet. He's a little busy doing something important for me right now. Besides, look what you gained from that little … endeavor. You are now more powerful than you ever could have imagined. Maybe you should thank him instead of trying to kill him. Imagine the team you two would make!"

"Fuck off," Dale said as he spun around and resumed heading for the elevator. He wanted to leave Ben, the Queens lair, and the entire northeast of the United States in his rearview mirror for a long time to come.

ABOUT THE AUTHOR

Shawn McHatton was born and raised in New England. When he's not busy writing, Shawn often hangs out where there's extra soundproofing so he can do plenty of double bass drumming without getting the cops involved. His fanatical passion for horror, fantasy, and German heavy metal may eventually require him to seek medical attention.